FINAL THERAPY

Also by Robert A. Burton

DOC-IN-A-BOX

FINAL THERAPY

ROBERT A. BURTON

JOVE BOOKS, NEW YORK

FINAL THERAPY

A Jove Book / published by arrangement with
the author

PRINTING HISTORY
Jove edition / December 1994

ISBN: 0-515-11503-7

A JOVE BOOK®
Jove Books are published by The Berkley Publishing Group,
200 Madison Avenue, New York, New York 10016.
JOVE and the "J" design are trademarks
belonging to Jove Publications, Inc.

PRINTED IN THE UNITED STATES OF AMERICA

10   9   8   7   6   5   4   3   2   1

FINAL THERAPY

ONE

ALAN FORESTER STOOD naked at his closet door. Had he been observing someone else, he would have made note of the irony of a famous psychiatrist indecisive in front of a half dozen suits of the same cut and color. Deep gray, as conservative as municipal bonds, the only variable the weight of the wool, the choice determined by the weather forecast. But Dr. Forester wasn't in an ironic frame of mind. Tonight he would be reading from his newest book, *Doctor on the Edge*. It would be a sophisticated San Francisco crowd, including several colleagues from the Institute.

He was surprised to find himself uneasy, even somewhat anxious. At the beginning of his career, twenty years ago, he might have been nervous about speaking publicly, but that had quickly passed. Each of his books had been modestly successful, and had gathered him a loyal following. There was no reason to be apprehensive. He would be reading to friends.

He fingered one of his suits, trying to recall the time when the suit and the life it represented would have been enough. Not that he was unhappy with his practice or his marriage. Quite the contrary. What was eating at him had nothing to do with externals, others, circumstance, economics.

He thought of talking to one of his own colleagues. Or to Joan. But there was no way that they could understand.

It was something he would have to lick on his own.

He eyed the suits as if choosing, trying to ignore the urge. No one would know, no one would be hurt. It was a harmless diversion. He told himself that there wasn't enough time, that it wasn't necessary, that he'd promised himself that he wouldn't, but there he was slipping into a pair of pitch black jeans and matching denim shirt, black Reebok high-tops and a black fedora. He kept them in a corner of the closet, hidden by the clump of suits, the high-tops carefully boxed and labeled slippers. An unnecessary precaution as Joan, not being suspicious by nature, allowed herself the slight conceit of respecting her faithful husband's privacy.

The choice of suits was suddenly irrelevant. Any one would do. He grabbed one at random and threw it, a fresh shirt and tie, and a pair of beige Hush Puppies into a garment bag. Minutes later he was parking his car in a side alley off upper Polk Street. He sat in the car a few minutes, until the last of the fall sun had spent itself and the evening darkness slid into place.

Normally he would have gone to a shop south of Market, or preferably in the East Bay or the Peninsula. He hated to waste time driving, but it was worth the guaranteed anonymity. On Polk Street he might be recognized. He stepped from his car, pulled his hat down low, and tilted his head downward, as though walking through some invisible storm. He was aware of his pleasure at merging with the surrounding blackness.

It was a balmy night. The street was lined with young boys who couldn't project their own future far enough even to worry about AIDS. Several smiled and one whistled as he passed. And there were the usual gritty young girls, smoking and lounging on a herd of Harley Davidsons gathered at the curb. Forester walked by quickly as though he had some destination down the street, then abruptly turned into the book and video store.

Rows of naked men gawked with frozen smiles sealed in cellophane. Black circles hid their groins, but not their faces. It should be the other way round, Forester thought as he averted his eyes. He reached the section on bondage, stopped, and turned to see if the store clerk was watching. She was a young woman in a cheap leather jacket. She was wearing two luminous green diaphragms for earrings. She nodded without expression. Her obvious indifference was comforting. He was safe.

He thumbed through page after page of women in high leather boots, brandishing whips and chains. The scenes were clearly staged, the models so uninterested that their faces threatened to kill with boredom. Then he found the picture of the young blond girl, loosely tied to a four poster bed with strips of pink lace. She seemed clean-cut. Forester looked for signs of intelligence and breeding in her high cheekbones and unblemished face. Yes, she might be from a good family, he thought, sliding his hand into his pants pocket.

He turned the page. A man kneeled over the woman, his erect penis lightly grazing her cheek. She was looking up at him with adoration. Forester looked closely, trying to judge her sincerity. The photos would have been taken in a studio. He tried to imagine the model coming to work, tossing her tote bag on a chair, stripping, playing with herself, getting all worked up, anxious to get it on. It was that way sometimes, young women who needed it that way. Yes, the woman wasn't acting, it was what she wanted, down deep. She was smiling at him, looking at him with those loving, adoring eyes.

Forester held his thumb and index finger around his penis, wrapping the bottom of the pants pocket around himself, feeling himself straining against the cloth. For a few moments he stood motionless, sensing the raw power smoking in his veins. Then he put down the magazine, walked to the general magazine section, and bought a copy of *Architectural Digest.*

The woman at the front counter took his money and slid the magazine into a bag.

"That won't be necessary," Forester said.

"Yeah," the woman said, as though noticing the magazine for the first time. "Habit," she said as she handed him his change. "By the way, if you're interested in the real thing, I have a friend."

"How's that?" Forester said.

"Light S and M. Nothing kinky or far out. A good friend of mine." The woman wrote down a telephone number—441-2987—on a scrap of paper and slid it toward Forester.

"No thanks." He turned and walked out the front door.

He repeated the number to himself as he drove to a gas station on Eddy Street. He changed into his suit and tie in the men's room and drove to Opera Plaza. He was the very essence of respectability. And why shouldn't he be? He was a good husband and doctor, and gave readily to a variety of charities. All his virtues were clearly in place.

■   ■   ■

Dr. Forester was a tall, slender man, with a heavily lined face and thick reddish brown hair. Somewhat stoop shouldered, he stood with one foot propped on a footstool. "My back," he explained to the audience of fifty gathered in the Opera Plaza bookstore. "Probably psychosomatic. We psychiatrists are the worst of all." He smiled briefly, fumbled through his pockets for his reading glasses, shrugged, repeated the motion of patting his pockets, his face puzzled. He checked underneath the podium, then with a look of surprise, saw that he was holding them in his left hand.

"Perhaps we should start with the chapter, 'The Psychiatrist as Buffoon.' "

There was considerable laughter, which was a good sign. The audience wanted to enjoy him.

"Just kidding. That wouldn't be fair. I have nothing against clowns." Forester spoke in deadpan, looking over his reading glasses at the mostly female audience settling in their seats. There was the usual air of expectation. Dr. Forester was about to start another evening of psychiatry-trashing. His local following was based on three slender novels that exposed the seamy side of therapy. *Doctor on the Edge* was more of the same, a tale of a middle-aged therapist's obsession with one of his patients. Each chapter of fiction alternated with a brief essay.

" 'The private life of the patient should be considered an epic poem, to be read slowly, cautiously, the therapist always on the lookout for hidden or alternative meanings.' " Several in the audience shifted in their seats. Forester heard the creaking sound of folding chairs sighing in boredom. He quickly switched to another chapter.

" 'I have sinned,' " he said, his voice shifting from forceful and resonant to soft and contrite. " 'I have desired my own patients, have found myself wishing to manipulate them for my purposes. I have had my fantasies.' " He looked out at the audience. He had their attention.

He believed what he said. His voice rang true in its confessional tone. He felt momentarily purged; his only sins were sins of the mind. Everyone had them. He couldn't be blamed for what ran unprompted through his brain.

Several of the women were smiling and nodding. One, Dorothy Lindholz, a fellow analyst from the Institute, was a good judge of character. She knew him as well as anyone, including his wife, and she openly admired him. Wasn't that proof? Weren't the nods and attentive eyes living demonstrations of his essential goodness? The audience heard the worst that he had to say, and they approved. He was confessing without being accused. Certainly this was a noble introspective gesture.

No, they have no idea. What I confess to is nothing compared to what I feel. I am scum. The very worst. He read with a quiet fury of a man anxious to blurt out everything. Except that he did not. He stuck with the awful but acceptable—desire, greed, malice. Ordinary vices. He stayed away from what ate at him, the horrible thoughts that would drive the audience from the bookstore, screaming and pointing.

Many times during meetings at the Institute, he contemplated what would happen if he just interrupted the presentation and blurted it out. And when he thought this way, he'd have a brief sense that there could be some absolution, or at least some diminution in the intensity of what was bothering him.

Let it all come tumbling out. Watch the searing fires race from his mouth and scorch the air around him. One second of true confession would make all the difference. He read with an intensity that had the audience riveted to their seats. He told them of desire in so many forms, leaning forward on the podium, looking right at each of them, letting them know with his supplicant eyes that it was himself he was talking about, not some imaginary antihero in his novel. He told them it was him, yet he swore the book was entirely fictitious, and any similarity to persons living or dead was purely coincidental.

There wasn't a soul in the audience who believed the disclaimer. They admired him for his honesty.

In the back row sat Kate and Owen Carbone, an attractive couple in their early thirties. Kate was dressed simply in a white turtleneck sweater and gabardine slacks. She wore little makeup; with her fair skin and jet black hair she was striking in a wholesome athletic way. She listened intently to Forester, her shimmering eyes indicating a certain guarded optimism as well as a suggestive undercurrent of sadness. Owen, tall and large-framed, slouched uncomfortably in the small metal folding chair, playing with the zipper of his weathered leather flight jacket.

He was dead set against "flannel-mouthed bullshit-artist therapists," but recognized that Kate needed to talk to someone. Last Sunday's *Chronicle* had carried a feature article on Dr. Forester and his public criticism of psychiatry. Owen felt that they might have something in common. He would rather trust his wife to someone who didn't believe in himself. Maybe such a person could have the lightness of spirit to help Kate with her recent depression. The Carbones had come to check out Dr. Forester.

Kate had her hand in his. Normally warm and strong,

today it was cool and light, somehow smaller and more tentative than usual. In some inexplicable way, there had become less of her, as though she had been turned down, her power reduced.

Owen felt sick and helpless. He wanted to make her better but had no idea what to say or do. He leaned over and kissed her softly on the cheek. "I love you," he whispered. He squeezed her hand.

Kate nodded. Dr. Forester paused to start another chapter. "What do you think?" Kate asked Owen.

"He seems sincere. I think it's worth a shot."

"You sure this is necessary?" Kate asked. "I think I can get better on my own."

"Give him a try."

Owen looked up at Dr. Forester. *I sure hope you can help,* he thought, at the same time as he had the strange feeling that he was making a big mistake. *It's your stupid prejudice against psychiatrists,* he tried to convince himself. Kate could go once or twice and see if he had anything to offer. Certainly one or two visits couldn't hurt.

TWO

IT WAS A WARM, COZY morning, the bedroom a blaze of early morning pink. Joan Forester kissed her husband on the neck, then ran her hand down across his chest. She slipped her hand between his thighs and began to tease.

Forester was uneasy. He propped his head up on a pillow to watch. He tried to imagine the old excitement, but he felt nothing beyond a frustrating pressure. Joan was handsome and sexy. She still caught the eyes of other men. And there was no question that she loved sex. On paper she was very desirable. Yet Forester did not stir. Instead he was unnerved by Joan's look of puzzlement and then irritation as she licked and stroked without success.

He ran his hand along the small of her back, up along her neck, and through her hair in a passionless attempt to comfort. Joan told him it was all right, these things happen, but he could see how hard she was trying. Her original tenderness and playfulness had turned to strained urgency mixed with a touch of desperation.

She covered herself with the top sheet. "Is it me?" she asked.

"Don't be ridiculous. I guess I'm going through one of those phases."

"It's been months. It must be me." She spoke with a

combination of humiliation and anger. She sat on the side of the bed, slipping on her robe.

Forester sat up and put his arm on her shoulder. "It's anything but. I'm stuck on ideas for a new book, I've got the lecture over at the Institute, it's a million little things. But honestly, it's not you." He leaned over and kissed her fully, at the same time aware of a dry, desolate quality to his wife's lips. He pulled away abruptly, as though he'd bitten into a splinter of broken glass.

"It's that bad?" Joan said. She twisted away from him. She rose from the bed and went into the bathroom.

"Tonight," Forester said. "We'll take a nice shower together, give each other a massage. I can barely wait."

"Sure. Me, too." Joan closed the door to the bathroom.

There was the sound of running water and another muffled noise. Forester wasn't sure, but it sounded like a sob.

Ten years ago, when they had first married, they made love with the abandon and special intimacy of a childless couple who had all the time in the world to dote on each other. It had been as natural as breathing. With Forester's sperm having officially been declared incapable of swimming upstream, there had not even been the intrusion of contraception.

In the last six months sex had become bathed in uncertainty and apprehension. Forester and Joan had become tentative with each other, but they did not discuss it. This morning, with the light streaming through the bedroom window directly onto his failed organ, highlighting his smallness, he'd felt it necessary to make excuses, knowing that each mumble and explanation drove the wedge of anxiety further and further into their relationship.

■ ■ ■

If only Joan didn't try so hard, he thought to himself as Kate Carbone, a new patient, entered his consultation room. His early morning embarrassment had now worked its way into a sullen irritability. He would have preferred taking the day off, but instead he was booked solid, eight hours of life gone wrong—expectations delivered to the wrong address, hopes trampled under the heel of pessimism, squashed under the humdrum of everyday. He was paid to listen, but today he would have been happy to forgo the money and hang a Gone Fishing sign on the front door of his home office.

Kate was quite attractive, with a broad, friendly face. Beneath her subdued manner Forester suspected a normally sunny disposition that had been temporarily derailed. Forester hoped her problems would be sexual, something juicy he could sink his teeth into. Besides, he hated to think of her having happy sex with her husband. Although she wouldn't know it, it would put them on unequal footing.

He enjoyed the moment of pleasant anticipation as Kate adjusted herself in the low-slung leather chair across from his desk. Kate's hour might be excellent distraction.

No such luck.

"I should have insisted that my mother see her doctor," Kate began. She was on the verge of tears.

Another case of situational depression, Forester thought as Kate began, her voice no more than a whisper.

"We had lunch together only a few days before her stroke. She mentioned her dizzy spells. I told her it was probably nothing. The next day she was unconscious in the intensive care unit. Dr. Powell, her neurologist, reassured me that dizziness wasn't a warning sign of a ruptured aneurysm. Without other symptoms they would have never done an arteriogram; it's too risky. Even if they had found the aneurysm, it would have been fifty-fifty. He told me all that. But I don't believe it."

"Dr. Powell is one of the best neurologists in San Francisco. He's telling you the truth."

"Maybe so. But it doesn't matter. I should have taken her to the hospital right then. Maybe she'd have been in the fifty percent that survives."

"No decent neurologist would have done an arteriogram just because your mom said she was dizzy. Even I know that."

"I don't know that."

Forester looked at Kate, then at his notebook. He made a few notes. Silence permeated the room. Kate toyed with the hem of her skirt, rolling it back and forth into a little woolen tube.

"I'm here because my husband insists. My talking to you isn't going to bring her back." It had been over a year since her mother's death, yet she felt as guilty as the first day. Kate looked down at her hands and began to massage the pad of her thumb with her other thumb. Forester said nothing, just watched. "She's gone, and it's my fault."

"Because you didn't tell her to see a doctor?"

"Of course I told her. I must have mentioned it ten times that day."

"So you didn't tell her it was nothing?"

"I did both. Mostly I tried to have her not worry. I wanted to brighten up our lunch. We didn't see each other that often and I wanted the day to go smoothly. She doesn't . . ." Kate paused, swallowed, and started again. "She didn't like to interfere. She was real independent and figured everyone else was or should be the same. She hated to phone or bother us. I should have driven her directly to the hospital."

"I'm confused. You said you told her it was nothing and you told her to see a doctor ten times during the lunch. Could you be a little clearer?"

"I wasn't forceful enough."

"And you think your mother died because you had the wrong inflection in your voice?"

"I knew this was going to be a waste of time."

"I'm just trying to understand your line of thinking. You did tell her, you just didn't say it the right way? Is that it?"

"No, that's not it. She was my mother. Don't you understand?" Kate's voice rose in exasperation. Forester was so unbelievably dense. Why was he acting as if he didn't understand? She would finish this one visit and that would be it.

"Tell me about her. You saw her regularly?"

"Not enough."

"She lived in San Francisco?"

"Sure. I was born here."

"Your father?"

"He died a few years ago."

"Your mother remarried?"

Kate shook her head.

"She worked?"

"She was a legal secretary in a patent attorney's office."

"She was smart and self-reliant?"

"Completely. No one told her what to do."

"And if she didn't feel well, she would go to a doctor?"

"My mother hated doctors. Her father was a pharmacist. He had stories. My mother was raised on dinnertimes filled with quack this and quack that, tales of near deaths from the wrong prescription. You name it, my grandfather had seen it. Once my mom had appendicitis. My father tried to get her to the hospital. She told him to mind his own business. It wasn't until she was delirious with fever that he was able to drag her into an ambulance. She nearly died. Afterwards she said she would have been okay with a shot of penicillin. She refused to pay the hospital bill. She often said she should have been a Christian Scientist except that she hated the words 'Christian' and 'scientist.' "

"Looking at it objectively, do you really think that you could have made a difference? You just told me your mother was stubborn and never listened. Why should she have behaved differently this time?"

"Maybe her not listening was my fault. If we'd seen more of each other, gotten to be better friends."

"You think being better friends with your mother would make her more rational?"

"Uh-huh."

"Without your support she didn't have enough common sense to phone a doctor if she thought it was important?"

"She couldn't admit that something might be wrong."

"But you did tell her to see someone."

"We've already covered this."

"But can't you see that you did all you could do?"

"I could have tried harder."

"No one can convince you otherwise?"

"She was my mother. I should have done more."

Dr. Forester made some notes. Then he leaned back in his chair. There was a subtle change of expression, as though he had remembered something that bothered him.

A mental taste of some bitter apple. "How would you know if you tried hard enough? I mean, what scale do you use to judge yourself?"

"I don't have a scale," Kate said. "I just know that it wasn't enough. If it had been, she wouldn't be dead."

"Are you this way about everything? Do you always feel that you've left something undone?"

"Not at all. You give something your best shot, then you forget it."

"But how do you know when you've done enough, as you put it, given it your best shot?"

"You know. What more can I say?"

"But that is a critical area, knowing how you know."

Forester's words were irritating. It wasn't *his* mother that had died. What did he know? On the other hand Kate had the sinking feeling that Forester could be making sense, and she didn't understand. The man was speaking in foreign tongues, certainly not in the language of her heart.

"Not knowing how you know is like being a scientist without a scale or tape measure."

"This isn't a scientific matter."

"No, it isn't." Forester paused, running his pen along his lower lip. "I get the feeling that you're somehow invested in feeling badly about your mom. I'm trying to offer you another way of looking at your feelings. All I'm asking you to do is think about why you should feel so strongly that you could have made a difference."

"I don't know. You tell me."

"Therapy doesn't work that way." Forester glanced at his watch. "I'm sorry, but the hour is up. We'll talk more about it next time." He looked at his appointment book. "Say Thursday at two."

"Sometimes I don't feel like living," Kate said.

"You think you'll be okay until Thursday?"

Kate's eyes filled with tears. She bit her lip and nodded. "I'll be fine. I'm just a little confused." She picked up her purse and walked quickly to the door. "Don't worry about me. I'm tough, like my mom."

Before seeing his next patient, Forester made some notes. He was surprised to find himself angry. Something about Kate had gotten under his skin. He ran over his own feelings during the hour. Midway through the session he had become impatient, then frustrated. Forester hated it when patients refused to see the obvious. But there was something else, some perverse movement of Kate toward her guilt. She clung to it with a vehemence that suggested deeper conflict.

His buzzer rang. Mrs. Siefert was leaning into her hour. Every second paid for must be accounted for. Forester recalled the day in medical school when he had opted for psychiatry. It could have been different, he could have been a radiologist or a pathologist, a scientist who dealt with facts and made specific diagnoses. But no, he had wanted to talk to people, listen, give advice, his advice. It had seemed so wonderfully intellectual. And now, as though to taunt his very decision, Mrs. Seifert, the veritable thesaurus of petty complaints, was warming up in the waiting room.

"This has nothing to do with my husband," Kate said at the start of Thursday's session. "We've been married seven years, but we've been together since we were freshmen at Berkeley." Kate's face momentarily brightened as she made a show of deliberately counting on her fingers. "Thirteen years, and we're more in love than ever. We even run our record and poster store together without arguing. And anyone who can work all day with me is an absolute saint. No, Owen's my buddy."

It was the first time that Forester had seen Kate smile. However the smile quickly faded as Kate continued.

"I've tried to see things from your perspective. You may be right, but it doesn't feel right. In my heart I know I failed my mother." Kate looked out the window, her eyes brimmed with tears. Then she turned and squarely faced Forester. "And that's something that I can't live with."

"You really mean that?"

"Sometimes I think so. I've heard about survivors from Vietnam who say they should have died, too. I know the feeling. My mom was only fifty-three. Too young to die. She wasn't even sick. She liked to dance all night, go to Reno, play the slots until her arms gave out. That's not someone who should be dead.

"My father's last words were, 'Take care of your mom.' I promised him." Kate put her hands to her face. In a muffled voice she said, "I feel so worthless."

Forester cringed. At the start of today's session Kate had struck Forester as being particularly handsome. But gradually, despite her good looks and pleasant manner, Forester felt a growing annoyance. It was something in her downcast look and air of defeat, as though she wanted to feel guilty, was volunteering for the role of victim. It made him mad, that kind of weakness.

That's not very kind, he warned himself. She's struggling with her grief. He tried to listen to her with an open, nonjudgmental mind, but the bad feelings started up, gathering strength. There was a dull ache at the base of his neck. He was aware that one of his hands was clenched.

He told himself that it was a different set of circumstances from that other time.

Though it felt the same.

Forester walked to the window that overlooked his garden. He opened it and took in some fresh air. It wasn't until he felt a little better that he realized that he had arisen from his seat while Kate was talking. And that he hadn't felt well. The nausea was receding before he was aware that he'd been nauseated.

"Are you okay?" Kate was asking.

"Oh, sure." He sat down at his desk, his note pad surprising him as it came into view. He had not remembered making notes. He felt disconnected, overcome with a brittle, metallic tremulousness.

"You say it's hard to live with the idea that you didn't help your mother. But you don't really mean that you want to kill yourself. Do you?"

"Not wanting to live is different than wanting to kill yourself."

"But suicide is something that you've considered?" Forester's voice was slightly more penetrating and forceful than usual. He leaned forward in his chair.

"That's hard to say. Sometimes I feel so awful."

"And no one can convince you that you did all that you could?"

Kate shook her head.

Without warning, the idea occurred to Forester. It was not something he had mulled over, weighed, given time to form and shape itself. Rather it came directly from the cool anger that lodged in his chest like some giant frozen heart.

"We could go on like this forever," Forester said, leaning back in his chair. He assumed a gentle, paternal air. "But I'd like to see you work through this as soon as possible. I've got an idea."

"I don't think I can do with any more ideas." Kate rose and tucked her purse under her arm. "I'd like to leave."

"Please, have a seat." Forester motioned to the seat. "At least finish out this hour."

Kate hesitated, then sat down again, still holding her purse under her arm. Forester sat on the ottoman next to Kate. "You're really not well enough to stop therapy."

"I don't think I need to be here."

"Trust me. It's in your best interest. No one wants you to feel better more than I do." Forester took Kate's hand in his. "This is a very tough time for you." He held her hand for a moment, then placed it in her lap. "Give therapy a chance."

Kate nodded. Forester's plan exploded inside his head. It was the essence of simplicity. He was surprised he hadn't thought of it sooner. But it would have to wait until Kate was ready.

The realization of a plan was a relief in itself. But the sense of urgency remained. He hoped she wouldn't take long. This kind of guilt was so annoying. He wondered how he could stand listening to it, day in and day out. Sometimes he thought it was his personal cross to bear. Well, this time maybe it would be different.

When Kate left, Forester took a short break. He walked through his carefully trimmed Japanese garden and tried to ease his mind into the neat, orderly dimensions of the bonsai trees and precisely raked sand and gravel pathways. Symmetrical dimensions and an even keel. He breathed slowly, taking in the smell of nearby eucalyptus trees and the low ocean fog.

But his mind could not be tamed by the ordinary pleasantries of nature. It was hungry, snapping its ugly gray jaws. If she wanted to be helpless, he would show her what helpless really meant.

Kate met Michelle Draper, her best friend, at a coffee shop on Van Ness, a half block from Channel Six. Tall and graceful, with finely chiseled features and an easy natural smile, Michelle was stunning. Her looks plus her short but impressive career as an investigative journalist at *Rolling Stone* had quickly made her the up-and-coming reporter at the local independent station.

Michelle rushed in, late and breathless. Last night the city administrator had been caught red-handed with a twelve-year-old prostitute. Minutes earlier Michelle scooped an exclusive interview with the administrator and his lawyer. She would be meeting them in an hour. She was sorry to cut short her lunch date with Kate, but she only had time for half a sandwich.

Kate began to tell Michelle about her last session with Forester. But Michelle was miles away, lost in preparation for her interview, wondering how she was going to ask the question. She couldn't simply blurt out, "How could you do it with a twelve-year-old?" Yet that was what she wanted to ask, if given the chance. She thought of the administrator's wife and imagined the shame and humiliation. For a split second it occurred to her that the wife might already have known, and somehow had been a silent accomplice. Michelle dismissed the thought, and tried to pick up the threads of Kate's meeting with Forester.

"Sometimes I wonder about my sanity," Kate said. "The way Dr. Forester looks at me. It's as though he sees right through to what's wrong with me."

"There's nothing wrong with you." Michelle put her hand on Kate's. "You're as solid as . . ." Michelle looked around the coffee shop for a comparison. But the shop was a flaky leftover from hippie days, decorated with concert posters of the Doors, Janis Joplin, Jimi Hendrix, and the Grateful Dead as well as a huge neon sign salvaged from a long-defunct head shop: High Aspirations. She looked down. The countertop was chipped Formica. The stools were worn maroon Naugahyde.

Michelle shrugged and gave Kate a comical grin.

"Go on," Kate said. "Solid as . . ." The two women looked at each other. Michelle laughed first, then Kate. But Kate's laugh was tight, arising from somewhere high in her throat.

"Come on. Lighten up," Michelle said. "You'll be just fine."

"That's what I said to my mom."

"But there's nothing wrong with you. How about you and Owen hitting Hawaii? Or Mexico? There's a cute little place in Cabo San Lucas. With clean water. It's very sexy."

"A week somewhere far away. Maybe you're right. Yeah."

"Sorry, but I've got to run," Michelle said. "See you in a few days?"

"Sure. I'm not going anywhere."

■　　■　　■

It took nearly a month before Kate was sufficiently involved and comfortable in therapy. Initially she was resistant, but most sessions seemed to go well. She actually began to look forward to talking about herself with Forester. He paid attention and seemed anxious to listen to her dreams and fears. He was trying to help. Even so, his observations sometimes made her feel dreadful, reduced her to tears.

The day of their eighth session she was particularly dispirited. Her face was lined; she looked awful. One of her fingernails was broken; she sat pulling on it, then, in a single motion, ripped off the broken rim.

Forester realized that long-term therapy wasn't going to be the answer. Kate wasn't making progress; she looked even worse than at the last visit. She needed some dramatic intervention, some irrefutable demonstration that she really wanted to live. Forester thought again of his idea. It was unorthodox and it smacked of showmanship, a trait that he despised in other psychiatrists. And it could be risky. Yet it made perfect sense.

Have Kate experience the feeling of near death and then offer her the choice. Then she would know, actually understand, that talking of being dead wasn't at all the same as actually wanting to be dead.

He began cautiously. "Let me run a thought by you. Consider the possibility that some of your feelings of guilt and failed responsibility are actually self-generated. In order to make some, albeit faulty, connection with your mother. Guilt is easier to acknowledge than the much more complicated mixture of ambivalent feelings most of us have toward our parents. Particularly when you have trouble communicating. Sometimes it becomes the one emotion that most closely binds the generations together."

"That's not true. I loved her."

"But you saw her so infrequently."

"That's because we were so different. It made talking difficult."

"The two of you irritated each other?"

"It wasn't intentional. She was originally from a small town, and had different interests."

"You would describe your relationship as close?"

"That's not what I'm saying."

"Has it occurred to you that you're creating this sense of guilt in order to establish a stronger bond with her, something more than actually existed? And that you're actually inflicting your depression on yourself?"

"You mean I'm making this up?" Kate looked at her hands, ran her index finger over her torn nail. "That's ridiculous."

"What if it isn't? What if you've boxed yourself into a corner where you have to feel guilty in order to have a real relationship with your mother. By being depressed you can tell yourself that you must have really loved her."

"That's pretty farfetched." Kate shook her head. "Unbelievable, actually."

"But you still feel sad, and think of being dead. Right?"

Kate nodded slowly, her head bobbing up and down in time with the pounding in her head. Forester seemed like a good man but he made no sense. She loved her mother; they just didn't get along. Millions of daughters had the same situation. No, she felt guilty because she had failed her. Because she had let her die.

Kate felt terrible. For a moment she had the thought that

she might throw up. Her hands were sweaty. She tried to concentrate on what Forester was saying, even if it wasn't true. Anything was better than what was running through her mind.

"Just imagine that whether you feel badly is within your control. That your guilt is, in large part, a false emotion. You say you'd like to be dead. I don't accept that. It sounds like so many words you've made yourself believe."

"How would I know?" Kate asked.

"Imagine submitting yourself to pain. How much would you want, and when would you pull away?"

"I don't want any pain."

"Then why do you torture yourself with guilt?"

"It's not in my control."

"Yes, it is. Try a mental experiment. Picture yourself submitting to various punishments, from mild to severe. Make the state of guilt one of the punishments. Play with the image, decide clearly how much you actually want, then discard the rest."

"It's not that easy."

"It can be if you want it to. Think of the act of submission as positive, in that it can demonstrate to you your own actual desires. Prove to yourself that you aren't really interested in being dead, that it's really only a figure of speech."

"Submit to what?"

"Submit to me. I'll show you your own limits."

"You?"

"You trust me? You know I'll do what's right for you?" Kate nodded.

"There's no hurry. Mull it over. If you agree, I think there's a way we can get you feeling better a lot quicker."

"I'll let you know." Kate's head was throbbing. She saw Forester trying to help. He must know what he was doing. She wanted to discuss it with Owen, but she knew how enraged he'd get. Perhaps she could run it by Michelle. No, she'd think it over, on her own. She was levelheaded. She'd make the right decision.

Kate's therapy was going nowhere. Owen watched his wife trudge through the days, her spirits at half-mast. It broke his heart to see her so listless. She no longer cried at night; he sometimes wondered if that wasn't an improvement. And she did manage to keep things going at the store. She even suggested the occasional movie. But Owen knew her heart wasn't in it.

Owen phoned Michelle. The two women had been roommates at Berkeley, and afterward in a Telegraph Hill apartment, now Michelle's apartment. None of the three had any siblings, and they looked upon each other as family. Better than family. Michelle knew Kate nearly as well as Owen, maybe better if one included woman things that he knew nothing about.

"Don't rush her. These things take time," Michelle said.

"I don't think Forester's doing the right thing."

"He's got a great reputation. Besides, how do we know what the right thing is?"

"Psychiatry is all hunt-and-peck, hit-and-miss. I should never have suggested it."

"It's only been a month. That's nothing. You've got to keep in mind that her mom was her only family."

"There's got to be something I can do."

"Try giving Kate some air. She doesn't need you constantly looking over her shoulder and asking her how she's feeling."

"Forester should be making her better."

"You already said that. For Christ's sake, psychiatry isn't like fixing a car," Michelle said.

"Very astute. I'll try to remember that."

"Hang in there. Try being a little less impatient."

"I don't know. I've got this bad feeling."

"Owen. It's Kate's decision."

"Just be cool. Right?"

"I'll take Kate to lunch later in the week. Maybe I can get a handle on how she's feeling. Okay?"

"Sure."

"I'll be talking with you."

Alan Forester's wife was a psychiatric social worker at Los Medanos Community Mental Health Clinic in the Mission District. Tonight was her evening shift. She wouldn't be home until eight-thirty or nine o'clock. Joan was usually in high spirits after work, full of self-esteem for providing bilingual therapy at low rates.

"I can fix them in Spanish and English," she would tease her husband. She saw her services as providing a proper balance to her husband's uptown, primarily long-term analytic practice. "Get them in and out, no lingering over the rough edges. Los Medanos could patch up a whole neighborhood before you could dissect one screwed-up childhood," she would often say with a laugh. It was a friendly rivalry, with Joan always ready to concede experience and training, but not necessarily results. It was a cute game that Forester didn't mind.

Forester rubbed a clove of garlic on a free-range

chicken—organically grown with free run of the roost—and sprinkled on some rosemary and basil. He stuffed the bird with red onions, then trussed it tightly with heavy twine, double knotting the legs. Twice a week dinner was his responsibility. It was only fair.

Forester smiled at the idea of a negotiated marital equality. Yet there was no objective measurement other than the division of chores, the choice of movies and vacation sites. The fair give-and-take of emotions—which was, of course, the real indicator of equality—was impossibly subjective. So many patients accused their spouses of taking more than they gave, and yet when they got out pencil and paper, the whole concept of equality seemed to swim away like some dark slippery eel.

He and Joan had a reasonable marriage, each carrying a share of the bargain. Except in sex. He tried not to think about his recent failures. He never would have predicted that he would be one of those men who would one day require props and special fantasies. But on balance he was better than many men his age who couldn't even get it up.

Forester's infertility had been partially responsible for the dissolution of his first marriage. He had been adamant against adopting. "The child wouldn't be mine, and that's it." His first wife had gone elsewhere to find her family.

Joan had wanted children, but that wasn't part of Forester's equation. Initially there had been periodic outbursts of resentment and accusations of selfishness, but these occurred less frequently as she established her own career. Eventually she laughed and said that even the idea of young children around the house was exhausting. "It's probably for the best," she told herself and Alan. And for the most part, she meant it.

Occasionally Forester would look over at Joan and sense a quiet sadness, even disappointment. From her point of view he had been selfish; he should have gone ahead and adopted a child or two. But it was too late. He would make it up to her in other ways. He would have flowers on the table tonight. And a good full-bodied chardonnay. He would tell Joan how much he loved her, how much she meant to him. She was a good woman and deserved a devoted husband.

The chicken would need to be basted again at eight. He would have nearly an hour for his films. He slipped the first of the videocassettes into the VCR and sat back on the couch in the downstairs living room.

It was liberation day at Auschwitz. Some of the stick figures smiled feebly at the camera. Others were as blank as the ground on which they sat. It was a familiar sight; Forester had watched this segment of the tape, as well as the filmings of other liberations, hundreds of times. He sat forward on the couch, the remote control in his hand, and carefully scrutinized the succession of wasted faces. Sometimes he would hit the pause button, study someone's features, before moving on.

One woman always captured his attention. Her hair was as pale and brittle as straw, but for a few frames it caught the meager, apologetic sun and gave off a single twinkle of light. The woman managed a slight baring of her teeth; sometimes it was a sneer; at other times Forester sensed a wry grin, a massive irony at being saved after there was nothing left to save.

Forester searched for a hint of class, but the woman was beyond social definition, her features no longer revealing anything other than a collective past. She was interchangeable with all the others. Forester, as always, found the face profoundly disagreeable, maybe even hateful. How could she? How could they just allow themselves to be herded into the camps like sheep to the slaughter?

Early in his career he had written a paper on the voluntary aspect of becoming a prisoner of war. After all, anyone with half a brain could have seen the Nazis taking over. There were months, even years, before escape was impossible. To stay on in a state of denial, believing that nothing might happen, was to be delusional.

Initially his paper had been accepted by a major psychiatric journal. Then a barrage of complaints from the editorial board had prevented publication. Forester had withdrawn the paper and reworked the ideas. Years later it appeared not as a theory, but as an aside, an idle speculation, in a paper on the interrelationship of guilt and masochism.

Forester changed the tape, now watching the fall of Poland, the Jewish section of town in flames, the Gestapo rounding up the men and women in their dark overcoats and hats. The black-and-white grainy film drained the people of any residual color or vitality. They moved like ciphers in a theory he would someday fully develop.

In the burning buildings there appeared some lost piece of architecture that would seem more than just vaguely familiar. He offered up his memory to the video, but there was nothing. It is denial, he would tell himself, but the words meant nothing.

A building collapsed; the camera closed in on a man running down the street. He was machine-gunned in the back. *Turn and fight, you coward,* Forester thought.

A group of German soldiers were laughing, standing by the side of a tank. Their sooty faces reeked of the youthful, headlong enthusiasm of the hunt, the kill, the triumph. They weren't afraid, not like the man running away.

There was a recent book by an Israeli in which the survivor of a concentration camp, on his first night after liberation, slept in a log cabin formerly occupied by Nazi soldiers. The young Jew found a pair of Nazi boots under the bed and tried them on. Then he spent the night marching around the cabin, naked except for the boots, imagining how it must have felt to be the aggressor. In the morning the man left the cabin, returned to town, where he changed his name, renounced his Judaism, and opened a candy store on the very street from which he had been taken years earlier.

Look at them lining up. They were all so pathetic.

It was eight o'clock. Forester punched the pause button and went to the kitchen. The chicken was nearly done. He basted it with a plastic syringe, at the same time as he admired the golden-brown twine that was now soaked in the bird's juices.

He returned to the den and started the film again. He had ten minutes before he started in on the vegetables.

THREE

"MR. CARBONE? I'M AF-
raid we have some bad news. It's about your wife." The
words reverberated. The remainder of the conversation
was blurry and difficult to remember. A week later would
come the final verdict from the medical examiner's
office—massive head injuries and cardiorespiratory arrest.
The position of the body on the rocks below the cliff was
most consistent with suicide.

Point Reyes had been Kate's favorite spot along the entire coast. They'd often hiked the trails through the woods
to the beach, and Sunday breakfast at Point Reyes Station
Café was her idea of heaven. Now some apologetic voice
kept telling Owen that his wife was gone. Just like that. "It
wasn't slippery and there was no sign that a piece of
ground along the edge of the cliff had given way. It's hard
to imagine how she could have fallen, but I'll leave it as
accidental. It'll look better."

"Thanks," Owen remembered saying to the voice on the
phone.

Owen was lost. Without warning the rest of his life had
been canceled. He wandered up and down Grant Avenue
and along the Embarcadero, oblivious to the glorious fall
weather and the steady stream of joggers running grace-

fully into their own futures. He kept coming back to their last few days together, replaying their final conversations, now looking for any hidden message, implication, innuendo. They never kept anything from each other. He hadn't heard suicide in her voice, but maybe he hadn't been listening.

It seemed impossible.

Just the week before Kate died, midway through a pepperoni-and-mushroom pizza at Calzone's, they had talked about starting a family. "Maybe it's not just my mom. Maybe it's baby time." They held hands and agreed to work on the next generation of Carbones. Kate smiled and traced her finger along the prominent veins of Owen's hand.

This wasn't a woman on the verge of suicide.

And yet there was no other explanation. Owen tried to imagine her state of mind, driving out to Point Reyes. And not even leaving a note. His mind kept coming back to the image of Kate getting out of her car, looking over the side, and then. . . . It was impossible for him even to think the word *jump*. Each time he would back away, only to return moments later.

He went from bar to bar, opening up the hard-hat joints on Third Street, before spending an abbreviated day at the store. Evenings were the worst, especially mealtime, when he and Kate would normally linger over coffee and wine, sharing little jokes and two-bit events of the day. Instead he hit a succession of neighborhood bars that he did not frequent normally. He stayed away from his regular haunts and his favorite bartenders. He couldn't face conversation. A couple times he tried talking to Michelle, but it was hard even to finish a sentence.

He walked the streets late at night, inviting the fatigue that would allow him to return to the apartment for a few hours' sleep. He passed through the heart of darkened Chinatown without fear of being mugged. Physical pain would have been a blessed diversion. A black eye or a broken nose would certainly be better than the emptiness that sucked away his very life.

What good was it to say to himself that he loved Kate with all his heart? She couldn't hear him. The words were a mockery. He had failed her.

He stayed in his apartment as little as possible. Every item, from the towels in the bathroom to the rainbow decal on the kitchen window, reminded him of Kate. Yet he often found himself holding something of hers—a hairbrush, her scruffy red slippers, even her checkbook. He read the entries, seeing where she spent her money. He was not snooping; he wanted only to be with her on her daily chores. At night, under cover of darkness and the alcohol, on her side of the bed, he cried and rocked himself to sleep.

Michelle stopped by Cala Foods and shopped for tomorrow's get-together. She had waited two weeks, until Owen finally agreed. She wanted to say "memorial," but the word stuck in her throat, tears welling up at the thought. Moments later she was home with her bag of groceries, peering into the darkness of her apartment. It felt different, like some abandoned stage setting that she had accidentally stumbled upon.

An hour ago she'd interviewed several adolescent prostitutes who came forward to speak out about the city administrator. One of the girls was eleven. Her face was a

mixture of street toughness and a peculiar innocence that
disturbed Michelle. The city administrator had paid the
girl seventy-five dollars and given her a vial of coke. The
thought of a sixty-year-old man with an eleven-year-old
girl made Michelle sick.

She wanted the police to throw the book at the administrator. But that was outside, in the street, at the station,
wherever public matters mattered. But now she was inside,
alone with the feelings that she sidestepped during the
day. Michelle sat in the darkened living room, thinking of
Kate, trying to understand what Kate might have felt. But
she understood nothing.

She dropped the groceries on the kitchen table, then
went and stretched out on the couch, exhausted and
vaguely disoriented. The darkness pushed in, claustropho-
bic and unfamiliar. The thought of preparing a meal for
thirty was overwhelming. She considered phoning a ca-
terer in the morning. No. This would be a family gathering. Which meant home cooking.

She forced herself from the couch and went to the
kitchen. She would spend the night by herself, preparing.
Thinking. Remembering.

Michelle had the small apartment softly lit, with candles
on the windowsill, the fireplace mantel, and each of the
side tables and coffee tables. Owen was acutely aware of
the flickering flames. He associated the candles with his
immediate postcollege years, when Michelle and Kate had
shared the two-bedroom apartment. The candles spoke of
so many romantic nights, Michelle out at a movie or on a
date, Kate and Owen snuggled up on the couch, comparing
his size to Coit Tower in the distance.

On the kitchen counter was Michelle's homemade lasagna, salad, roast turkey, and stuffing.

Several couples took turns telling humorous stories about Kate. Each finished by offering a toast and a silent prayer. Owen was aware that many of the stories about Kate did not include him. He had anticipated that everyone would be a bit uncomfortable, but there was an additional conspiracy of averted eyes and abbreviated conversations that he had not expected. Several of the women seemed to flash glances of hostility, and preferred chatting with each other.

Owen was halfway through his third scotch when he realized the awful truth. Wives commit suicide when their husbands fail them, or worse yet, drive them to it. He saw it in their eyes. They held him responsible.

That's not it at all, he wanted to shout. *God only knows that I adored her. We were happy. We didn't have pretense and bullshit like most of you who are staring at me like I'm some sort of killer.*

Cool it, Owen, he said to himself. *These are your friends. Sure. Then why are they all avoiding me, and looking at me like that?*

He motioned to Michelle. They stepped into the kitchen. "I don't think I can take much more," Owen said.

"I know it's tough. Give them another half hour, then I'll say that you're not feeling well." Michelle gave Owen a hug, her cheek pressed against his. He could feel her body shaking and her tears running down his cheek. They held each other for some time, until Michelle pulled away and dried her eyes.

As though reading his mind, she said, "They don't understand. I know how much Kate loved you. It wasn't your fault."

"We'd started reading the Sunday want ads, even considered buying a small condo. And kids. We were talking about Carbone juniors. We got along fine. Honestly."

Michelle punched Owen lightly on the shoulder. "Come on, soldier. Give them another few minutes. Then you slip out and I'll carry the ball. Tomorrow we'll talk."

Forester awakened with a start, his heart pounding. It was three in the morning. Joan was curled at his side, deep in sleep. A window rattled, a floorboard creaked. Every sound was magnified. Forester slid out of bed, careful not to awaken Joan. He went to the bathroom, drank a glass of water, then returned to their bedroom. He sat on the edge of the bed, his feet dangling.

In a few weeks he would be giving the keynote lecture at the annual Institute meeting. It was an honor usually reserved for one of the prominent senior analysts approaching retirement. Forester felt particularly honored to be chosen at his tender age of fifty-seven. He considered speaking on a wide variety of topics from medicine and literature to various aspects of memory. Normally he would be enthusiastic, even excited, over having a captive audience listen to his ideas. But none of the subjects seemed particularly appealing.

It was probably just a case of nerves, something he often experienced while struggling with the beginnings of a new book. He was glad he had blocked out some free time in his morning schedule. It would allow him to think without interruption.

But it wasn't that type of anxiety. It was a more generalized disquiet, a sense of apprehension. Kate Carbone's name popped into his mind. Forester flinched. The *Chronicle* had not specifically mentioned suicide, stating only that Kate Carbone had fallen to her death. But there was no mention of an accident, either, so that the article read as a suicide. Joan and Forester had had a single discussion about Kate the day her death was in the newspapers. Since then Joan had not mentioned it, the absence of any reference to Kate's death in their daily conversations as damning as a direct confrontation. In her eyes Forester saw reflected the knowledge that he had failed his patient.

And she was right.

Worse still, he knew that Joan's condemnation was fueled by his failures in the bedroom.

The word *impotence* came to mind, but Forester immediately dismissed it. But he had to admit that it had been over two months since they had made love. Joan continued to act as if it were temporary, nothing to get alarmed over, but now and then Forester saw worry and concern, even bitterness, poking through her uneasy pretense. Forester knew he had to get over whatever held him down; then a good unself-conscious fuck or two could right everything between them. He would put his mind to it. But right now, the less said the better. One day he would be his old self again.

Forester stared out into the darkness of the bedroom. He was surprised to note that the digital clock read four o'clock. He didn't remember having enough thoughts to fill an entire hour. Perhaps he had drifted off, though that seemed unlikely, as he remained sitting on the side of the bed, his slippers still dangling at the same angle. He sensed an unaccounted-for period of time preceded by some thoughts of Kate Carbone that he could no longer recall.

Someday soon he would have to go over all of their sessions and find out what had gone wrong. He considered going to his den and getting out his notes, but he didn't feel that well. He was vaguely nauseated. The prospect of going through his observations frightened him, as though he had no idea what he had written or what he might find. One day soon he would definitely look. He owed it to himself and to his patients.

"There's something I must tell you," Michelle had said to Owen over the phone. "I'll meet you right after the board of supervisors meeting. It should break by midafternoon."

The two of them sat across from each other in a booth at the Cigar Store, one of the few remaining original North Beach coffeehouses. "There were things she didn't want you to know," Michelle began. "Woman things."

"Maybe we'd better have a drink." Owen motioned to the bartender, who brought two glasses of Chianti. Owen downed the glass and ordered another. Across the street, in the park, two old women in black sat on a bench and knitted. Behind them a boy and a girl played with a Frisbee. The girl was laughing; her blond hair caught the late afternoon sun. North Beach was Kate and Owen's neighborhood. It was a weekend ritual to walk from their one-bedroom apartment on Telegraph Hill to the Cigar Store for two double espressos. Then they might walk to the Embarcadero, look at the row of freighters, and imagine steaming off to see the world. Dreams and plans and home again.

"I think you're right. I think her problem started with Dr. Forester."

"How's that?' Owen asked.

"We had lunch just before . . ." Michelle paused, took a deep breath, and started again. "She said she was feeling a little better and had told Dr. Forester that she was going to quit therapy. And do you know what he said?"

"She didn't tell me much about her sessions. She knows how I feel about shrinks in general." Owen was acutely aware of mixing past and present tense when speaking of Kate.

"He came over to where she was sitting, sat down on the ottoman, and told her, 'You're not that well.' Those were his exact words." Michelle picked at a crumb of French bread. She finally flicked it on the floor.

" 'Do you think there's any truth to that?' " Kate kept asking me. " 'Do you really think I'm sick?' "

"She never told me," Owen said.

"There's more." Michelle looked away, at an old man hunched over his coffee. With a long curved fingernail he picked at a spot on his ancient coat. "Boy, it's times like this that I wished I still smoked." She reached out and lightly touched Owen's hand.

It was just the two of them. He looked at her hand on his as a gesture of friendship.

"I've debated not saying anything. But in the end I knew I'd tell you, so I might as well get it over with."

"There was another man?" Owen asked.

"Of course not. It's not that simple, and nothing more than suspicion. The day before she died, she phoned me at the station. She was in a panic. 'I think I might be losing my mind,' she said. 'Especially if any of what Dr. Forester says is true. He wants me to come three days a week, or more, if I can afford it. He says it's very important.' Kate insisted on discussing it further over lunch. A half hour later she phoned back and canceled. She said everything was just fine and that she had forgotten that she had an appointment with Dr. Forester. It was her tone of voice. She sounded different, so distant. That was the last time we talked."

"Did she say anything else, drop any hints?"

"Apparently Dr. Forester told her that a trial separation might allow her to get more in touch with her grief and sadness. He felt that you were treating her feelings too lightly, and that she should have some time alone."

"Trial separation? Are you sure?"

"Kate was as floored as you are. But apparently Dr. Forester is quite impressive. Even when she told me how shocked she was to hear him talk like that, there was a note of awe in her voice. She kept telling me how he was so well respected in the community. I told her that he was full of shit."

"And?"

"And she said that she wished she could believe that."

"So what do you think happened?" Owen asked.

"I think that bastard got her so mixed up that she couldn't cope. That's what I think."

"You know," Owen said, his jaws set, his voice as dead as steel, "If I thought that there was any truth to what you're thinking . . ."

"I know. That's why I hesitated to tell you." Michelle

was looking directly into Owen's eyes. "It's probably nothing, just my imagination."

"Yes or no? You think Forester's got something to do with Kate?" Owen's voice was all business.

"I'm not sure," she said.

"There's still more, isn't there?" Owen's face was flushed, the redness spreading into his neck and upper chest.

"Honestly, it's mainly this gut feeling that I can't shake. It's like sensing that something horrible happened. But there isn't any more."

"Kate was strong. No one could have pulled the wool over her eyes."

"She was different after her mom died. More vulnerable."

For some time Owen stared out the window, watching the traffic stream down Columbus Avenue. Nothing made sense. He was so tired. Maybe his mind was playing tricks on him, telling him that Michelle was suggesting more than she was saying.

He looked up at Michelle. There was something in the way she was looking at him. He tugged at his collar, as though straightening his shirt might right his tipped mood. But he felt as off-center as before—confused, angry, sad. He belted down the rest of his Chianti, then reached over and finished off the rest of Michelle's. If only he could get a good night's sleep, he thought as he kissed Michelle good-bye and headed over to the store. It was too early to go home, and the idea of a good night's sleep was merely something to get him through the day.

Owen's store was a converted souvenir and post-card shop on upper Grant Avenue. The high walls were covered with posters from the twenties, large photos of the opening of the Golden Gate Bridge, bread lines on Market Street. The three aisles were stocked with hard-to-find jazz records. Bins of seventy-eights sat virtually untouched, victims of the new electronics that removed surface noise. CDs were making the seventy-eights worthless. There had been a scavenger collector who offered Owen ten cents on the dollar, wholesale, but Owen wanted to be surrounded by real history, not sanitized, scratch-resistant discs that didn't even smell like records.

In the back, Owen booked sports. It was a penny-ante cigar store operation, with Owen avoiding any big bets that were likely to attract attention. His rule of thumb was one week's salary. A man lost more, he was liable to stiff you, or make a scene, or blow the whistle. And all the business was referral. First Owen met you, made a quick character assessment, and limited the action to less than a hundred dollars. You had to have your own track record before you could do four digits. Caution was his motto.

His father had been one of the biggest bookies in Chicago. Then a competitor got him three years in prison. It broke his father.

Owen had never intended to get in the business. At heart he wanted to play music, but his college days had taught him the inverse relationship between aesthetics and economics. He played portable keyboard in a high-stepping high-decibel rock and roll band at a Telegraph Avenue beer joint and made fifty dollars a night. For continuously recycling five chords. Ten bucks a chord. Sundays he played the local jazz joints for tips only. In his high black zippered boots, oversized second-hand tweed jacket and a porkpie hat he had found at a thrift shop, he was in pauper's heaven. His goal was to master the poly-rhythms of Tristano and Bartok, and the chord changes of Monk and combine them into his own unique style.

Years later he realized that uniqueness never arose through emulation. But by then he was disenchanted with public performances, limiting his piano playing to the occasional gig on upper Grant. Mostly he played at home, in jeans and tee-shirt, on his electronic Yamaha that fit into a corner of the cramped living room. Sometimes he'd slip on the jacket and porkpie hat, à la Mingus, and entertain their friends.

And he'd accompany Kate. She'd also been a music major and had sung in a few local productions, mainly Cole Porter and Gershwin. She had a clean no-nonsense style. Owen normally wasn't much on popular music, but he loved playing for her, listening to her. Being with her.

One day, as a birthday surprise, Owen brought home the keys to the store. *You sing to the customers and I'll make ends meet.*

Owen opened the front door and looked around. "What's the point?" he said out loud, standing in front of the light switch. Either way it was still darkness.

He did not flip on the lights. Instead he locked the door behind him, went to the back counter, pulled out Gershwin's *Porgy and Bess*, found the track "Bess You Is My Woman," and blasted the music into the empty store. Gray muted light filtered through the poster-covered windows, hanging heavy in the aisles like some personal unshakable fog. Tears streamed down his face.

Kate had danced naked in front of the bathroom mirror, singing through the open bathroom window. It was North

Beach, and no one cared. She would sing her way into bed. Afterward she would hum, no words necessary.

He had brought the record back to the store the week after she died.

He looked down at the ancient jacket cover. There were smeared fingerprints. Some might have been Kate's. She would stand staring at the cover and imagining herself at some speakeasy. She wasn't wild about Owen's booking, but at least the crime was manageable and wasn't any worse than investment banking or creative financing. Owen reassured her that no one in San Francisco was busted for the kind of small-scale operation he ran. The cops in North Beach were cool. Besides, it was a family tradition.

Kate agreed to look the other way.

Owen added that they took bets at the Cotton Club.

She would hold the record jacket and dream of them together, the perfect hip couple.

This was not a woman who would kill herself.

Owen positioned his fingers over each of the fingerprints, as though holding a seance. Afterlife was nonsense; he and Kate were separated forever. Still, he wondered whether or not somewhere out in the infinite darkness she might be looking in on him. It wasn't even a thought or a belief, but rather a feeling that gave him a momentary vague sense of comfort.

And obligation.

He owed it to her.

Underneath the counter, in a drawer marked "seventy-eight needles," Owen kept the pearl-handled revolver his father had left him. Owen never knew whether or not it had been fired. Sometimes when he tried to understand his father, he would sniff the oiled barrel and guess. But the gun was as clean as a whistle. It could have been ornament or implement. Owen wasn't even sure which he would have preferred.

Owen held the gun in his hand, a hand remarkably similar in shape to his father's, and saw his father's fingers wrapped around the grip, his index finger against the trigger. Perhaps it had been in jest, just to threaten. Or had it been the real thing? In college English Owen had learned to beware of the smoking gun. Introduce a gun into a story and it had to serve a purpose. But that was drama and this was real life. All over the country there were storekeepers with loaded guns under their cash registers. If they were lucky, the guns weren't fired. They went from generation to generation with no more meaning than having a security alarm.

Or they were fired and history redirected itself.

Owen tried to imagine putting the gun to his own head and pulling the trigger. It was the most personal and violent of crimes. Worse yet would be jumping from a cliff. He started to imagine how Kate might have seen the rocks below, the waves, the beach . . . He steered his mind away. He loved her. He told her so every day. That should have been enough. He had failed her.

Owen pointed the gun out into the darkened store. He had the urge to shoot. Forester's face loomed up. It would feel good, as though confronting Forester could somehow discharge the ache in his heart. The gun wasn't traceable. One shot through the forehead, or the temple, or at the base of the neck. But first Forester should know why, and that would mean face to face.

Owen spun the empty chambers. He had the gun exclusively for show. He didn't even know how the safety worked, or what size bullets the gun held. He could go into an ammunition store and say, "Fill 'er up." Truth was, the only weapon he had ever fired was an air gun at the Cook County fair; he had missed the largest target.

But, if there was any truth to what Michelle had said. . . .

For some time he held the gun, feeling its weight, its power, wondering. Then, reluctantly, he slipped the non-smoking gun behind the seventy-eight needles.

FOUR

WITH HIS NEW REFER-
ral—Michelle Draper, the TV reporter—the day promised
to be interesting. If he could get through the hour with
smirking Jim Van Allen. Van Allen was a prominent San
Francisco internist. The man had it all—a privileged upbringing, a thriving practice, a good family, community respect, even supercilious good looks.

For no apparent reason Jim Van Allen had begun to
abuse his female patients. At first it was subtle innuendo,
then he began to make overt and often demeaning comments about their underwear, their figures, their breast
size, or their personal lives. There was the hint of proposition, but mostly the comments were thinly veiled sarcasm. There had been multiple complaints to the medical
society.

Several of his former office staff also came forward, relating with a mixture of embarrassment and bitterness their
own tales of harrassment and office sex. Many of the
women's accusations were undocumented hearsay. Conse-
quently none had filed civil complaints. Instead they
salved their humiliation with a barrage of sordid details,
including allegations of a variety of Van Allen affairs at
his hospital.

It was a sticky situation. The medical society concluded

that his behavior had been reprehensible, but there were no claims of malpractice or other formal charges that required official investigation.

He was referred to the medical society division that handled the unclassified complaints. They decided that he would best fit the category of impaired physician, a slot normally reserved for drug and alcohol offenders.

The committee and the women settled on Van Allen receiving counseling; Van Allen had reluctantly chosen Forester.

Forester had originally balked at the idea of trying to provide therapy to someone against his will. The medical society asked him to give Van Allen three months. If there was no progress, Forester could terminate treatment.

"It's not treatment," Forester said to the committee. "Not unless someone wants to change." But despite his initial protestations, Forester agreed to working with the "impaired physician."

Van Allen came twice a week, filling up Forester's consultation room with his gassy demeanor. Not once did he admit to anything more than possibly making some mildly off-color remarks. "Naturally it was foolish to think that they would all share my same sense of humor. I should have known better, and if you call that a mistake, I guess I'd have to agree. Sometimes you think someone is on the same wavelength as you, so you make some little innocuous comment. Then they get all upset. If anything, my fault is not reading people as well as I might. Of course, what would you expect? I'm only a humble family doc. I'm not trained in the intricacies of the mind."

As Forester had predicted, nothing in Van Allen's behavior changed. After two months he was as abrasive and offensive as ever. Forester hated the sight of him—it was invariably a dreadful, useless tug-of-war hour—yet he persisted.

He couldn't explain his motivation to himself, but sometimes Forester had the distinct sensation that there was some greater reason behind his persistence. Some as yet unrevealed purpose.

Today, as usual, Van Allen was sitting in the leather chair as though he were astride some stubborn beast. Forester was impatient, another hour turning into hide-and-seek.

"I know you think these sessions are a waste of time," Forester said. "But can you honestly tell me you're pleased with the way you've treated your patients, your staff, and particularly your wife?"

"What about my wife?"

"Try for a moment putting yourself in her position. How do you think she feels?"

Van Allen paused, as though weighing his thoughts. "My wife understands," he said.

"Understands what?" Forester braced himself for another snide remark.

"I am an evil man with evil thoughts." Van Allen looked down at the rug, an uncharacteristic gesture suggestive of some element of remorse. For the first time in their visits he did not attempt to stare Forester down. He kept his eyes averted and remained silent. Forester was stunned, even moved by Van Allen's sudden reticence. He waited for what he presumed was going to be the first insight, perhaps even a confession.

"Yes," Van Allen repeated in a matter-of-fact tone. "I

am an evil man with evil thoughts." He kept his head down, his hands folded in his lap.

"Take your time," Forester said after another lengthy silence.

"There's nothing more to say." Van Allen's face was grim; his voice was flat and had an uncharacteristic ring of honesty.

"I realize this is difficult. Maybe you could explore how you're feeling right now?"

Van Allen looked up at Forester. He was smiling that old inflammatory shit-eating grin. At the same time his body drew itself up into his familiar self-confident pose. The transformation took only an instant; it had the quality of a mime shifting roles. Van Allen had reconstituted himself.

"The Lord Jesus understands. We are all evil." Van Allen let out a small blood-curdling laugh.

"I'm afraid I don't understand," Forester said. He was enraged to have been so easily duped. Van Allen was looking at him as though it had been a one-move checkmate. He fully expected Van Allen to say, "Gotcha." Forester hoped that Van Allen could not see the anger rising in his cheeks.

"Sure you do. Original sin. We've all got it. I struggle against it, as I'm sure you must. Sometimes it gets the best of us. My wife and I pray every night. She knows exactly what I've been through. I guess it's just something I'll have to live with."

Van Allen went on to describe his religious conversion. He and his wife held weekly Bible readings in their home. "The human condition is sinful. And therapy isn't going to help. It's a matter of prayer and forgiveness." Van Allen did acknowledge that his interest in religion was relatively recent. Forester calculated that it began at about the same time as Van Allen's personality began to change. Forester put two and two together. The doctor had seen himself changing, knew he needed an explanation that he could use with himself and others, including his wife. He became a "born-again" and stocked himself with clichés to ward off the cold of his behavior. "We are all evil" was not a confession, but a diversion, the interposition of a canned phrase shutting out any light of self-revelation.

Beside Forester's hatred of the man huddled a separate, contrary emotion. There was the subtle hint of some delicious pleasure. Of course. Just like that, he had the subject of his lecture at the Institute. How wonderful was the unconscious, extracting some unexpected value from this slimy greaseball.

It would be called "The Elmer Gantry Syndrome Revisited."

Perhaps that was inaccurate. Gantry had been a phony who had used religion for exploitation. Van Allen was different. He was using religious vernacular as an alibi to himself. As much as he detested organized religion, Forester acknowledged that it wasn't formal religion's fault that the doctor was making his patients completely undress and then forget the examining gown. Formal religion had not inspired Van Allen to tell them they needed dieting or exercise, as he flashed his flirtatious, goading smile that said that if they lost weight or toned up, he might be personally interested.

The man was a complete sociopath. Everything compartmentalized. Fuck your secretary, home to the wife and kids, slip out to the peep shows, tie up some woman in a motel room—each action disconnected from the others, explained away in some simple phrase: "I am an evil man." The words were as meaningless as mindlessly singing the "Star Spangled Banner."

He was evil personified. There was no doubt. And he was hiding under the skirts of religion. Religion, original sin, domination, humiliation—the permutations were endless. Forester felt he could free-associate a lecture on the spot.

Forester knew it was beyond his control, but he wanted to see Van Allen punished. It was truly offensive to realize that he'd go on teasing and taunting the women who came to him with trust. They should take away the man's license. He didn't deserve to be a doctor.

After he had completed the lecture he would tell the medical society committee that Van Allen had not responded to treatment.

Through the bay window in Dr. Forester's home office, Michelle could see a well-tended Japanese garden. The shrubs and trees were neatly pruned, the dirt path recently raked. The consultation room was similarly uncluttered. One wall was lined with books. Included among the rows of psychiatry books were several volumes on forensic medicine. The top shelf was devoted to the works of Camus, Sartre, Kierkegaard, and Heidegger. Another contained a collection of books on the Holocaust, including several by Primo Levi. On the shelf below were the complete works of Kafka. On the opposite wall was a single black-and-white photograph of a young mother cradling an infant child.

Dr. Forester motioned Michelle to a well-worn black

leather armchair. Michelle looked at the matching leather ottoman and saw Dr. Forester sitting beside Kate and telling her she wasn't well enough to stop therapy. But Forester, conservatively dressed in a plain gray suit, was on the other side of the room, seated at an antique desk, his body at an angle to her. His voice was low and soothing, friendly in a nonintrusive way. Contrary to her expectations, he was without airs.

Since Kate's death Owen had become obsessed with the possibility of Forester's involvement. He couldn't say why or how, but it had to be. Michelle felt responsible; it had been her offhanded comment that had started Owen's mind lurching in the direction of Forester somehow manipulating Kate. During their daily talks she tried to downplay her original assessment of Forester, but she wasn't convincing. Or entirely convinced. Kate was the last person on earth Michelle could imagine throwing herself off a cliff.

Last week, toward the end of a bottle of wine and a late snack across from the TV station, Michelle had come up with the idea of going to Forester, simulating a depression similar to Kate's. "We could see how he responds. If there's any hanky-panky or unprofessional behavior, anything suspicious, we'd know. And I'd shove his face on the ten o'clock news, make him public enemy number one."

"Fix his wagon, bust his balls, then we'd fucking ruin him," Owen said.

It had been Michelle's spur-of-the moment attempt to lighten Owen's mood. But once out in the open, the plan seemed to make sense. It developed a life and a logic of its own, with Owen's face brightening as he and Michelle traded opening lines for the news spot.

Now, uncomfortable in the leather chair, Forester the very picture of propriety, Michelle's schemes felt ridiculous. It was another of her harebrained judgments, imagining Forester had anything to do with Kate's suicide.

Michelle reminded herself of the sound of Kate's voice the last time they had spoken. It was Forester's fault, she told herself. Something bad had happened.

"Begin at the beginning," Forester was saying. He looked at her intently.

Michelle wondered if the look was practiced or genuine. She tucked her legs beneath her, wrapped her arms around her knees, and made herself small in the large armchair.

"I feel lost," she said, her voice barely audible. She watched Forester for any change of expression, but Forester was distant and clinical. He jotted notes on a pad he balanced on one thigh.

"Maybe it's early burnout, too many hours at the station, the rest of my life on hold, that kind of thing. Take the news. It seems so repetitive. What's the point of chronicling the inevitable? Crime, corruption, war, famine—you name it, I flesh it out."

Michelle and Owen had spent two lunches deciding on the best opening, as though it were some chess match. They had settled on the what's-the-use? gambit. It was an easy mood to slip into. It would allow for infinite detail and wouldn't require Michelle to dredge up any major personal issues. Michelle was just warming up when Forester sidestepped her complaints and asked about her parents.

"They're not the issue," Michelle said.

"I understand. But I need a little background information."

"There's really nothing to say. My father left when I was seven. My mother's in Oroville, preying on her fifth husband. He's a wholesale butcher. Hopefully he's a good match." Michelle gave Forester a slight smile. She didn't feel like saying more. There was so much unresolved bitterness. She never knew what mood might pop up when she talked of her mother and her alcoholism and her four unraveled marriages.

Michelle saw her once a year, when she remembered. Out of sight, out of mind. For the purposes of these sessions, it would have been preferable to create fictional parents, but using her own mother would require less effort. Besides, it would be illuminating to watch Forester sort through her mother's self-destructive behavior.

Forester continued, his voice calm and unthreatening. She kept reminding herself why she was there. She shifted in her seat, allowing her skirt to rise above knee level, her long sculpted legs available for viewing. Forester did not seem to notice.

"I gather you don't think much of your mother."

"No, but that's not why I'm here. It's a job thing, I'm sure of it. Maybe it's a premidlife crisis. I was always a bit precocious."

"It's that hard talking about your mother?"

"Not at all. But not on my dollar. She's a problem, but not my problem."

"Your present discomfort has nothing to do with her? You're sure?"

"Absolutely."

"A simple question. How do you know you're sure?

You seem to have so much emotion invested in not having any emotion about her."

"I'd really prefer not discussing her. It'll take forever."

"I've got time."

"Well, I don't. I was hoping you could give me some sense of direction, and that doesn't mean toward the past."

"She's that bad?"

Michelle nodded. She hadn't counted on her face flushing and her eyes welling with tears. She could feel herself veering in a direction not of her choosing. Forester was asking more about her mother, and she wanted to leave. She shifted in the chair, suddenly impatient for the end of the hour. He was raising questions she should have dealt with a long time ago.

She examined his expression; it was one of genuine concern. "Tell me and I'll make you feel better," his softly lined, gentle-featured face said. "That's not why I'm here," she wanted to say as she found herself blurting out long-repressed details of her mother's bourbon-soaked attacks on family life. She wanted to tell Forester that Owen and Kate were her only real family, and now Kate was dead. That was why she was in tears. But she found herself condemning herself for not having seen her mother in over a year. One phone call every few months, never more than a few minutes, have to watch the phone bill. And the following chill of defeat, of a mother-daughter relationship that had ended in mutual bitterness and sense of failure.

To her surprise Forester interrupted, concluding the session. "It looks like we have a lot of ground to cover. Don't worry, the first few visits are always the toughest. Be patient." He stood up and walked across the room and shook her hand. It was cool and dry and light in her hand. He gave her a slight formal nod. "Till next week."

And Michelle was out in the street, blinking and squinting in a sun that seemed too bright, almost painful. Like leaving the movie theater in the middle of the afternoon. She found herself looking at her feet as she walked to her car, not quite certain of her footing.

After Michelle left his office, Dr. Forester saw a succession of marital problems. Routine stuff related in dull, self-important urgency, each problem so monumental in its personal implication, yet nearly identical to the person who followed. He listened politely and daydreamed of Michelle. He kept coming back to the wonderful sheen of her legs. While middle-aged Mrs. Seifert sobbed that her husband was spending too much time playing golf, Forester imagined Michelle in her shower, one leg braced against the shower stall, as she shaved. Then she would run her hands over each leg, enjoying the smoothness, the satiny texture rising up over Forester's cheeks as he ran his face up between her thighs.

Mrs. Seifert stopped crying and looked at Forester. "Am I boring you?" she said.

"We've been over this ground before," Forester answered. "One of the reasons you're coming here is to learn new ways of looking at old problems. No, I'm not bored. I'm frustrated. And a little disappointed. You're a smart woman, capable of seeing a bigger picture."

"You think I'm smart?" the woman said. "If I'm so smart, how come I've been coming here for almost six months? I can't see any improvement." Mrs. Seifert reached for her purse, as though she were considering walking out. Forester said nothing, turning to his notepad and making a few scribbles.

"What's that supposed to mean? I threaten to walk out and you make notes." The woman dropped her purse onto the rug. There was a dull thud and a sigh. The woman fell back into the leather chair. Forester tapped his pen on his front teeth, his mouth filling up with a loud clicking sound. Outside an occasional car passed. The woman looked at him. "That's the problem, isn't it? I don't have any balls. My husband treats me like dirt, you treat me like dirt, and I take it, like a vacuum cleaner. I should be out the door, phoning the medical society to complain about your outrageous bills, but no, I just look at my date-book and plan the next visit like some perfect masochist."

"Good. Now we're getting somewhere." Forester put down his note pad. "Try thinking this way for a bit and let's see where this takes us."

Michelle would wait.

The last patient of the day, a young Korean woman, described her fear that Japanese cars were somehow invading the country. "Most people think they're here just to destroy the economy, but there's more. Just read the papers and see how many accidents involve Japanese cars. They're going after the people." Otherwise the woman was normal. Idée fixe, Forester thought. The woman went on to describe the pounding in her chest, the sweaty palms, the difficult swallowing. She was sure she was going to die. And it was the fault of the Tercels and Celicas and Subaru sedans.

Forester took copious notes. How wonderful was the human mind, the biology of agoraphobia and panic attacks shaped by a centuries-old clash of civilizations. The woman spoke quietly of her increasing inability to leave the house—Hondas and Toyotas were everywhere. This woman would make a good character in some short story. The desk in his study was filled with old notebooks stuffed with scraps of paper that he browsed through when starting a new book. It was the only area of his house that was not neatly tended. He looked upon his drawer as being a metaphor for the human unconscious, thus it was pointless to tidy up. The rest of the house and garden were neat reminders of what he could control.

He never wrote about actual patients; rather the drawers of quirks and odd comments served as catalyst, his mind bending histories into anonymous anecdotes.

She was so interesting that Forester forgot to be angered by her helplessness.

After the Korean woman left, Dr. Forester opened the window to let out the cloying scent of garlic. Pickled kimchee, he presumed. His home was three miles from the ocean and a half mile from the bay, but he could almost see the fresh ocean breeze responsible for the brilliant blue freshly scrubbed sky. No, San Francisco wasn't New York, but who cared. It was clean and light and people's problems seemed to carry less sense of foreboding. After his residency he had practiced for two years at Harkness Pavilion, but the filth and noise and constant aggravation of daily life had driven him west, away from 168th Street. He smiled—in New York stating your address was like revealing your astrologic sign. East Fifty-fourth, Bleeker Street, Central Park West, Aries, Pisces.

Moving was like changing your birthdate.

He took off his coat and tie and walked down the back stairs to his garden. He had spent several hours over the weekend cutting and pruning. Now he was double-checking, on the lookout for the occasional scraggly, protruding branch. With a methodical precision he whacked off any unevenness, enjoying the knowledge that the shrubs at both ends of the garden were at exactly equal heights. It was nature controlled, a queer balance of growing things. Dr. Forester stood with his clippers at his side, looking for something else to cut. But the garden was essentially geometric now, and he reluctantly put the clippers back in his toolshed.

The problem is one of too much free time, he said to himself as he walked back into the house. *If I played golf or poker or bridge, or believed in community affairs, or could find a cause. Some hobby that soaked up the hours.*

He was stalled in his writing. Normally, after completion of a book, he would spend his mornings gathering ideas for his next novel. But it had been over six months since he had seriously sat down at his desk and organized his thoughts.

He toyed with the idea of working on something completely different—maybe a medical detective story, or a good old-fashioned psychological thriller. The thought frightened him. All his books had been about psychiatry, with major components of thinly disguised autobiography. He was not sure he had it in him to write a completely imaginative work. He promised himself to think harder about a plot line, or a character—some beginning thread that would work itself into a routine of morning hours at his desk.

In the meantime each day was an eternity, the minute

hand of his life weighted down with this rising sense of unreality that he could not shake. He checked his watch; bedtime was far over the horizon, somewhere where they were manufacturing those scary Hondas.

For two weeks he had debated calling 441-2987. He enjoyed rolling the number over and over in his mind. It was like having foreplay with a secret friend, someone out there in the darkness. Sometimes the number had more substance than his carefully chosen furniture or the arbitrary geometry of his garden. The harsh edges of the shrubbery were suddenly irritating. He should let everything grow wild, one large organic mess. But he couldn't; it wasn't his disposition. No, everything had to be in its place as though his life were carefully filed in a succession of manila folders.

It could be different, it really could, he told himself as he went inside. If only he knew what to do. He thought of Michelle curled up in the chair, saying she was lost. She had no idea what that really meant. He wanted to laugh, but it wasn't funny. Instead there rose in his throat a low, stifled growl. It was the sound of some enraged animal straining against his leash.

He could not remember getting angry, but there it was, that awful rage welling up again. It was as though his moods fell unannounced from the sky.

He went into his study, a small oak-paneled room with a skylight, a writing desk, and a leather couch. He lay on the couch, his feet dangling over the arm rest, and balanced the phone on his chest. He dialed the number.

"Yes?" The woman's voice was husky and tough. Forester imagined her to be tall and thick in the shoulders. She would stand with her feet apart, hands on hips, in a defiant stance. The voice said she didn't take shit from anyone. With her it would be give-and-take.

"I understand you like to be tied up and treated badly, like someone who's done wrong and deserves to be punished." Forester spoke slowly in a low gravelly voice, letting his words resonate in the receiver.

"Who is this? Am I supposed to know you?"

"Not yet. I was referred."

"I'm sorry to be short with you, but I've got a whopping headache. Perhaps you could phone back tomorrow. Just for tonight you can put pain on hold." The disconnected line hummed in his ear.

She was so free and easy, the voice of experience. He would phone back, crawl up inside the receiver, huddle against her words. She could be what he was looking for—a woman who was comfortable with pain, no, not comfortable, desirous. Someone who could understand the descending movement of anger—the fist traveling downward, like some flaming star from another galaxy, crashing to earth in a thud of bruised flesh.

Forester debated steering his mind away toward safer thoughts. But he didn't want to be distracted. He wanted to slide deeper into the feeling, down into that spiral of anger and resentment, the silvery thrill of retribution slithering up the back of his neck. There would be pain and they would understand, they would see his eyes and know it was worse to have done nothing.

Usually a few minutes of conjuring up atrocities was enough. But tonight he felt charged up, and he spent the next hour lying on his couch thinking of colleagues who had done him wrong, patients who continuously annoyed him, anyone who he felt had it coming to him, and he marched the condemned individuals through the fires and the poisoning and the injection of potassium, succinylcholine, barbiturates, digitalis, distilled water, insulin, the shooting in the head, the emptying of brake fluid from the master cylinder. The litany of methods was routine by now, the way you might count sheep before dropping off. Only it was stronger than usual, more protracted than the chance thought or two.

Forester read the danger signs in his mind. He tried to think of something else—his upcoming lecture at the Institute, plans for a vacation, whether or not he should get a new car. But he was like an animal who smelled the hunt; there were no gears in his head to shift.

He walked to the kitchen and downed a double shot of Crown Royal, the burning in his throat offering the promise of imminent distraction.

Standing at the kitchen sink rinsing out his glass, Forester returned to the woman at 441-2987. He would fasten her arms to the bedposts, and then her legs. She would be helpless and begging him to hurt her. He would begin by calling her by the wrong name, or better yet, by no name. He would ignore her by sitting between her legs, his back to her, and watch the Giants game. In the dark, the lights out, the baseball images would flicker over her glistening skin.

And then, as though he had found her lying there quite by accident, he would start in on this anonymous woman in the dark.

"It's no big deal," Joan said to her husband. "We can try again in the morning." She rolled away from him, her back now rising up to shut off further conversation.

If only he had had time to prepare, to get in the mood. But she had surprised him. Wednesday was usually PBS night—Bill Moyers and Joseph Campbell. He had not planned on the station holding their annual auction, the regular programming preempted. He had not noticed her slipping into the bathroom. He had been in the study trying to outline his upcoming talk at the Institute.

He was as soft as a slug.

Forester curled up alongside his wife and kissed her between the shoulder blades. Her skin was smooth and smelled of expensive soap. He was moved by the extent of her continuing efforts to be a good wife. "I love you," Forester said quietly, his words echoing from her back, flowing around him. Joan murmured. Maybe she heard, maybe she was already asleep. He did love her, he really did. It was just that there were things working at him that were beyond his control.

A floorboard in the hallway creaked. It was a big house, large enough for each of them to have their own private areas. Maybe it was too big. Being solitary was what Forester enjoyed, most of the time, but it drew him more and more into himself. Maybe if he and Joan lived in a small apartment, where they were constantly bumping into each other, getting in each other's way, making noises that interfered, telephone calls that you couldn't help but overhear. Then their lives would be more of a unit, like a ballroom dancing team. But instead he danced by himself, with his typewriter and his patients. And the desires and thoughts that he could not share. Not with Joan, not with another therapist. Not even with himself.

His mind drifted back to his upcoming lecture and his observations on Van Allen. He despised the man and all he stood for. *Think of something else,* he told himself. *Clear your mind. Use some will power.*

He held his cheek against his wife's back and tried to enjoy the pleasure of contact with her body. Instead he noticed that his feet were in constant movement under the blankets, as though he were horizontally pacing the bed. He might as well get up.

Forester rose, slipped on a terrycloth robe, and went to his office. The garden was bone white with misty shadows; the full moon poked through a loosely knit fog bank. Behind him were the accumulated books of his profession. And the rows of philosophers neatly arranged. The office suggested an order echoed in the Japanese garden. But it was illusion. He was operating with a short fuse, which was lit. He could feel the heat creeping toward him, could hear the sizzling. It was building up again, as surely as night follows the day.

He sat down in the leather chair his patients used. Michelle crossed her legs like so. He hung one leg over the other. It was a strange sensation, as though his leg had turned feminine. He flexed the ankle, arching his foot like some model in a stocking or shoe ad. His leg was well muscled, even a little beefy. It was ludicrous. He tried to feel what a woman might feel, being seductive and in control, but the sight of his leg made him smile. Maybe he was sick, but he certainly wasn't gay. Not getting it up had nothing to do with that.

He watched the leg dangling, the limb disarticulated and waving on its own. It was posing for him, perhaps even suggesting that all things were possible, even things unconsidered by the mind. A colleague had once said that the brain is nothing but a knot at the top of the spinal cord to keep it from unraveling. Then the brain would be nothing more than another appendage, not the body's master. Separate from the soul, said Descartes. Separate from the mind, said Wilder Penfield, the Pulitzer Prize-winning neurosurgeon who first mapped the various functions of the brain. Imagine a lifetime of stimulating the brain, your hands on the very substance of thought, and concluding that the mind was somehow different.

He repositioned himself, now leaning back in the chair. A draft of cold air shot up between his legs. It was masculine to sit with your legs wide apart, exposed, welcoming everyone. Women crossed their legs and were selective.

He recalled his mother sitting in the kitchen. He couldn't have been more than three or four. She was so beautiful. She smelled of honey and fresh fruit. The evening's potatoes were balanced in the wide lap of her skirt. Her legs were wide apart. He had snuggled up to her and she had pushed him away.

"Careful," she had said. "Can't you see that I have a knife in my hand?" And she went on peeling the potatoes.

The knife had been small, for paring. But in his dreams the wonderful light had magnified the shining silver. His real mother guarded her sacredness with a silver sword, little Alan dreamt.

With his adopted mother, Mrs. Forester, it wasn't the same. She tried so hard. She would have never pushed him away. She treated him as though he were so fragile that even a little shove might break him. You couldn't blame her; little Alan had been a precious flower suddenly dropped onto her barren body. She and Mr. Forester had tried and failed; they had waited, and finally, in the desperation of middle age, had trundled to the agencies. It was wartime and babies were in scarce supply.

Yes, they would take a foreigner, even a Polish boy. And it would be temporary. Probably a few years at most. Mr. and Mrs. Forester looked at each other, assessed their own futures, and assented. Temporary was better than not at all. Alan came with a dozen other children he did not know, first by boat, alone with his bags and teddy bear, then traveling from New York to Toronto by train, a kindly black porter watching over him, helping him down the steps of the train to meet his new parents.

His new mom had a round, common face, with puffy, grainy cheeks and small sad eyes. Her hair was already graying and shot out from her head like small spears. Mr. Forester stood to one side, steam from the train rising up around him. He remained at a distance for a second too long, the instant magnified through the years. Then he rushed forward, pulling Alan to his burly chest. The steam hissed behind him, swirling in the damp sooty diesel air. His new father smelled of train, dust, dampness, and a sweet cologne. Something like English Leather, Alan would later conclude. An inexpensive scent.

His new home was overheated and smelled of old people.

"It's okay to cry. It'll take time to get adjusted," Mrs. Forester had said. "And you don't have to call me Mom unless you want to." Tears formed at the corners of her small brown eyes. "I'd like it," she added, softly, not sure what to do with her hands.

He had arrived by Canadian Pacific, complete with an

observation car. Through the glass dome he could see giant trees and open blue sky. Suddenly the sky had closed
up, turned gray, then black. Lightning stabbed at the train,
the sky alternating between a dense black and a ferocious
light that threatened to dissolve the young boy. He wanted
to go back to his seat, but he knew there was something
special in the sky, something he should watch and one day
understand.

To this day he still shuddered and thrilled at the sound
of thunder. He would drag Joan to a promontory at the
Presidio so they could watch the lightning crash down
on the Bay. "It's scary," Joan would say, snuggling up
against him, the two of them secure in the Jaguar sedan.
"Scary and wonderful," Forester would say, pretending
that he had conquered his own fear, holding his wife
closely against him. "It's like the sky is opening up to
reveal its true self, letting us know that behind the lovely
blue is this." Forester would wait for the lightning to begin his observation, knowing the thunder would punctu-
ate the end of his sentence. Sometimes he would even
count the seconds and extend his arm outward, as
though orchestrating the crashing sound of the heavens
descending.

He caught sight again of his naked leg. He was startled.
In the chalky light it seemed almost translucent, as though
the bloody corridors beneath the skin were nearly visible.
It was a mass of muscle, arteries, and veins, wrapped in
parchment skin, like knockwurst. He wiggled his toes; the
sausage came to life. *It's my leg,* he said, as though scold-
ing himself. *Sartre said it all, in* Nausea. *You are being de-
rivative and self-indulgent. You are allowing this to*

happen to you. It's all a game that you can stop any time you wish.

He wiggled his toes again. *See. You are in control. And your thoughts about Michelle Draper are no more than fragments in the game. Idle thoughts. They don't mean anything. Everyone has them. Where do you think the phrase "fuck her brains out" came from? From tenderness, warmth, and devotion? Michelle with the wonderful legs and devastating smile. How many men have had the thought? And the other thoughts?*

For an instant he saw Kate watching him, listening to him, nodding, her wide eyes closing as she consented. It was all for her benefit. He had wanted to make her better. Make her see that she didn't really want to die. How her insisting on feeling guilty was unnecessary and ugly—a sign of weakness of character. And a willful desire for punishment.

Accidents happen. It wasn't his fault.

Forester pulled his robe tightly around himself. There were thoughts and there were thoughts. With Michelle he could be a real tiger. He would be a man again. The words "fuck her brains out," came back, uninvited. No. Make love. Tenderly. But there was the number, hanging in the air like some black thunderous cloud, 441-2987. He tried to keep his mind on Michelle and how she would feel, but he kept hearing the number. He had the senseless urge to phone, hear that husky voice breathe into the phone. Breathe again into his ear. He picked up the receiver and was staring at it when he heard his wife in the hallway. He put down the receiver.

"Who are you phoning at this hour?" Joan asked.

"Just getting the time."

"You've got the time right there." She pointed to the digital clock on his desk.

"I was double-checking."

"You sure you're okay?"

"A little worried about my talk."

"Come on. Let's have a cup of cocoa. Nothing like hot chocolate to drive away the demons."

Obediently Forester turned and trudged after his wife like some slightly sick child. He heard his slippers pad along the hallway carpet; they were the sounds of an old man shuffling through time. For a moment he caught himself wondering if he could tell Joan, let it all just gush out like pus from a wound. But she was standing in the kitchen, the kettle in her hand, pouring hot water into two cups. He loved her and you don't tell someone you love. . . .

If only he could, Forester thought as he sipped his cocoa and tried to clear his mind.

Joan chatted on about how a single lecture wasn't everything. She was stroking his inner thigh. There was a pleading look in her eyes.

Get hard, he said to himself, looking into his cocoa and thinking about the woman who had answered 441-2987, reciting the number over and over, at the same time seeing the woman in her room, tall and broad-shouldered, in black nylons that stopped at her upper thigh. He saw her dark, shiny hair and high cheekbones, admired her slight Connecticut accent.

Did she really smell of honey and cinnamon?

Joan was leading him upstairs by the hand. The woman would pinch her nipples until they were hard. It was working. Thank God. He was inside her and it felt good. "I love you," he said into her ear.

"It'll be okay," Joan said. "We've got each other, and that's all that anyone can ask."

"Yes, we've got each other," Forester said, his eyes closed, grateful.

FIVE

IT WAS MONDAY, AND A rare weekday away from the station, compliments of Dick Winters, the station manager. Michelle sat at her cluttered drafting table. Stacks of memos, unfiled notes, and tape cassettes of unused interviews crowded in from the perimeter, while scribbled-on Post-It notes stuck to the sides of the table and along the nearest wall. There were three coffee cups to one side, one steaming, the other two from yesterday. Michelle wore faded jeans and a loose-fitting red-and-green flannel shirt; her bare feet curled under the wooden rung of her stool.

Doing the illustrations for childrens' books had started as a lark. Winters's sister, a pediatric cancer specialist, wanted to create a series of short books that would help children prepare for the hospital. The woman had been down at the station, visiting her brother, and the three of them had had lunch. Michelle had sketched some line drawings of kids while the doctor was discussing the book's format with her brother. "Why don't you have Michelle do the drawings?" Winter had suggested, pointing to the gang of wine-stained kids on the table cloth.

Neither of the women had much free time, so the book had progressed quite slowly. Michelle enjoyed drawing, but was resentful of yet another commitment, particularly one that dragged on. She wasn't in the mood, but felt that a finished drawing or two might make her feel better.

On her drawing pad a doctor was squatting, his face at eye level with a little black girl holding onto an IV pole. It was the first of a series of drawings intended for children receiving chemotherapy. Michelle worked on the doctor's expression. It should reflect friendly concern. Michelle had difficulty with the mouth. She drew and redrew the corners, yet there was always, to her eye, the sense of a sneer. The doctor seemed uncaring, even threatening.

It was the long white coat. Michelle wanted the doctor to be at eye level with the child. But when the doctor squatted down, his white gown draped over his feet. It was too much pomp, like the flowing robes of popes and medieval religious figures. She erased the coat, drew the doctor in rolled-up shirtsleeves. He was immediately friendly. But most of the doctors wore the long white coats, especially on the cancer service. Michelle remembered vividly; she had toured the pediatric ward, then spent a week making preliminary sketches.

The medical center wanted a book that reflected what the children could expect, and that meant the doctors should look like doctors. She could draw the doctor standing upright, but then he would be talking down to the child, which was also scary.

She compromised by putting the child on an examining table, with the doctor seated on a tall stool, his shoes clearly visible beneath his white coat. She drew in black-and-white saddle shoes, like the ones Archie wore in the cartoons. The doctor looked silly. She drew loafers; he looked preppy and supercilious. Wing tips made him pompous. Sandals made him unwashed.

Nothing worked. Worse yet, it suddenly dawned on her that she hadn't even considered making the doctor a woman. But then she'd still have the problem with the right shoes—pumps, loafers, high heels, high-top tennies? Every style had negative implications.

It's just a fucking drawing, Michelle thought. *What's gotten into you?* But she knew. Dr. Forester had thrown her off-balance. The bastard was *good.* He was already giving her new insights into her mother's addiction to self-destruction. And he was respectful, except for that occasional stare that suggested something not yet revealed, or even hinted at. It was hard to fake softness in the eyes. Either Forester was a master con man, or she was wrong about him screwing up Kate.

She drew clay feet on the doctor, then ripped the drawing from her pad and tossed it onto a pile of abandoned sketches lying beneath the drafting table. She would take the drawing to the elementary school in North Beach and ask the kids. There was no point getting all steamed up over a pair of shoes. The kids would know.

Michelle stood at the kitchen window. Coit Tower was visible beyond a succession of rooftops. A white cloud hung over the tower, making an upside-down exclamation point. To what? What was the sky punctuating?

She had seen Forester four times. He had graciously accommodated her work schedule by squeezing her in over the lunch hour. Six hundred hard-earned dollars and she was no further along than the first day. She would push harder. She slipped out of her jeans and flannel shirt. She would give it her best shot. And a time limit. One month more.

She went to her closet and chose a pale yellow silk blouse, white stockings, and a tightly fitting but tailored blue gabardine skirt. She patted on a few drops of Chloe. *We'll see what this man is made of,* she thought, not smiling, her jaw clenched. She looked at the phone, as though she could ring up Kate and report on her progress. The sight of the portable phone was upsetting.

Before leaving her apartment Michelle watered her ficus and a barrel cactus that squatted under the bay window. A dust ball was caught in the spines. Michelle carefully pulled it free, then blew away some other specks that had gathered on the cactus's face.

Single women dote on cats and plants, Michelle thought as she locked the door behind her.

The effect was not lost on Dr. Forester. After all, it was his profession to look and observe. He was the pathologist of the soul. Not to look was like closing your eye while peering into the microscope. There were reasons behind her dress; it was not by chance alone that she showed up at her psychiatrist's office looking so absolutely ravishing.

Dr. Forester had seen it before, many times—the seductive patient who hoped to win him over, have him grant absolution. If the psychiatrist says you're okay—and who would be a better judge?—then it must be so. And what's better proof than having him slobber all over you like some drooling maniac?

Seduction was the great equalizer, the psychiatrist no longer in charge.

He was reminded of the woman who came with the

complaint that her vagina was numb. He asked her if she had been examined by a neurologist. She said there was no reason; if he had any doubts he could feel it himself. "Go ahead and touch me; then you'll be able to see that I can't feel anything."

"And if I don't touch you?" Forester had said.

"Then you won't be able to know whether or not I'm telling the truth."

He had gotten a big laugh when he told the story at an Institute meeting. A cheap shot, but then the woman had asked for it.

Michelle shifted in the leather chair. She was talking about her mother. Forester realized that he hadn't heard a word she had said.

"Tell me the worst time the two of you had together," he said, reestablishing his presence.

Michelle stared out the window. Thinking of a bad time with her mother was no problem. If their relationship had been a professional fight, both sides would have already thrown in the towel. That is, if the referee hadn't already stopped it. But she stalled a minute, as though thinking. If Forester liked vulnerable women, he would love this silence of pain. Then Michelle began, as though recalling an ancient dream. In reality it had happened the summer she had come home from her freshman year in college.

A new boyfriend had moved in with her mom, and, as Michelle's mother put it, he was prone to "little outbursts." "Honestly, hon, it would be better if you found yourself somewhere else to live. Just for the time being. He gets nervous in new digs. Come on, I'll help you pack."

"There's nothing to pack. I've got everything I need

right here," Michelle had said, pointing to her two suitcases filled with everything from school.

"What? No argument?"

"Mother. You can go fuck yourself." Michelle had
started down the path between the apartment buildings.

Her mother hollered after her, from the doorway, "It's
nice to see that college has given you some sense. You're
getting to be a real chip off the old block."

"And?" Dr. Forester said.

"And we didn't see each other for two years."

"Did your mother's boyfriend beat her?"

"All the time."

"And you think you might have made a difference
there?"

"I doubt it. She loves to get knocked around. Her whole
life she's led with her chin."

"Did she beat you?"

"No more than any mother would. The usual spankings.
Nothing more that I can remember." Michelle decided on
being evasive. There was something lighting up in Forester's eye. He had turned toward her and was more erect,
leaning forward slightly. Something was definitely on his
mind.

"I'm afraid that part of my childhood is pretty vague."

"How would you know that you had that part of a childhood unless there had been something?"

"I just meant that I don't remember anything out of the
ordinary."

"That's not what you said."

"I said I don't remember."

"Okay. We can come back to it later, when you're more
comfortable."

"I'd appreciate that."

"It must be difficult skating around all the unpleasantness."

"We had good times, too. It wasn't her fault that she was a sucker for the good-looker with the bad temper. My grandmother was the same way."

Dr. Forester looked at Michelle and said nothing. The silence was uncomfortable. Michelle spoke first.

"You wondering if it's familial, whether I'm the same?"

"It crossed my mind." Dr. Forester smiled faintly. "What do you think?"

I think you're probably right, Michelle said to herself. The story about her mother was true and unembellished. And her grandmother had run off with a man from the circus—he rode motorcycles around the inside of a large barrel. The women in her family had a genetic screw loose, some chromosomal defect that made their romances into a combination of tragedy and comedy, depending on who was telling the story.

Michelle, too, had an unblemished record of unsuccessful relationships. A stock broker with his computer running while they made love. A lawyer who swore that guilt or innocence was not the issue, that every man deserves the best advocate that money would buy, ethics being nothing more than lip service to feeling guilty. The poet who sat around all day playing with his mental blocks. And most recently, the orthopedist who subspecialized in arrogance and self-centeredness. Michelle had stopped seeing him a few months ago. To her personal embarrassment, it had taken her six months to make the decision.

All had been good-looking, sometimes fabulous in bed, and collectively as empty as solitary sin.

She referred to her romantic past as collecting pretty shells.

"Maybe it is familial." Michelle flashed a killer smile. "I've always been a sucker for the wrong man."

"I think you need a lot more treatment. There's more here than meets the eye." A bad choice of words, Forester thought. Not at all what he meant to say. "Dysfunctional family circumstances take time to unravel." He concentrated on looking serious, yet compassionate. He wanted to laugh and clap his hands. She was so beautiful and she was looking at him as though she truly needed him. And wanted him to take control of her life.

He would have to be careful.

Forester finished with his last patient and wearily stepped out of his suit. He slipped on a pair of gym shorts and rode the stationary bicycle in Joan's study. It was Wednesday evening; Joan was scheduled for an aerobics class. Afterward she was going to the bookstore. It was a glorious Indian summer night; Forester and Joan would grab a bite at Max's Opera Plaza. She would be home around eight o'clock.

Forester worked the pedals furiously, as though pumping out the venom acquired during a day topped off by the barking dog—Mrs. Seifert—followed immediately by poor, innocent, mistreated Jim Van Allen. Seeing them back to back was a bad idea. He should shift his schedule, interpose someone decent, like Michelle.

One of the rubber pedals slipped off. Forester's foot hit the metal bar of the bicycle, scraping his ankle. He replaced the pedal, repressing the urge to kick the bike. He pumped even faster, the wheel humming like some crazed metal beast. Neither Seifert nor Van Allen had a shred of insight. Mrs. Seifert paid to have her complaints acknowledged, even if it meant that she might be accused, in some psychoanalytic jargon, of being an accomplice to her problems.

"Go on, say it's my fault. I wish sadness and grief on myself. I go to bed at night and pray to be struck by lightning and my family."

Forester had suggested that she might try another therapist (he suppressed a laugh at his choice of words). Mrs. Seifert ignored him, lancing the air with her vicious, disagreeable voice, sucking the very life out of the air around her.

Forester saw the human eye as being able to see forward and backward. Seeing backward meant being able to look inside the dark recesses covered over by skull and expression, and actually see the inner workings. Blind people could not see outward. They were handicapped. Those who could not see inward were doomed.

He couldn't abandon Mrs. Seifert; she wouldn't go away.

And that perfect bastard, Jim Van Allen. One of the complaints to the medical society had been from a former employee who'd wanted to sue him for mental cruelty. She told the story of being invited to Dr. Van Allen's home in Kentfield and going swimming. Dr. Van Allen had stood at the edge of the pool with a boa constrictor, his son's pet, and had thrown the snake in alongside her.

"You guys can do some laps together," he had said, tossing his head back and emitting that high-pitched scary laugh. At the hearing he had answered that the snake was harmless.

He had no more insight than a ball bearing.

On the surface.

That horrible smile suggested that he knew exactly what he was doing, and that he loved it. It was the smile of the class bully, the drill sergeant, the postal clerk who closes the window in your face, apologetically announcing that the hours are nine to five and that the post office would be open again on Monday.

They were living examples of the bumper sticker that reads: Don't Get Mad, Get Even.

It made Forester angry to think that there were so many hostile, unenlightened people. The answer certainly wasn't in psychiatry. After a few visits you could divide the patients into those who were open to suggestion and introspection, and those who had developed elaborate mental dance steps to avoid themselves. Sometimes Forester saw the mind circling itself in some jerky exaggerated tango, the mind bending backward, almost double, to avoid contact with itself. Unfortunately psychiatry seldom shifted anyone into the introspective category. You had it or you didn't.

Van Allen had gone through ten different secretaries—an average of one per year. He had slept with nearly all of them, according to reliable testimony. He denied all but one. That one had been a sin of the flesh, he had told his wife, dropping to his knees and begging for forgiveness. He had made that affair public knowledge, wearing his mea culpas to weekly Bible class, and letting everyone know that he was a failed man, a man of sin. There had not been any others, according to him. It was their word against his, and he was a man who had confessed to his sins. There was no point in lying to the Lord.

He was evil for what he had done, and what he thought. *But honestly, I swear to God, all the others are fabrication.*

The tone of today's session had been particularly unpleasant. Van Allen had started the hour by producing a month-old clipping describing Kate Carbone's unexplained fall. The tone of the article strongly suggested suicide. The *Chronicle* article had referred to Dr. Forester as Kate Carbone's prominent treating psychiatrist. The word *prominent* was underlined. Van Allen dropped the article on Forester's desk like a hot smoking turd.

"At least my victims are still alive," Van Allen said. Then he strutted across the room to assume his usual arrogant pose.

Forester realized that there was no hope that Van Allen would change. The two of them danced around a null point of neither's choosing.

Forester had worked up a full sweat. His wrist watch said he had been pedaling for twenty minutes. That was plenty. He took off his shorts, carried them to the hall laundry chute, and folded them in half before dropping them down the chute. The folding was wasted effort, but it seemed right.

After his shower he had at least an hour before Joan would be home. He pulled a robe from his closet, felt the coarse terrycloth fabric, and put it back on its hanger. He double-checked his watch, then pulled out his black kimono. It was so smooth, the silk a thousand tongues against his skin. Moments later he was in the living room watching a videocassette of a PBS documentary on a World War II Lithuanian Resistance movement.

The program began with a debate among survivors as to

why they had or had not joined the Resistance movement in the woods. Forester had heard all the arguments. He fast-forwarded the discussion among the men. It was the women who counted. Most of the women were broad-faced, a combination of Slavic and Scandinavian. One woman talked of living in a forest near Vilna, of carrying arms and joining with the Lithuanian partisans. The woman was quite plain, with short-cropped dark hair and the face of a shopkeeper or a baker. She was ordinary and she had resisted.

The woman spoke eloquently, though it could have been the work of the translator. Forester chose to believe it was the woman speaking directly from her heart. She talked of responsibility to her faith, and if that meant embracing death, so be it. She described the exaltation of the moment in which she knew she was going to die, and it was going to be a good death, she and her friends going down to-gether, fighting to the last. She spoke with reverence of the leader of her outfit who had died instantly from a bullet wound in the neck.

"He fell at my feet. His eyes were glazed, not with pain, but with the joy that he had died for his God, and for his people." The woman dabbed at her eyes, the camera freez-ing the image, the program over and the credits running.

The woman's face burned in Forester's mind. What gave this woman her strength? How much better it would be to have had a mother who had died fighting than one who had lived an extra day or two in cowardice. If she were still alive, he'd tell her a few things. If he knew where she was.

His mother would be in her midseventies. She would carry the badge of the martyrs on her arm, numbers that tallied up her suffering. There had been no moment of exaltation, only the sensation of backward motion, perpetual backpedaling until there was nowhere left to retreat. Yet she would feel no need to apologize. She had been tortured, brutalized; they had plucked out her heart. She had suffered enough.

If he were to see her, what could he say that she would understand?

Forester removed the cassette from the VCR. It had been a special tape; he would save it and sometime again would look at the woman who had done what his own mother had not.

Be reasonable, he told himself. *You might have done the same.*

No. Never. Never.

You owed more than passivity to your only child. Rising above self-preservation was what separated man from the animals. That and memory. Not thinking. Animals thought. Memory. The ability to carry a grudge.

Why now, why when reaching fifty-seven? He had been bothered before, but never with such insistence. Each week was worse, the thoughts more intrusive and distracting. He couldn't remember how they had taken this shape. He could hear his rage like some bedeviled train hurtling down the tracks of his mind. Its headlight was as bright as the sun, hot and brilliant, pure and white, scorching everything in its path. Electricity raced down to his fingertips, into his spine, into his groin. He was on fire, the anger now a white light overflowing from every pore. He would never have abandoned his own child, given him away to strangers in some distant land.

There was no punishment equal to the crime.

He knew it wasn't a good idea bringing home the videos. So far he had kept them in a locked bottom drawer of his desk. The owner of the Hayward store had said that they were first-rate, live and unrehearsed, not some staged performances. The owner had taken them out of his back room; they were unlabeled and unboxed. On the side of the cassettes were numbers that corresponded to a list that the owner kept under the front counter.

Forester went to his desk in his den. He took one from his desk drawer and slipped it into the slot vacated by the woman from Vilna. Somehow the video seemed staged, though the amateurish lighting and poor camera angles suggested that it had, as the store owner promised, been photographed in an L.A. sex club. There was a close-up of a woman's hand struggling against its restraint, the hand opening and closing like some confused flower not certain of the presence of the sun. Forester played this back and forth, the motion the same in either direction, the opening and closing and the struggling somehow an elemental comment on the human spirit. The female spirit.

He watched closely, scanning the sucessive women's faces to see the actual moment of resignation. It was important to understand precisely. To know what the women felt, and why. Though it was impossible for him to accept, Kate Carbone had made the choice.

Sometimes he thought he saw her face in the video. He tried but he could not remember her expression. His lack of specific recall frightened him. So did the women on the TV screen. It made him sad to watch the women submit. And angry.

To his surprise, he was aroused.

Forester did not hear his wife coming up the stairs and

standing in the hallway. He did hear the scream of surprise and turned to see Joan rushing into the room, her face twisted in horror, her eyes announcing the end of innocence. She stood over him, in her navy blue sweats and gray high-tops, pulling at his kimono, which was open to the waist, revealing his erection. She was screaming and tugging and hitting him in the chest with her fists.

"Oh, my God," she said again and again. "It was this?" She walked past him and stood at the window. "You bastard," she said, looking out the window.

Forester was speechless. He had been uncovered, the lid lifted off and the snakes, worms, and demons jumping out. He approached his wife and tried to stroke her arm.

"Don't touch me," Joan said. She swatted his arm away. There was nothing he could say. He turned off the cassette.

Joan continued staring out the window for what, to Forester, seemed like hours. When she finally turned to looked at him, Forester was startled by the pain in her red puffy eyes. The look on her face frightened him. It was as though he had come upon her unexpectedly and was seeing her for the first time. And how she saw him. He wanted to comfort her. He wanted to hide. He did neither. Instead he moved behind the couch, to the doorway, where he stood bracing himself for what was to come.

"So many nights I've watched you sleeping, wondering what had gone wrong. I've imagined everything—another woman, even that you didn't love me. I thought maybe it was my looks. So I've busted my ass exercising, dieting, trying new perfumes. I knew it was something, but I never imagined. . . ." Joan shook her head. "Never."

She gathered herself together, and walked to the kitchen. Forester followed.

She poured herself a glass of water, then threw the water in the sink. She filled the glass half full of Chivas Regal and took a large gulp. She was leaning against the counter.

"Sorry," Forester said. "I think I need some help."

"You couldn't have talked to me about it?"

Forester shook his head.

"What about someone from the Institute? Nate Giles? Someone you trust?"

"It's not that easy. I can't even figure out what the problem is." Forester was relieved that Joan was still talking to him. She was such a decent, sensible person. He could tell that she wanted to smooth this over. He ran quickly through a potential litany of excuses. All sounded hollow. No, he would tell her the truth. As much as he could. For a brief moment Forester sensed a way out of his condition; he was buoyed up with the lightness of hope. He would bare his soul and she would forgive him.

"Are there more?" Joan asked. She took another large swallow.

Forester nodded. "There're two others."

"More of the same?"

"I guess so. I haven't seen them."

"Sure. You're saving them for some special occasion?"

Forester shrugged.

Joan walked to the doorway of the kitchen. She turned back to Forester.

"Are you going to join me?"

"You're not serious?" Forester said.

"Absolutely. I need to know what we're dealing with."

"You haven't seen enough?"

"Believe me, I've seen too much already."

"I'll go into therapy." Forester's eyes were pleading.

"Get the others. Oh, and I suppose we should play civilized. You want a drink?"

"I can get it," Forester said. He took a matching glass from the overhead cabinet, and an equal amount of scotch. He went to his den and came back with the other two cassettes.

At first, as they sat far apart—Joan in an upright chair, Forester at the other end of the couch—he thought she might be able to recognize that this wasn't the real him. It was just a foreign corner of his soul. Everyone had them. Certainly she was psychologically sophisticated and could understand weaknesses.

His hopes faded as the women groaned and begged for mercy. Joan's face was frozen white and bloodless. Her hands were clenched in her lap; her knees were jammed tightly together. They were on uncharted ground, their history wiped clean. She looked at him as though he were a stranger. Yet she insisted on seeing all of the tapes in their entirety. Forester said it wasn't necessary, but she motioned to the last cassette.

He swore that he did not know that the last video was a snuff film from Argentina. He might have guessed because of the five-hundred-dollar price of the cassette. But he swore up and down, may God strike him dead, that he had no idea.

"Certainly it must be staged," he said. His voice was childlike and distant. Joan watched as a young woman was gagged, then bound to a wooden kitchen chair. Abruptly she ran to the TV and punched it off.

"I don't know you," she said. She ran from the room. Forester could hear the sound of gagging and water flushing in the bathroom. Then there was the sound of closets opening and closing. She was packing her things.

"Please don't," Forester said. He stood in the doorway of their bedroom and watched as Joan jammed some clothes into a suitcase.

"I don't know you," Joan said again.

"Where are you going?"

"Somewhere clean."

"Just like that, after ten years? Without an argument, a disagreement, anything?"

"I'll try to understand. I'll give you that. But in the end I won't. I wouldn't know where to look inside myself that could forgive a man for this."

"I'll see someone."

"Of course you'll see someone. But this isn't ordinary neurotic stuff we're talking about." Joan finished packing and closed her suitcases. She walked downstairs and grabbed her car keys. "I'll give you a call and let you know where I'm staying. Probably at Sarah's over in Berkeley. But don't phone. I'll get in touch with you." She stood in the doorway, her bags in one hand, her car keys in the other. "I'll try, Alan. I owe you that. But I don't know. I never imagined. I'm so sorry."

A minute later there was the sound of Joan accelerating into the twilight. Forester was alone.

It wasn't fair. Maybe he couldn't explain, but she should give him another chance. It wasn't like finding him in bed

with another woman. Even then there was room for discussion.

Forester thought back over their relationship. It had
been good. They were happier than most couples. Other
than his trouble getting it up, there was nothing to complain about. He wasn't really even sure that their diminished sex life had particularly bothered her. She always
seemed so chipper.

He flinched. Of course she wasn't happy. The defensive
coolness had been coming on for some time. He thought
of Joan, for the first time in their marriage, going to bed
in a high-necked nightgown. He heard her explaining that
she was chilled. How awful it must have been. And how
little she complained.

Forester felt his face flush with private embarrassment.
I'm sorry, he wanted to tell her. *You didn't deserve this.*
But, at the same time, he heard himself begging for for-
giveness. Most of all he wanted her back.

They were just films, nothing more. He hadn't done
anything. But that was how women could be. Get an idea
into their head and that was it. She was being cruel, which
was something he might fantasize, but no, never, would he
intentionally hurt her. That was the difference. He could
never hurt anyone. He just wanted to watch.

Forester's hopes collapsed when Joan brought over a
college student with a small pickup truck. They took the
big items that she hadn't been able to fit into her car. She
timed their visits so that Forester would not be home. It
took nearly a week to move the heavy pieces.

The house was gigantic without her. Every room echoed
of lost love. Joan had taken most of the artwork, the mem-

ories of the departed images hovering dimly in the empty spaces like ghostly decorations.

He phoned for several nights. Eventually Joan agreed to talk. She was civil, but there was a new protective edge to her voice. The conversation went nowhere. Though she promised to give it more time, Forester knew by her tone of voice that they were finished.

During the following week he kept busy, accepting two new patients and working on his talk. The hours filled themselves. Friday night came. It was movie night. Normally they would go to the Lumière and see some foreign movie. Joan was cultural minister of the house and scoured the reviews, choosing the best films. Forester considered going alone. Routine was important. But he wasn't interested in sharp dialogue and great camera angle. He'd rather stay home and watch his own movies.

He became aware that something was different. Beneath his loneliness fluttered some other sensation. Not sadness, not pleasure, exactly. It was hard to say what it was, but with it came a keen sense of excitement.

Gradually it sank in. He was free to pursue what ultimately he knew he must. Joan's leaving had put an end to pretense.

So Alan Forester put the last of the cassettes in the VCR. He could watch, go downstairs for a sandwich, leave the cassette on pause, return, take his time, there was all the time in the world. He didn't need to explain or worry about being caught. He had been caught and he had survived. He was still eating and seeing patients and carrying on normally. He had come out into the open and had made it.

There was nothing he could do about Joan. He hoped she would come to her senses and see that he was a good man. He certainly meant well, which was more than you could say for most people these days. He settled down in front of the TV, a sherry in one hand, the remote control in the other. It was a small universe that he inhabited, but at least he was in charge.

SIX

"IT'S A CLOSE CALL,"
Dr. Setledge said. "It could be accidental. With a gag
properly positioned you can breathe through the nose. But
if it's too far back, it shuts off the entire airway. The guy
gets all worked up, he doesn't notice, and the woman can't
scream; then afterwards it's too late. He panics and leaves
the body for someone else to discover. It looks like a homicide, but maybe it isn't."

"Are we through?" Detective Lockhart asked. He was
tall and well-muscled; in his gray trousers, open-necked
white shirt, and blue blazer he looked like a successful ex-
linebacker turned Secret Service agent. In truth his football
career had been cut short his sophomore year in college. It
wasn't much of an injury—a broken nose that healed perfectly. It was the idea of pain that made Lockhart quit.
And now, the smell of antiseptic and chilled flesh made
Lockhart swallow forcefully. Five years in homicide and it
was only a little easier than the first time. He had learned
to play mind games, think of redwood trees and flowers
opening. But, at the same time, it was important to pay attention. Medical examiners had their own perspective, and
Setledge was notorious for a brilliant mind and lazy disposition. Find a cause and wrap it up. He hated the minute
dissection.

Dr. Setledge dictated into the overhead microphone. Bobby Lockhart sat on the aluminum stool, only inches away from the autopsy table, and wondered how a young woman could allow herself to be tied up and gagged and whipped. He stared at the ligature burns on her wrists and ankles—she must have squirmed and struggled. But was it in pain or pleasure? Earlier Dr. Setledge had shown him the rows of whip marks on her back. Bobby knew he would have the usual bad dreams. It was the type of information that could be acknowledged but not assimilated.

Lockhart figured there was a part of the brain that registered war, the possibility of nuclear catastrophe, mass murder, torture—all the unthinkable subjects. This section of brain would be like the closet in the haunted house that bore the warning: Do Not Enter. If you were lucky there was nothing in the closet that you needed.

Working in homicide was like throwing the closet door wide open.

"Asphyxia during sexual bondage," Dr. Setledge said, concluding his dictation. He turned to Lockhart. "Not conclusively accidental or homicide."

"Off the record, do you have an inclination one way or the other?" Lockhart asked.

"Not from the body. But there is something that bothers me. This woman was a professional. Her apartment was filled with all kinds of gear. Her friends say she was very careful about what she allowed and where she drew the line. A woman like that would be cool; she'd be sure the gag was loose enough. She probably wouldn't be tied up until she was certain. The accidentals are usually the amateurs or those on drugs. Her friends said that she didn't take anything, not even pot. She was into health foods and aerobics. Which is another thing. She taught exercise classes. She wouldn't want people to see her wrist and ankle burns. She would have taken more precaution, like greasing her wrists and ankles with lotion or Vaseline."

"But you've got nothing definite."

"Nope. You're on your own."

"Thanks, Doc."

"Anytime."

Lockhart turned to leave, then turned back to Dr. Setledge. The pathologist was a half foot shorter than Lockhart, stocky with thinning sandy hair and a reddish gray mustache. His loosely knotted tie hung halfway down his chest. He was the epitome of slovenliness, yet his eyes were dancing smartly. "One more time, let me ask you the same question," Lockhart said.

"Shoot."

"How can you stand it here?" Lockhart motioned to the large scrubbed tile autopsy suite.

"You know Mahler's Second Symphony?" Setledge asked.

Lockhart nodded. Setledge was one of the few department superiors who knew that Lockhart had once taught philosophy at a small Pennsylvania college and that he was an educated man. Normally Lockhart downplayed his background, but with Setledge he enjoyed being the existential detective, the man with nothing to prove.

"What's that got to do with working here?"

"Nothing. I thought you'd be above asking about reasons. Listen to Mahler. I do, when I'm not down here tolerating stupid questions like 'Why are you down here?' "

"Setledge. You are one worthless piece of bullshit," Lockhart said. He gave Setledge a tired smile. "In the future remind me to keep our conversations strictly professional."

"Sure. By the way, you know that Mahler's Second Symphony is subtitled 'Resurrection.' " Setledge motioned to the other room. A burly assistant appeared and began to suture up Kelly Caldwell—8900189. As Lockhart walked through the polished aluminum double doors, he couldn't help thinking what a sad little man Setledge must be.

But at least he was alive. Kelly Caldwell wasn't as lucky. How could she have gotten into such a mess? Lockhart decided to wait until the toxicology reports were in before making a final decision. And poking his nose around. Something didn't smell quite right, but maybe it was his imagination.

He could have stayed on teaching. He had already made tenure, and, being only thirty-five, was young enough to have had a chance for a chairmanship somewhere. But one day the study of philosophy seemed irrelevant and altogether too precious. Besides, philosophy was no longer a matter of scholarship—not when United Airlines, the State Department, George Bush, Oliver North, and Tommy LaSorda all had "philosophies."

His father had been a cop before he was sidelined by a bullet through the knee. And what was good enough for his father was good enough for him. Bobby had not been encouraged by the police recruiter. Five years later he was assistant in charge of vice, and now at forty-five was one of the top three in homicide. Not bad for a college kid, his boss, Sam Spagliano, would say, hitting Bobby lightly on the side of the head.

So ten years ago it was searching for the flaws in Kant. Now it was trying to decide if the gag in the throat of the pretty young girl with the high cheekbones and trim figure was there by intent.

As he walked to his car at the back of the lot, Bobby Lockhart had two simultaneous thoughts. Was Mahler's Second Symphony titled "Resurrection" to symbolize the emergence of music from silence or the solemn beauty of death and transfiguration? And was today's grim little dissection only an accident, or was it the work of some sickie? Which meant as sure as the sound of violins rising from the silence, that there would be more to come.

Mi Mi ran a frame shop on lower Columbus Avenue. She was in the back room, polishing a strip of ebony wood. There had been a time when she would have commanded three fifty an hour, fifteen hundred for the night. And there would be lines from here to the Bohemian Grove, where she specialized in senators and power brokers. Tall and sleek, half Chinese and half French, she was better than a dream. But the years had made her into a businesswoman, complete with reading glasses and sensible pumps. She was still gorgeous, looking up over her glasses and flashing that smile. Bobby smiled back, glad that he had never had to bust her when he was on vice. Women that beautiful should be given special license.

"Careful," Bobby said, "or you'll rub the starch out of that frame."

"The black ones always take longer," Mi Mi said. "How's it going, Detective Inspector Lieutenant Lockhart?" She held out her hand.

"I'm not in the women's division anymore. I just thought I'd drop by and say hello." Lockhart stood on the other side of the worktable.

"I no know nuttin'," Mi Mi said. "I fresh off boat." She held the frame to the light, put it back on the counter, and lightly sanded one edge.

"You got time for coffee?"

"Personal or business?"

"Business."

"Yours or mine?"

"Department."

"*Merde.* I thought you finally came to your senses." Mi Mi walked to the front of the store and handed the frame to an assistant. "It needs three coats of lacquer." She turned to face him from the other end of the store. "It's kind of weird, being legitimate. You ought to try it sometime."

They grabbed a coffee at La Rocca's. Mi Mi traced her fingernail along the rim of the cup. Lockhart was past the age where hormones muddied mental waters, but he could not help staring.

"It's not a sin, looking," Mi Mi said. "Sometimes I stand in the mirror and take a gander myself. Now I need bifocals. And I see some of the petals drooping. But it was good while it lasted."

"You completely shut down?" Lockhart asked.

"Sure, now whenever I'm out with a man, he introduces me."

Lockhart reached into his jacket pocket and pulled out a photo of Kelly Caldwell. "You ever run into her?"

Mi Mi looked at the photo, her eyes clouding up. She handed the photo back to Lockhart. "I had her with me up at the Grove a couple years ago. But it was a bad idea. Some junior senator wanted to play rough. He gave her a bruised cheek. Kelly gave him two black eyes. She was second degree black belt." Mi Mi looked down at her coffee. "I read about her in the paper. You think it was an accident?"

"I thought you might be able to tell me."

"The answer is yes, she got off on the thin line. Having these powerful men tie her up, at the same time capable of knocking any of them silly, or worse. She loved the illusion of being helpless and knowing differently. She showed me how she had them use granny knots. That way she could get herself loose with a simple twist of her wrist."

"You ever try it?"

"Sure. I use them to tie the bows in my hair."

"I don't mean granny knots."

"Well, what do you mean, Lieutenant?"

"I mean, have you ever . . ."

"Please. What do you take me for?" Mi Mi flashed a smile that was not all mirth.

"Sorry. I just thought that if you knew the actual mechanics, you could guess whether or not she might have accidentally choked."

"Not Kelly. Even though I really liked her, I stopped hanging around with her. There were complaints that she was a little scary. After the senator incident, she seemed different, more intense and into martial arts. Sometimes she seemed like she was turning the corner. Too bad. I tried to talk some sense into her. Last I heard she was hanging around with a south-of-Market crowd."

"Got a name?"

"They're not your type of people."

"I'm in homicide. Everyone's my type."

"Don't say I didn't warn you. You think you've seen it

all. Well, you're still a first-grader." Mi Mi finished her coffee. "R.V."

"R.V. what?"

"You wanted a name. R.V. Recreational vehicle. There's no last name. People like this don't have family names. Now, if you'll excuse me."

"I'm glad to see that things are working out," Bobby said.

"They'd be even better if you'd come around again." Mi Mi melted his heart with a smile that was as old as time and as fresh as you wanted it to be. "Maybe you have someone you'd like to frame." And she was gone, back at work, waving at him through the store window.

Bobby Lockhart could remember when south of Market meant wholesale distributors of whatever it took to run the rest of the city. Dozens of wheel alignment and brake shops, restaurant equipment stores filling an entire block, giant ovens and ranges sitting foodless in the industrial sunlight. Tires stacked up in fenced-off yards. Thousands of trucks double parked, hard-working men sweating their way through days of thankless, boring routine as stock boys of the universe. In the blocks closest to Market Street they shared the road with the armies of winos stumbling through their own hazy, endless days. The paddy wagons made daily runs, randomly picking out a few, trying to make a point, never succeeding, but keeping up the pretense. They might as well have had Carry Nation go storming down Mission, poking the bums with her pamphlets. But that was years ago.

Now bums were called the homeless and they'd spread out through the city as though distributing their own ill-conceived messages. Mission and Sixth still had its collection of shattered men, but cheap muscatel and fortified port were no longer the predominant pharmacological agents. The doorways, alleyways, and low shrubs were cluttered with syringes, needles, empty vials. The gutters were living proof of the advance of science, technology in the veins of all but the very poorest.

Now port was decanted by yuppies and served to smiling couples on art deco leather couches.

During his college years Bobby had spent the better part of a year hitchhiking, seeing America. So he was familiar with flophouses and cheap hotels; for him they still held a faded sense of glamour and adventure. He had to remind himself that the homeless were not the same as the bums he had met along the way, that these battered men might be low on Thorazine or con men fresh out of a clean shirt, or so gone on angel dust that the street looked like some jungle path and you were the enemy. The sidewalks and people's parks were filled with all that could go wrong with the human spirit, all mingling together trading stories and techniques and a crazy affirmation that all men really want is warmth and friendship. And to live out their deepest fantasies.

R.V. was listed in several of the sex newspapers. She wasn't hard to find—she lived in a loft above a brick-and-glass-fronted bar called So Far Inn. Bobby walked up the flight of rickety wooden stairs, not sure what to expect. Certainly it was anything but the woman in a straight tweed skirt and loose-fitting green sweater who appeared at the top of the stairs and motioned him inside. She was in her midthirties, with clear, nearly white skin and short-cropped kinky coal black hair. A single blue vein ran under one eye, suggesting a fragility to her broad, flat face. She was someone's sister, someone else's secretary, an intake worker at some social welfare agency.

"It's standard policy. First we meet and get to know each other. You tell me your dreams and I'll give you mine."

"Me first?" Bobby said.

The woman looked around the sparsely furnished loft. "You see someone else?" She flashed a deceptively open, friendly smile. Beating each other up was like arranging for a tennis partner.

"You really want to know?" Lockhart said. "I'd like to see the Giants take the series in four games."

"They're not even in the play-offs yet."

"Just testing how good you are. Mi Mi says you can arrange most anything."

"There's a difference between beating and winning. God herself couldn't help a team with zero pitchers. They should start a ball machine." R.V. looked at her hands. The palm of her right hand was heavily calloused. "Or me."

"You play in the city softball league?" Lockhart asked.

"Not play. Star. The last three outings were shutouts."

"You guys ever play the police team?"

R.V. looked at Lockhart, her eyes narrowing, her smile fading. "I knew it was too good to be true. Some nice guy walks into your life, his face all clean and shiny, like some Norman Rockwell soda jerk, and he turns out to be, correct me if I'm wrong, from vice. Watch the pretty young things hunker after each other, then lock them up for giving in to life's baser urges." R.V. walked to the front door and opened it. "Sin's out there, where you live."

"I have a few questions."

"I'm sure you do. Like, What's a nice girl like you doing? . . . Or, Do you really get off on whacking little kids? Or, Who's the local distributor of snuff movies? You got questions, I'm sure."

"Easy, a minute ago we were talking baseball and hitting it off like two old cronies."

"Well, times change."

"It's not vice. It's homicide." Lockhart pulled a picture of Kelly Caldwell from his jacket pocket. "Ever work with her?"

R.V. closed the door. Her eyes brimmed with tears. She walked across the room to a low couch and sat down, her head in her hands.

Lockhart stood at the edge of the couch. It was an ordinary living room, a stage setting for an ordinary life. But Mi Mi had told him about R.V.'s special interests. He looked down at the crying woman and found it impossible to imagine nipple clips, cock rings, whips, and all the paraphernalia. He knew he could open her purse and see snakes and rats come streaming out. She carried her unconscious in her bag and decorated her apartment in contemporary conventional, as though that made it all comprehensible.

"Kelly and I did doubles. She was very careful. She even gave seminars on how to prevent injuries. She was strictly fantasy. I never even knew her to have a bruise. Not like these." R.V. pulled up the sleeve of her sweater. There was a nasty purplish brown blotch on her forearm. "She'd never have let some bastard hit her like this."

"Does this happen often?"

"First time in months. He promised he'd use his open hand."

"I meant, someone dying during a session."

"Never. I've been in town five years, and, no, never." She shook her head for emphasis, and as though dislodging the news of Kelly's death. R.V. gave a feeble smile. "We lost our best third baseman."

"What kind of seminars?" Lockhart asked.

"Over at the Institute on Sexuality. Talk-throughs for sex therapists. She even gave an hour demonstration at the American Psychiatric Association annual convention. I'll bet she showed those bow ties a thing or two. But it was always in fun. 'Hit Me with Your Best Shot,'—that old Pat Benatar song—was her favorite line. You like Pat Benatar?" R.V. asked.

"She's okay."

"Okay? You sure you're still alive?" R.V. took a handkerchief from her purse and wiped her eyes. "It makes me sick. She was so beautiful. And she made me feel this"— R.V. started to make a motion with her hand, but let it fall back in her lap—"that this is all okay. Just a fun game to blow off a little steam."

"It couldn't have been some guy getting overheated. You're sure?"

"We're professional. You think you'd drive Indianapolis without a seat belt? Kelly was so careful she put rubbers on her dildos, even when it was just with us girls."

"You have any suggestions how to proceed?"

"Not unless you have a strong stomach. Then I'd suggest you answer the ads, all of them, but not as a cop. Or better yet, get one of your lady cops to place the ads. That way, in about a hundred years you could have screened half the city. Which leaves out the East Bay. Fremont, Hayward, San Leandro—all the biker towns where pain is a good head on your Friday night beer."

"You've been a great help," Bobby said.

"You find the bastard, let me cuff him. It's the least you can do."

The phone rang. "Yes," R.V. said. "You've been a naughty boy? And you want Mistress Diana to put you back on the straight and narrow. Well, you've called the right place." R.V. looked over at Bobby and shrugged her shoulders. "A hundred dollars a session. More, if you need more extensive punishment." R.V. listened for a few seconds, then said into the receiver, "Fuck you, you pervert." She hung up. "Phone freak," she said to Bobby. "The town's full of screwballs with loose quarters."

And the tears began, silently, R.V.'s shoulders rising and falling. Bobby tried to close the door quietly behind him. He found himself almost tiptoeing down the stairs, as though he could sneak out of R.V.'s life. The Greeks said to shoot the messenger. They were right. And homicide was like being the Western Union of sadness.

Which was still better than the emptiness of philosophy. Better to bring sorrow than nothingness. A thousand griefs to fill your empty basket.

Bobby peered in the downstairs bar. It was nothing but men sitting around drinking, watching the afternoon soaps, fighting urges and the knowledge of AIDS that made every outing a dance of the devils. Wasted stick men in black, with walking sticks and hairless skulls atop glowing skeletons. And at other tables, the healthy who refused to check their blood for the enemy.

Forced laughter, neither masculine nor feminine, pierced the air.

Upstairs, a woman who beat others for a living sobbed. Her friend was gone. In the alley between the bar and a laundromat, a filthy black man, his hair in dreadlocks caked with dirt and bits of fluff, snored contentedly, dreams of a better life being shown in seventy-millimeter living color on the insides of his flickering lids.

Take away this man's drugs and alcohol. Sure. It would be like not giving a dying man his pain medicine. "Just say no," Nancy said. Bobby leaned down over the sleeping man and said softly, "Just say no. It's your civic obligation, your moral responsibility, if we're going to build a better America." Bobby took a dollar from his jacket pocket and slipped it in the man's hand. The man stirred slightly. Bobby took the dollar from his hand and shoved it gingerly into one filthy coat pocket.

Across the street, at a sports bar, two construction workers watched him, the two men laughing to each other. Bobby walked away, nursing the feeling that he was always on the wrong side of someone else's street.

SEVEN

DR. FORESTER LEANED slightly forward in his seat, his face attentive and concerned. Here was a man who was intelligent, sensitive, stable, and nice looking in a gaunt, beardless Abe Lincoln sort of way. In fact, in other circumstances, Michelle could have seen him as attractive. So far he hadn't been out of line, and his asking her about her sex life was certainly done tactfully and in a cool, clinical way.

Michelle focused on the pain in Kate's eyes, the unmistakable blush of confession. What was the truth about Forester?

Dr. Forester had a bemused expression. "The questions a psychiatrist asks about your sex life always seem contrived. But they're necessary."

"Of course a sex life is necessary." Michelle smiled, for the moment her assignment clear. "But that's not why I'm here."

Forester said nothing. For a brief second he flashed a tiny enigmatic grin. It could have been amusement or the acknowledgment of her nervousness or embarrassment. Michelle disliked the ambiguity of every word, every silence, every movement, even the rug beneath her a finely woven Persian quicksand. "Insinuendo," one of her friends once termed therapy. Michelle had the mixed sensation of being patient and prey, Forester the healer also being Forester the predator on his leather perch.

She reminded herself that she was neither. But being in his quiet office wasn't at all what she had expected.

"Do you think discussing your sex life might shed some light on your feelings of sadness?"

"Good grief, no."

"Very funny. But not an answer."

"Sex and love go together and right now I'm in between engagements. By choice, I might add."

Michelle was aware of being defensive and immediately saw that Forester recognized this. But it was true. Her job at the station exposed her to a wide variety of decent men who would give their right arm to be with her—her boss, two of the newswriters, one of the attorneys for the station. But none of them grabbed her heart.

She wanted to tell Forester that her sex life was wretched because she chose powerful self-important men too busy or otherwise self-absorbed. She was on the verge of saying that she understood that it was a special type of weakness, like drinking or drug addiction, and that she had given it a great deal of thought, and wished that it were different. But she wasn't here for therapy. Besides, just because her own affairs, in retrospect, tended toward the self-destructive didn't mean that she couldn't tell the difference between a good and a bad man. And that's what this was all about. Judging Forester, not her sex life, *not* working out some perfectly obvious shortcoming that she could correct on her own, if she put her mind to it.

When not personally involved she was a very shrewd judge of character. When the city administrator had been at the height of his popularity, with everyone writing feature articles about this self-sacrificing nonpolitical public official, Michelle had seen a certain shifty, wandering, perhaps troubled look in his eyes, even in his well-modulated restrained laugh. She was sure the real person was hiding behind a mask of deceit; she had told Winters so at a station staff conference. Winters, a savvy former newspaperman, had disagreed.

When the scandal broke, Winters's first words were, "You were right." Music to Michelle's ears. And a big plum, getting assigned a one-week, five-minutes-per-night, blow-by-blow account. The viewer response had been dramatic, a real break for her career.

Which meant that she *was* insightful, could read men. Would make the right call on Forester. But how long would it take? Maybe she was presenting herself the wrong way. She was sorry that she had not stuck with her original idea of presenting a story similar to Kate's. But she had been certain that Forester would have been suspicious of a reporter showing up on his doorstep with Kate's exact circumstances. She settled for a generic unhappiness, a mild, only partially acknowledged, depression. But this had uncovered nothing.

Michelle remembered the last few lunches, with Kate being downcast, uncertain, biting her nails, looking away, not at all in control. Maybe she needed to act more like Kate. Michelle slumped in her seat, stared at her shoes, and tried to slip into Kate's body language.

Forester was watching, and taking notes. *This is for Kate, not for you,* she told herself, trying not to assert herself.

"It's been really hectic at the station—sixty-, seventy-hour weeks. I guess that hasn't allowed much time for romance."

"You must have had plenty of offers for marriage. Your being alone, you say that's by choice?"

"Marriage isn't the issue." Michelle's voice rose unexpectedly, more harsh and insistent than she had intended. *Relax, stay cool.* "At least I don't think so," she said softly, as though conceding a small point. She watched closely to see if Forester's expression registered any minor victory. It didn't.

"When you were a little girl, did you playact, or imagine being married?"

"Of course." She sighed, fluttered her eyes, and flashed a slight girlish smile. It wasn't her style. Forester would see through her, she was sure of it. But he remained distant and analytic.

"Tell me about him."

"My knight in shining armor was tall, blond, gentle, romantic, brilliant, intuitive, understanding, and he needed me. In other words he was totally imaginary." She watched for his response, but found herself remembering the dreamy sensation of twenty years ago, of a magical childhood time when all was possible. She was annoyed. She hated responding to her own daydreams as though they were real.

Michelle realized that she was picking at her cuticle, a habit she had dropped years ago. She drifted off, remembering how hard it had been to break the habit. Now the urge had returned, along with her imaginary man. Perhaps the two went together.

"Did this dream include having children?"

"Sure. Ten kids and a hundred grandkids, like the old lady who lived in a shoe."

"And now, do you think of having a family?"

"Eventually. But there's no urgency." Her voice quivered, and though she said what she thought was the truth, she felt as if she were lying. She folded her arms across her chest, then dropped them to her lap. To her surprise, her eyes filled with tears. If she wasn't careful her cheeks would soon be hot and smeared, and there would be hand-sized blotches on her neck. All at once she was both angry and sad. She concentrated on the anger, trying to will the tears away. Other than crying over Kate's death, she couldn't remember the last time she had been this out of control.

Forester reached into his desk drawer, pulled out a box of Kleenex, and handed it to Michelle.

"You'll have to excuse me." Michelle wiped her eyes. Someone was pulling on the rug beneath her feet. She looked down and thought she saw time tugging away. She always imagined herself with a little girl and boy. She tried to visualize how they would look, but couldn't. Too much would depend on the father. She imagined Owen, and saw two tall, strapping children, quick and bright, energetic and yet wistful.

Owen. He had chosen her roommate. After the freshman dance, Kate and Michelle had sat up half the night, Kate talking about wonderful Owen this, and marvelous Owen that. Michelle had been pleased and secretly hurt. He could have chosen either of them; he had fallen for Kate. And because she genuinely loved Kate, she came to love Owen, not for herself, but as her adopted sister's boyfriend, and then, husband.

They would have had smart, handsome children.

Michelle was amazed at the direction of her thoughts. She tried to look away from her spinning mind. "Do you have children?" she asked Dr. Forester.

"We were talking about you."

"I was just asking."

"Right now we should concentrate on your feelings."

"I'm not married. Kids are out of the question."

"That's not exactly what I asked."

"Just because I got momentarily upset over the thought of having children is no reason to think that it's a problem. I cry at TV commercials—that doesn't make me depressed." *Kate was depressed. Say you're depressed.* But Michelle didn't, couldn't.

"I can understand your wanting to avoid the issue, but that's not the solution."

"A woman without a man and a dozen babies is by definition unhappy? Is that it?"

"You were the one who mentioned the old lady who lived in the shoe. Please, Michelle. You came here because things were bothering you. You bring them up and then say, no, not me. Be sensible. The whole point of therapy is to pull back the curtains so that you can get a good look at yourself. Then you can make the necessary changes."

"Changes? I came here because . . ." Michelle stopped. She almost blurted out that she was here to find out what had happened to her friend. And to destroy Forester. Instead she had been reduced to tears and excuses. "I thought it would be a simple matter of talking it out, and picking up my spirits. I really don't think I need a complete overhaul."

"It's up to you. But I'd suggest two to three times a

week, for now. This is important information you're bringing up." Dr. Forester was looking at her. There was no hint
of sarcasm or manipulation. He wasn't speaking in veiled
hostility or with the leer of domination like so many men
she knew. Yet it was the same pitch he had given Kate.

"You need some more?" Dr. Forester asked, holding out
the Kleenex box.

"No, thanks. I'd rather use my sleeve." Michelle
straightened up in her seat and looked directly at Dr. Forester. "Being alone by yourself is better than being alone
with someone, so don't give me this you'd-be-better-off-
married crap. I'm here because I've been having problems
dealing with my work. Period. You think you can help or
not?" *Not so harsh. Say you're depressed. Admit you're
depressed. Give him Kate's words.*

She said nothing.

"I gather having children is a big issue with you."

"I asked you a question."

"You're the patient. Believe me, I'm on your side."

"You sure of that?"

"Yes, Michelle. I'm sure." Dr. Forester looked at his
watch. "I'm afraid our time is up." He was standing at her
side, escorting her to the door. There was his hand on her
shoulder, gently patting, a gesture of comfort, and then his
hand pulling away, Dr. Forester standing with his hands
clasped in front of him. "See you Thursday, the same
time?"

Michelle nodded grimly.

After Michelle left, Dr. Forester sat motionless in his
chair, trying hard to keep his mind clear. It was different
from meditating, when he might actively think of nothing.
Rather he sat trying to fend off the thought that jabbed at

his brain and groin. The picture of the young woman with the penis against her cheek floated in and out of view. The woman had high cheekbones. So did Michelle. The woman had been on her knees, in the posture of supplication, as though praying to the male organ—an act of communion. Her hands had been tied, only her face rising from the bed to meet her captor.

Give it to me, she said. *I am yours.*

No. Forester shuddered. That wasn't exactly what the woman would say. It was what he imagined. She would say something like "Oh, my God." Her eyes would be so large. Then she would squeeze them closed. That wasn't necessary. It wasn't necessary to be afraid.

There was a buzzing—Mrs. Seifert was ready for her session. Poor whining Mrs. Seifert, a professional sad sack, a first-rate complainer, now forced to pay someone to nod and commiserate, her husband feigning partial deafness and her children forever out for the evening. A hundred fifty bucks to rattle over the same godforsaken terrain, and drill in the same barren field.

Complainers had a singular lack of imagination. They could annoy a stone. And he was to heal her, or at least comfort her. It would be easier to climb Mount Everest in a wet suit. He should send her to someone fresh in practice. They could use the money and they might have more compassion.

No, he would try harder. *We are all in this together,* he reminded himself. Each with our pain. She deserved his best efforts if for no other reason than to affirm that he was a decent man who cared.

He looked down at her Birkenstock sandals. One great

toe was bent inward. Mrs. Seifert had asked him on four successive visits whether or not he would recommend podiatric surgery. Forester had told her that he knew nothing about feet. "But you did go to medical school. You must have an opinion." He knew it was just a matter of time before she appeared in those ghastly lace-up open-toed shoes that podiatrists use postoperatively. She would wear them for six months, or longer, and he would have to stare at her silent suffering. She would say nothing and let her bandaged feet do the talking, another burden to be woven into the fabric of disappointment that she cynically referred to as "my life."

She is a human being, a suffering soul. So don't be so smug, Forester again reminded himself as he screwed himself down into his seat and tried to listen. *She doesn't wish to be what she is any more than you do. If you can forgive her, maybe someday someone will forgive you.*

Forester made a ten o'clock appointment with Mistress Diana. By then the street would be dark and he could pass in shadows. He had found her name in the San Francisco *Nighttime Express*, a cheap tabloid that specialized in advertisements for massage, telephone sex, bondage, and so on.

He walked up the wooden stairs, trying not to look into the So Far Inn. The men would be staring; they certainly knew what went on upstairs.

R.V. was dressed in a navy blue gabardine skirt and matching jacket. She could have been a loan officer. She was introducing herself as Mistress Diana. Her voice was matter-of-fact. Forester suspected that she would use the same tone of voice talking about enemas or low-risk mutual funds. She motioned Forester to a seat facing the front window.

Forester was reasonably pleased. The woman obviously had education and was sophisticated. He would have preferred her to be blond, but the woman who called herself Mistress Diana was at least light complected. In a photograph, particularly a grainy black and white, she might appear blond. She offered him a glass of wine. It was a Kendall-Jackson chardonnay.

Forester found himself having an imaginary conversation with Joan, saying that there were intelligent, cultured women who understood. He had the momentary fantasy of having Mistress Diana phone Joan and explain how all men liked to dominate. It came with the genetic territory, man as hunter. "Listen, hon, just humor him. It's in their blood."

"So, what specifically interests you?" R.V. asked.

"Did you ever read *The Balcony*, by Genet?" Forester asked.

"Sure. It's required reading in our business."

"You know how one man dressed up like a general, another like a priest?"

R.V. nodded.

"Those men had specific fantasies. I don't think I do. I just want to see you tied up on the bed. I'm not interested in hurting you or anything like that. I just want. . . ." Forester stopped. He realized he was repeating himself.

"That's it? No dirty talk, no costumes?"

Forester shook his head.

"If you change your mind, I've got closets full of dreams. Uniforms, maid's outfits, you name it. And it's all included. So don't be shy."

"I'm not shy." His voice was a little too loud. He took a gulp of the wine.

"Don't rush. We've got plenty of time. I just got back from dance class. I don't mind sitting here for a few minutes. If you want, you can tell me a little about yourself."

Everyone is a therapist, Forester thought. He saw the look in her eye, the inquisitive, comforting, practiced gaze. The woman saw herself as a professional. He tried to enjoy the irony, but realized that he was so nervous that his legs were shaky. She was pouring him a second glass of wine and telling him to relax. How maternal. And condescending.

"You sure you don't mind?" Dr. Forester asked.

"Mind what?" R.V. sipped from her glass, her lips full against the rim. She smiled at him through the glass. It was a game. Life was a game. There were winners and losers, victors and victims.

"Being tied up and helpless."

"Mind?" R.V. let out a gutsy laugh. "Why, that's what a woman is all about, isn't it? Laying back, spreading her legs, the man on top, letting him do whatever he wants."

Forester suspected a note of sarcasm, but he wasn't sure. Perhaps this was verbal foreplay, what she thought turned him on. "No, I'm serious. It must be something that you genuinely want to do."

"Trust me. There's nothing more delicious than giving yourself up completely to some handsome man like yourself."

"This is something you dream about?" Forester asked R.V.

"You bet. Lots of women feel this way."

"Don't let Gloria Steinem hear you talking like this. She'll take away your sisterhood card."

"You've been in Gloria's bedroom? Who knows what Gloria digs? This is sex we're talking about. Just a variation on the old in-and-out. It's not a matter of principles, or of life and death."

"True." Forester took a large gulp of wine. "It's very important that you enjoy yourself," he said. The wine was working. He felt lighter, less of a burden to himself. In the back of his brain pieces of memory bumped against each other, lightly, jockeying for position. Each one was a highly polished opalescent pearl, rubbed bright by rumination, bubbling up into the crisp yet fruity chardonnay buzz.

Suddenly he became aware of a horrible thought, which quickly became more than a thought, a realization. In that other time, long ago, the tall slender blond woman with the finely sculpted neck and the smell of cinnamon and honey had stood at the basement door, whispering to him that it would be all right, that he would be going away for only a short time, that she would come to Canada and take him home again soon. *Yes, I promise, very soon.* And she had stayed on, waiting for them to take her away.

Wanted it. Wanted them.

Dreamed of them.

Opened her door and let them in.

After first sending away her only son.

He swilled down the last of the wine. R.V. refilled his glass and hers, then offered Forester her hand. They walked down a narrow corridor that smelled of old rug. R.V. stepped out of her skirt and blouse. She was naked. Her body was firm, her skin strikingly white, chalk white, like some cold, distant moon. R.V. pulled out four lavender scarves from a bedside nightstand.

"Be careful."

"Don't worry," Forester said. "The main thing is that you enjoy yourself." And he set to work tying the knots.

If he could see the expression, catch the moment, he would understand.

On the way out Forester carefully washed out his drinking glass. He was the perfect guest. *Always leave everything the way you found it,* his real mother had said. *You are a boy of good upbringing.*

EIGHT

BOBBY LOCKHART looked down at R.V.'s blanched face. Her skin was smooth, unlined by any signs of terror that must have marked her last moments. She was turned on her side; the lower border of one breast was a mottled purple. Bobby recognized the residue of the old bruise on her inner arm. It was now a pale yellow emblem of a woman who rented her body to strangers. Bobby couldn't imagine being that trusting. He realized that the ultimate motive was sexual, that she must have gotten off on the thrill of danger, but it was impossible to look at her and have those thoughts. Somehow it was blasphemous.

Other than some reddening on the wrists and ankles, there were no signs of struggle. Dr. Setledge indicated that they could have been from earlier in the day, or even the day before. The apartment was neat and tidy, everything in its place. There wasn't even a dirty drinking glass or plate in the sink. It was as though the woman had fallen from the sky. The lab boys stood around with empty evidence bags.

Dr. Setledge had one of the technicians sit R.V. up. He inspected the sheet underneath. He was wearing a magnifying loop over his glasses. "Hair today, gone tomorrow," he said to Lockhart, without turning to look at him. For

some time he stood bent at the waist, scouring every inch
of the bed. Finally he stood up, his hand in the small of his
back.

"Nothing. It's like the guy vacuumed the bed." Setledge
pointed to the corners of the bottom sheet. They were precisely tucked underneath the mattress. The bedroom had
two matching straight-backed chairs, one on either side of
the foot of the bed. Both were arranged at the same forty-
five-degree angle to the corners of the bed. "Must be
Navy," Setledge said. "Like he knew there was going to be
inspection."

"You mean like she's on display?" Lockhart asked.

"It's a thought."

"You going to tell me this one's accidental, too?"
Lockhart motioned to one of the lab techs to dust the windowsill.

"It's possible."

" 'It's possible. It's a thought. There's a chance.' Come
on, Setledge. Gather up your wits and say something specific." Once Lockhart thought that medicine was a science
and that pathology was the answer book to questions of
disease. Certainly an autopsy would give the final answer.
But there had been no last word on Kelly Caldwell. Her
blood alcohol level was consistent with a few drinks—a
social level, as Setledge put it. Average for a San Francis-
can in the evening. There also was a modest amount of
barbiturates. Enough to cause drowsiness, but certainly not
coma or death. Setledge still hadn't signed Kelly Caldwell
out one way or the other.

"There's no point in creating false certainties. This isn't
philosophy. This is real life." Setledge did some quick
bending exercises, his hand still in the small of his back.

"Back-breaking details that don't mean shit in the big picture."

"There isn't any big picture," Lockhart said. "Only detail. And this isn't real life. This is real death." Bobby sat down in one of the straight-backed chairs. "She seemed like a decent sort, despite her trade."

"You knew her?"

"She was a friend of Kelly Caldwell. They played softball together."

"I can imagine batting practice. They probably started a half hour before the ball arrived."

"She could be your daughter. Have a little respect."

"No need to get nasty. Sooner or later there'll be a clue. Then we'll get out the retrospectoscope and piece it together. You and I will sit down over coffee and cold danish and speculate, formulate, disagree, make blind assumptions and false starts, and by some stroke of luck that others might term intuition, we'll figure it out. We'll shake hands and feel, for a moment, like old buddies. If you were smart, you would forgo the initial accusations that will make you want to apologize later on. This is twenty-five years speaking." There appeared in Dr. Setledge's eyes a momentary muddying, a cloud of emotion scudded quickly by. "This type of death brings out the worst in all of us."

"You think this is number two?" The lab technicians were finished now. They packed their suitcases and were waiting to be excused. Setledge nodded his head. Suddenly Lockhart and Setledge were alone with the dead woman. She had only been dead a few hours, but Lockhart was sure there would soon be a bad smell in the room. He went to the window and opened it wide. Up drifted snatches of

Edith Piaf. She was singing a duet with someone in the bar below.

"It's number two, all right. It's number two in my face, deep doo-doo. If I don't come up with some half-truth about the Caldwell woman, Spagliano will mumble that old Setledge is slipping. But I can already tell you that this one isn't going to be any easier. For example, her nails are as fresh as if she had just been manicured. If there had been any struggle, any fight at all, we'd see something. A hair, a piece of fabric, a fleck of skin. Sure we'll look with the microscope, but there's not going to be anything."

"You'll be nice and thorough, like you expect to find something. Right?"

"Absolutely, but he's a professional."

"So that's reason to yawn your way through?" Lockhart looked over at the man that he sometimes liked, sometimes wished would shape up, and sometimes suspected had seen some bigger picture and moved right into it. But today Setledge seemed out of his element, over his head in a way that Lockhart had never seen before. Cocksure Setledge seemed uneasy. "There're going to be more, aren't there?" Lockhart said.

"Sorry, Bobby. This isn't your ordinary fratricide, patricide, lover's quarrel, drug shooting—with ordinary motives like hatred and revenge. Not this one. I'll lay twenty to one that we're looking at a message, not a motive. This woman is laid out like a telegram."

"Maybe we should call Western Union."

"A word of advice. Don't take it personally. The last time we had a serial murder it destroyed everyone connected with the investigation. Especially the inspector in charge. He might as well have been one of the victims."

"There hasn't been one here in town since the Zodiac, has there?"

"Not that we've recognized. Most aren't, you know. Drifters moving from town to town, or different MO's. We can only recognize patterns, and only obvious ones at that. For all you know, there could have been twenty so-called accidental deaths during bondage in California over the last few years. Each would be classified differently, according to the county and the coroner. For example, if I wrote down that Kelly Caldwell was an accident, we'd still be at number one."

"I thought you didn't write down anything."

"I was waiting for number two."

The coroner and his assistant had arrived. Lockhart watched as they slid R.V. into the body bag. The assistant unfolded the aluminum gurney. Moments later they were descending the stairs. Several of the patrons of So Far Inn stood at the bottom, watching. As they parted to make way for the coroners and the gurney, one man, his arm around the waist of another, spoke. "Treat her gently. She was a friend." Another said, "I hope you catch the sick bastard." Several others nodded in agreement. Edith Piaf was still singing, this time by herself.

"You have a wife?" Lockhart asked Setledge. They were standing between their two cars parked diagonally on the sidewalk. Lockhart's side police light was still tossing red blotches on the bar window.

"The answer is no, I don't tell her what I do. And I don't ask her advice. I wear plenty of cologne and say the same thing each night. 'Tough day at the office. Only four million days until retirement.' Why? You feel like telling your girlfriend? Forget it. She isn't interested. Not unless she's as sick as us."

"My ex-wife thought philosophy was sick." Lockhart went halfway into falsetto. " 'You draw up imaginary assumptions like a shopping list. But a banana is real. You can't eat Kant. Everyone knows that pure reason is pure bullshit. Do you hear me? Everyone. And we don't need five hundred pages to prove it.' " Lockhart's voice descended again. "She left me for an investment banker with a two-page portfolio."

"You can't blame her. We're breast-fed on numbers. Reality is keeping score. Just watch the papers heat up. Today it's two. Tomorrow or next week, or whenever, the headlines will read number three. Not Kelly Caldwell or whomever, just *number three*."

"When are you going to issue your final report?"

"You still have a few days. Then it'll be the papers, and you can forget about the rest of your life."

Michelle angrily drove across town, winding her way through what seemed to be intentionally slow traffic. The day was designed to aggravate her. The last thing she wanted to do was to sit in that charged room and talk with Forester. The whole plan was ridiculous.

But she arrived five minutes early. For the first time she noticed that there was a slightly stale odor in the waiting room, and that two of the pictures were gone. Normally the magazines were updated weekly, but not today. Even the waiting room was out of sorts. Michelle slumped in the chair nearest the front door. *Collect yourself,* she said. She closed her eyes and tried to imagine something pleasant. A Caribbean beach with gentle blue waters lapping at her feet. But she couldn't. Even the imaginary sand was hot and got under her clothing.

Dr. Forester opened the waiting room door to invite Michelle in. He looked tired and haggard. His suit was wrinkled, as though he had slept in it.

Dr. Forester noticed Michelle staring at him. "My wife's had to go back East. Her mom's sick. I'm not much of a bachelor."

Inside, in the near corner of the corridor leading to the consultation room, an antique umbrella stand was missing. There was another empty spot on the corridor wall. It had been a seascape. Now there was only a square patch of unfaded paint. Michelle couldn't remember if the picture or the umbrella stand had been there the last visit. How observant, she chided herself.

As Michelle sat down for her session, she watched Dr. Forester watching her. He looked like a wreck. She felt she should be giving him therapy.

"I hope your wife does better with her mom than I've done with mine."

"She'll be okay." There was a note of resignation in his voice, perhaps even a hint of anger. Michelle added up the clues. Though it was only a sudden hunch, she felt sure that his wife had packed it in. Why? She should be interviewing Mrs. Forester. She'd know the real truth, or at least some aspect of it.

The session was going poorly, with Forester repeating himself several times. He was clearly out of focus, as though the slightly sweet odor of the room was coming from his mental state. Meanwhile he was taking her for another hundred fifty dollars, and she was no further along than the first day.

She had just about tapped out her rainy-day kitty, her prospective new couch already deep in Forester's pocket. Shortly he'd be into her grocery money. Dick Winters kept promising a promotion, even a chance at anchoring weekends, but he never mentioned numbers.

She wanted to quit, admit defeat. Get on with her life. But the signs of Mrs. Forester's probable departure nagged at her. You don't leave a prominent, well-off, outwardly decent man without *some* reason. Especially after what Michelle assumed to have been many years of marriage. Conclusion: Some women learn slowly, Michelle thought, putting herself at the top of the list. Which also meant that at that rate she would be in the poorhouse before she got her first clue.

She was pissed, and Forester was groping to find the thread of the last session.

"The last few meetings you've been exploring your feelings about having children. We seemed to be getting somewhere. Don't you think so?"

Michelle had trouble remembering her most recent point of view. She had cried, been defensive, even, reluctantly, privately considered her feelings on children. Which had led her to thoughts about Owen. It was a blind alley she didn't wish to enter again. She had always been a poor sport about voluntarily playing no-win games. Which was what her scheme about Forester was turning out to be. She felt emotionally drained, indifferent. Most of all she wanted to leave.

"Sometimes my biological clock sounds like a bomb about to go off. Other times I can't even hear it. Maybe I should wear earplugs." She didn't mean to sound so tough, but she couldn't find a comfortable mood. At the same time it made her mad that Forester would so easily see through her protective sarcasm. She looked up at Forester, expecting a stern judgmental countenance. Instead she saw a kindly middle-aged man, a little frayed at the edges, anxious to help and to please. And be acknowledged. Michelle couldn't imagine him intimidating Kate. Her tone softened. "Of course you're right. It has been on my mind. I guess it's hard to admit."

"I can understand your being angry. The whole dilemma of career versus family is blatantly unfair. Posing the question suggests that there is an answer. Which we both know isn't so. But it's a big step forward for you to admit—"

Michelle interrupted. "You've been very helpful. Given me a lot to think about." *Give it one or two more sessions,* she told herself. *Maybe something'll turn up. No. Not one more minute. I'll face Owen, tell him it was all a mistake. Finished. Done with. Over.* She stood up and draped her jacket over her arm.

"You're not considering stopping therapy, are you? There's much more you could accomplish."

"I'm sure there is. But first I've got to let this soak in. If I change my mind, you'll be the first to know." As Michelle slipped on her coat, she saw a pained, sad look in Dr. Forester's eye. His shoulders were hunched forward, his hands hung forlornly at his side. To her surprise, she started toward him, as though to give him a hug. She stopped herself, instead touching him lightly with her left hand on the sleeve of his gray suit jacket. Both of them seemed startled. It was a brief gesture, quickly covered up in the shaking of hands, but the moment would be burned into both of their minds.

Michelle stepped back again. "Thanks for everything,"

she said, being the perfect grateful patient. Later she would ask herself why she had started to hug the man.

"Is it the money? We could work something out."

Michelle shook her head.

"Instead of just terminating like this, why don't you give me a call in a week and tell me how you're doing." Dr. Forester glanced down at his hands, which were now folded in front of him. "There wouldn't be any charge. It'd be my way of knowing that you were doing okay."

"Sure enough. I'll call you next week."

"Thanks," Dr. Forester said.

"You did what?" Owen screamed into the phone. "I thought you were my friend."

"I am. But I made a mistake. Come on over. We'll talk about it."

"What's there to talk about? You told me that Forester drove Kate crazy, and now you say he's such a swell guy."

"He is," Michelle said. "I must have been wrong. Maybe I wanted to believe that he confused her. It's a lot easier to think that than to believe your best friend . . ." Michelle hadn't meant to be so direct. She had no intention of hurting Owen.

"So you think she just up and killed herself?"

"I'm not saying that."

"Then what exactly are you saying? Don't be shy on my account."

"It was a childish idea, trying to seek revenge on her psychiatrist. We were both grasping at straws." The image of Mrs. Forester, bags in hand, came to mind. And Kate, biting her nails and pouring out her heart, telling her about

Forester. Maybe there was some deep dark secret to Forester's treatment of Kate, but what more could she do? It was better to let Owen ventilate than to perpetuate this limbo of maybe Forester this, Forester that. She and Owen both needed to shift gears.

She thought of Forester's sad eyes as he said good-bye. There wasn't a trace of evil.

And she had wanted to hug him.

What had gotten into her?

"Childish? That's perfect. You seem to forget that Kate is dead. Dead! Do you hear me? She was fine before, now she's gone, and you fall for the very guy that did her in."

" 'Fall for'? You must be kidding. If there was anyone I'd fall for, it'd be you. But you never even notice." There was silence. Michelle wished she could reach into the phone line and intercept the disloyal words. And she hoped that Owen would hear her loud and clear.

"You still there?" Owen asked.

"Sorry. I didn't mean to be disrespectful. Forget what I said. I've got to go. Let's have dinner, maybe a decent home-cooked meal over here. God, I didn't mean it to sound like that. I'll talk to you soon."

Michelle wandered through her apartment, assessing. Three rented rooms equalled her life to date. She couldn't get the idea of children out of her mind. Before seeing Dr. Forester, kids had been a back burner item. Dr. Forester had seen right to the heart of the matter. *Why do you think you spend your valuable spare time illustrating children's books? Do you have any favorite kids among the drawings? Do you draw mostly boys or girls, or is it pretty much even?* A handful of questions and Forester had the entire picture by the second visit.

He had been anything but suggestive. All he had said was to think about it. There had been no coercion, nothing off-color. In fact he had been the picture of propriety. In her mind's eye she saw him as a lonely man who would slip out of his suit after-hours, pad around the house in robe and slippers making soup and coffee, waiting for his wife to return.

Michelle thought back to the last lunch with Kate. It could have been entirely Kate's imagination. She walked to the phone, as though to telephone Kate and ask her. She fondled the receiver, having the sense of Kate's presence. *She's dead,* Michelle told herself, though she continued to hold the receiver. Then she had the curious thought of talking to Kate about Owen. *Would you mind?* she wanted to ask. *You wouldn't hold it against me? I never said a word while you were alive.* But it didn't make any difference. Owen saw her as a friend, period.

She was glad to pull an evening shift at the station, doing a brief piece on alleged auto repair fraud at Sears. Not exactly an earthshaking revelation, but it got her out of her apartment, out of today. At least at the station she could keep busy, keep her mind distracted. Out of trouble.

Since Kate's death Owen slept in little restless chunks, a couple hours here and there, on the couch at home, or on a futon that he kept in back of the store. Liquor helped. So did the dream of Dr. Forester being publicly humiliated. He saw Forester being stoned, then run out of town, his psychiatric diploma dragging between his legs, bumping along like an old tin can. In his dreams he gathered up the stones. Each night they piled higher. He could feel the tension building as he waited for Michelle to confirm their suspicions.

Now there wasn't going to be any word. All he could conclude was that Michelle had fallen for the bastard the same way as his wife. Forester must be a regular Svengali.

He purposely ignored what she had said about him, as though Kate were watching. He felt embarrassed even contemplating Michelle, and cut the thought short, returning to visions of Forester undone.

An hour later he was at the San Francisco Gun Exchange, buying two boxes of bullets for his father's revolver. "You've got yourself a wonderful old piece," the middle-aged salesman said as he rang up the register. "A Colt twenty-five. Haven't seen one of these in years. They were hot in Chicago in the twenties."

"I don't think it's ever been fired," Owen said.

"Sure it has. Look here." The clerk took out a magnifying glass and held it over the barrel. "Look closely and you can see the scoring of the barrel. There, that purplish sheen."

"It was my father's."

"I'll bet there's plenty of history down there," the man said. "That's the worst part of our job, not being able to hear the stories. If only metal could talk." The clerk winked as he handed Owen the bag of boxed bullets.

Owen considered going to a standard range and getting some instruction. But the less public exposure the better. Instead he drove up the coast to Guerneville, and then toward the coast. He stopped near Cazadero, at a densely wooded area, mostly redwoods, and some madrone and manzanita. It was mid-October and the leaves were crisp and chattering under foot. He hiked up a steep hill. At the top he could see all the way to the ocean, the blue sliver of water barely visible between the trees. There was no one for miles.

He loaded the gun and aimed at a nearby flower. He started to pull the trigger but changed his mind. The flower hadn't hurt a soul. He took a handkerchief from his pocket and fastened it between two branches of a tree. He thought of drawing Forester's face on it. Instead he made a fist-sized circle in the middle. He stepped back and fired. Again and again, until he finally hit the target. By the end of the first box, he was able to hit it consistently from ten feet. Longer distances were questionable.

He took down the shredded handkerchief and stuck it in his pocket. He lay down on the bed of warm crisp leaves and watched the sun stream down through the redwoods. Dappled light fluttered across his face. He put out one arm, expecting Kate's shoulder. His hand struck a rock. The blow wasn't painful, rather there was a hollow discomfort, the stabbing sensation of emptiness. He pulled his arm back, now resting both hands on his chest.

Streams of light hung in the woods. The light had traveled all the way from the sun. It was a wonderful autumn day, yet there was an aching under his armpit and across his chest. Kate would have had her head nuzzled against him. She would have been laughing, humming, or snoozing. His skin ached for her touch as though the very cells of his body were drying up without her, his skin becoming brittle and threatening to crack open.

He reached down to his hip and picked up the gun, holding it in the flickering sunlight. So it had been fired. Had it been his father pulling the trigger? And what had been the target, an old Heinz 57 Varieties bottle or someone's face? His father had been a man of quick temper, but never violent. Had there been another side?

Holding the gun in his hand made Owen forget the aching. But did he plan on using it? Had his father really shot at someone? Was this more childish daydreaming? He had no idea. For the moment he would enjoy the cool of the metal and the possibility.

It was his first decent sleep, the gun weighing on his chest and anchoring him to the spot. He awakened to the evening fog and a rapidly gathering darkness. To the west there was a thin wafer of rust-colored dusk; overhead it was already the blue-black of evening. He couldn't remember the last time he had spent the day in the woods. It must have been as a young boy, his father pointing out the enormous variety of insects and spiders and why it was better spending summer in the city.

There were strange sounds everywhere—the crackling of limbs and leaves, the cries of fog-bound birds, his own breath. He thought he heard a voice. He turned in the direction of the sound, but saw nothing but the trunks of trees shrouded in mist. He heard the sound again, not loud enough to be understood. It was Kate, calling to him. *Owen. Owen.* He was sure, yet not sure. The beating in his chest was too loud, drowning her out. *Ssssh,* he wanted to say to his heart. *Keep still. Let me hear her.* But his heart pounded louder and he had the sense of failed opportunity.

The gun was heavy in his jacket as he started down the steep hill. He double-checked the safety. He didn't want to be an accident statistic. He was without a flashlight and proceeded slowly, cautiously. He would do the same with Forester. There could be no mistake.

It was almost completely black now, and in the distance,

between the shadowy tree trunks, was the road that led back to the main highway. Owen was reluctant to leave the woods. Kate was here, he was sure of it. Back in his car her presence would be laughable, some hokey California joke that smacked of reincarnation and hovering spirits. Out here it was different. He would remember this moment. In addition to his great longing, it gave him a sense of hope.

He reconsidered. There was no urgency to get back to the city. He was safe, he had a gun to protect himself. He found a level area beneath two massive redwoods. Some said the trees were thousands of years old. They would watch over him. He patted one tree on its furry bark, then slid down and secured himself in a bed of leaves. He pulled his down jacket tight around himself, and waited for the light.

He had all the time in the world to deal with Forester. Right now he would open himself to the possibility of Kate. He cocked his head, listening to the sounds of the earth beneath him, and the forest above. Hearing her again would be unequivocal proof. Not hearing her would be just like a woman, playing cat and mouse. Either way she was there. Very definitely. Absolutely. With certainty. Please.

NINE

DR. FORESTER RUSHED into the kitchen when he smelled the burning. His pan of soup was scorched; the kitchen was filled with smoke. He quickly turned off the gas flame and opened the window. He put his burned dinner in the sink, added some liquid soap and water, and left it to soak. He could not remember having put the soup on the stove. Judging from the empty can, it was Pepperidge Farm vegetable. He must have chosen it from the shelf of canned goods. He walked to the pantry and tried to recollect. Nothing came to mind. He was frightened. So many things he could not remember now. Twice this week he had forgotten appointments at the Institute. He ran into an old friend on the street and could not place him. Only later did his name pop into mind.

He had heard of Alzheimer's disease beginning this way. A little forgetful, a little less interested in what was going on, the next thing you knew, it was babble city with attendants and leather straps around your chest.

But he knew better. There was nothing wrong with his brain. It was only natural that he would have difficulty concentrating. His wife had left him right when he had a major paper to present at the Institute. He had tried contacting Joan several times recently, but she wasn't interested in conversation. This week she had retained a lawyer.

Strangely, like the smoke that was rushing out through the open window, Joan's presence was becoming less palpable. Before, Joan was everywhere. When she first left, Forester couldn't imagine how the various rooms of his life could be so completely emptied. Now the smoke was thinning out, barely visible against the background of the garden. He missed Joan, but more and more his failed marriage was becoming a matter of a sense of incompleteness and embarrassment. Forester was certain that he wanted her back, but couldn't tell if it was out of love or loneliness. That he might make the distinction carried its own sad implication. Maybe he was too selfish for real love.

Forester took out another pan and another can of soup. While dinner was heating, he went through his mail. The telephone bill had come. Local numbers weren't listed, yet the name Mistress Diana came to mind. He would phone her again. The last time she had served Kendall-Jackson chardonnay, but he wasn't sure what she had worn when they went into the bedroom. It was the difference between verbal and visual memory, he reminded himself. He was better with words than images. Perhaps that was why he had such difficulty conjuring up her face and body.

"Tie me up good and tight," she had said. It was too bad he couldn't remember her expression.

"Use your tongue. Right there. Yes. And your fingers. Yes."

He would dial her again, after dinner. But first he would eat.

He took the bowl of soup and went into the den. On his

desk was the outline of his address. He had planned on talking about the Elmer Gantry syndrome. He was going to use Jim Van Allen as the subject. But the outline yawned up at him, flat old ground recycled. It was rehash. The lecture was next Thursday. It was too late for a new subject. Or was it? He had learned so much in the last few weeks. But how do you organize unrelated observations into a single presentation? He gave a short laugh. He could call his lecture "Notes of a Madman." But it had been done before.

His soup was getting cold. He ate quickly, the spoon loud against his teeth. Sounds of solitary sustenance echoing in the empty house. He had been doing fine until he had looked at his phone bill. The local numbers not listed pried loose other fragments of shrouded recollection. Forester furrowed his brow, squeezing as though he could bear down on the unformed memories. There was the creaking of bedsprings, a heavy musk-based perfume, the sound of footsteps on hardwood floors, or wooden stairs. And a wisp of fog passing beneath the street lamp, his breath escaping into the pink neon night.

He looked down at his outline, hoping for the fog to clear, his thoughts to sort themselves.

First things first. You work out a decent lecture, then you have plenty of time to think about the other things. He finished his soup and put the bowl on the far corner of his desk. It was surprising; Pepperidge Farm was about as good as home-cooked. Certainly it was quicker and demanded nothing. Hooray for vacuum packing.

The medical society had shown him the statements of Jim Van Allen's former employees. They all said the same thing. Initially he had been extremely pleasant and courteous. They were glad to be working for him. Once they were comfortable, the nasties began.

One worker, who had a background in psychology, said that his primary goal was to humiliate her. At first she thought it was going to be old-fashioned hot office sex, with plenty of laughter and good feelings. No big deal. She was single, this was San Francisco. But it wasn't. They would have sex after work, on one of the examining tables—he was too cheap even to cough up motel money—and then, before the paper of the examining table was dry, Van Allen would complain about her slowness with dictation, that the waiting room wasn't as tidy as it might be, that she was making too many personal calls. He threatened to put her on probation if her typing didn't improve. Then he would be recharged, ready for a second round.

"At first I thought he was kidding," the woman said.

Another woman told of Dr. Van Allen "playfully ordering" her to lie on the waiting room floor, her wrists and ankles tied to the legs of the waiting room chairs. Then he took photographs, saying it was important for her to understand her position in the office. The following day he gave her a bonus of a free weekend at Lake Tahoe. On Valentine's Day he put copies of the photos in her office mail. In the space between her legs he had written: "Thanks for keeping an open mind." A week later he threatened to pin the photos on the office bulletin board if she didn't work late an extra night each week. The next late evening he told her to get down on her knees alongside him in the unlit waiting room and pray to God for forgiveness.

"We are all sinners," he had said, holding her hand

tightly in the dim waiting room light. The woman said that the sight of Van Allen rocking and praying in a room filled with back issues of *Today's Health* and *Preventive Medicine* had made her laugh. Van Allen became livid. "This is no laughing matter. This waiting room is the Devil's playground." Afterward he had invited her to Bible readings at his house. Yes, his wife would be there. They were a very close family. He loved her very much. They read the Bible each night. Yes, they had a wonderful sex life, better than she could imagine. Much better.

"Then why bother with me?" the woman asked.

"Because you need me to teach you about the ways of the Lord, about sin and redemption."

"You are a crazy motherfucker." And the woman had turned Van Allen in. To her surprise, there were a dozen complaints already filed.

On the top of his note pad Forester wrote: "religion, power, sex, humiliation, domination." He drew arrows between them, aware of the many permutations and combinations. Somewhere in the arrows lay his lecture. He drew a large circle around the five words, then an arrow pointing to the right—the male symbol. Below he drew the female figure, a circle with a cross hanging below. A cross? Funny he had never noticed that before. The woman was the hollow womb and the crucifix. From a row of books to his left, he pulled out a volume dealing with symbols.

According to Jung, the cross signified inner urges. The circle indicated the process of rising above urges. But that was just Jung's opinion. The symbols were ancient, dating back at least to Greek times, and probably earlier. How was it that woman had come to be universally symbolized by the circle and the cross? He read from his reference books, but found nothing useful.

Perhaps it was because symbols could be static representations of motion. The cross might represent the unfolding of the arms—the movement toward the position of openness. Jesus giving himself to God. Woman giving herself to the arrow that was man.

The cross was the symbol of inner urges.

Dr. Van Allen down on his knees, his black onyx cross to his lips. "Taste the cross," he had said to one woman. "Kiss it."

Forester saw Jesus stumbling through the streets, the thorns deep in his flesh, the crowds jeering and throwing stones. Public humiliation was the first step. And the final one? It was so obvious that it needn't even be mentioned. Just walk through any major museum; the Louvre had hundreds of Christ figures carrying the cross, and on the cross, moving toward, then arriving at the moment of purification.

It was in the relinquishing of himself that Jesus became God on earth. The ultimate yielding was the way to godliness. It was how man reached God.

Van Allen had said to several of the women that he wanted to show them the way to Paradise. Right now he was just tying them up and humiliating them. But it would be only a matter of time before he would go further. His agenda was obvious.

Van Allen must be stopped before someone got hurt.

Forester would begin by documenting carefully, meticulously, in his notebook. In addition he would record their sessions. He had a small powerful Lanier that he used for taping lectures. The Lanier could sit in his desk drawer, unseen, without affecting the quality of the recording. It was important that he had absolutely unequivocal proof, beyond a shadow of a doubt. Of course it was unethical, an invasion of privacy. And the recording couldn't be evidence in court. But Van Allen must be uncovered. Defrocked, to borrow a term from another discipline. He could unofficially play the tape to the head of the medical society profession relations committee. It need not be public to have its effect.

And he, Forester, would have the goods on him.

The lecture would be about the religious aspects of masochism, the spiritual nature of yielding. It was a sensitive topic; he would have to be very careful not to offend. He would emphasize that he was presenting the logic of the disturbed. His ideas about the cross would be the musings of an undisclosed patient. He would be above the ideas, presenting them the way an oncologist presented the critical information about a terminal patient. Ideas of the disturbed were no more than lumps of a cancer patient; they should be seen in the same neutral, nonjudgmental light. That was what the Institute was all about—the advancement of understanding of the human condition.

Forester was tingly and excited at the possibility of their response. Freud hadn't touched symbols. Jung made a career out of them and still hadn't seen the crucifix hanging down from the woman's body. How could they have overlooked what was so patently obvious?

Self-flagellation, hair shirts, and pebbles in the shoes along the road to heaven. Suffering, masochism, spirituality. One need look no further than Joan of Arc. He thought of the representations of Joan of Arc smiling suggestively as the flames licked at her feet. She was one of the great heroines in history. A woman true to her word. Saint Joan.

Had his real mother yielded herself so that her son might live? No. Forester specifically recalled that she had told him their separation would be temporary, a few months at most. "This will pass," she had said with a wave of her hand. Forester still recalled the gesture. She wasn't dying for a cause, nor setting an example. No. She had none of the purity of spirit that made Joan of Arc embrace the flames her eyes rolled heavenward. No, his mother had no claim to authenticity. She was a coward. So were the others, those who simply gave themselves up. They were all the same. They weren't messengers of higher purpose. Quite the reverse.

If I had died with her, resisting, then my life would have had meaning, Forester thought. *I could have held a gun, thrown a rock, done something. But no, it was a finger to the lips—ssssh—and being handed through a basement window. It was too dark to turn and see her expression. She said I was too young, that it was better this way.* Forester reached up and felt the deep wrinkles on either side of his mouth. They were the creek beds of former tears, the dry, hot landscape of adulthood. Tears were not the answer. *You're a grown man, and at some point you have to overcome your past.* That's what he told his patients.

Success in psychiatry required a peculiar quirk of memory. Uncover the bad stuff. Take a close look, then try to forget, repress, deny that which can't be acknowledged. It was a crapshoot. You never knew what would pop up— whether it was tolerable or overwhelming, intrinsic to the fabric of personality—until it was too late. Depth analysis could be the worst example of wishful thinking, like doing an exploratory craniotomy and cleverly cutting away only the bad tissue. Easy in theory, not so in practice. Some memories were too caustic and leaked out of their storage bins, washing over and eating through the dikes of repression and denial. It was the battle of the mind over what matters.

Ultimately successful therapy required a failure of memory.

Forget it, Alan. You're getting all worked up over nothing—but it wasn't nothing. If it was, then it meant that there was nothing.

Which made life as expendable as the exhalation of a breath of stale air.

Nada.

Rien de tout.

Zip.

He folded up his notes and put them in the top drawer. He took a blank note pad with him and he went back to his bedroom.

The bed was larger than usual, its edges ill defined in the darkened room. Forester was naked, his note pad, a penlight, and ballpoint pen at his side. Now that he had the skeleton of the talk, it was only a matter of his muses fleshing out the details. He was pleased at the idea of presenting his ideas as the product of a disturbed patient. At last he could explore without fear of criticism.

He sat bolt upright in bed. He would be talking about himself, which meant that he was disturbed. Forester was instantly covered in dampness, sweat jumping from every pore. *Me? No. It's Van Allen. Don't be ridiculous, Van Allen is going to be your patsy, but it's you you'll be discussing. So what? They're just ideas, and there have been so*

*many great minds that weren't appreciated in their own
time. Better the lecture be anonymous than I wake up on
Monday with no practice.*

But that's not what's bothering you. It's the other thing.
Forester looked out into his darkened bedroom. There
were so many ways of seeing yourself, ranging from pretty
good, on the whole, to horrible, wretched, the devil incar-
nate. It was just a matter of choosing the proper perspective. He had done nothing. There was no reason to be
down on himself. The sweat continued. He was not terribly convincing.

He wondered if it wasn't his recent fascination with
bondage that had led him to suggest Kate's disastrous
treatment. It was as though, in some way that he had not
previously considered, he had put her to the test. Which
would mean that there had been more to his motivation
than just trying to make her well.

That's not true. Not true at all.

Forester switched on the radio. Larry King was interviewing the Grand Master of the Ku Klux Klan. Now,
there was badness. The type of man that should be publicly castrated, then hung for all to see. Like Van Allen.
There were so many sick people out there. Maybe his lecture could shed some light.

Dick Winters and Michelle were standing next to the
water cooler at the far end of the newsroom. On one of the
overhead monitors an apartment building in Mexico City
collapsed in slow motion. "You have a strong stomach?"
Dick Winters asked.

"I'm talking to you, aren't I?" They both laughed, then
Winters's face turned serious.

"You can say no, if you want. But you'd be perfect."

"And I have a choice?"

"Word from the coroner is that the two bondage deaths were possible murders. I talked with Dr. Setledge myself. He's still hovering over noncommittal, cover-his-ass double-talk, has to wait for more tests, conclusive evidence, but unofficially he's given me the nod."

"The police have any leads?"

"Absolutely nothing. And Setledge is sure, unofficially again, that there will be more. It's going to be hot, a real opportunity for the right person. But sordid won't be the word."

"There'll be a raise to cover the nausea?"

"I was getting to that. It's a slam-dunk, no-lose proposition. The police don't find the killer, you've got a story on murder stalking the streets. If they do, you have interviews, maybe even a half-hour special. Either way you bring in a good story, we'll start you at anchor on weekends."

"I guess I'm a little hard of hearing. You didn't by any chance mention numbers, did you?"

Winters grabbed his throat as though choking.

"Is that a yes?" Michelle asked.

Winters nodded.

"How sordid?" Michelle asked.

"It could get pretty ugly. You've been to the coroner's office?"

Michelle shook her head. A juicy crime story was just what she needed to keep her mind off Owen and Forester. But she was naturally queasy. In high school biology she'd fainted the first day of cat dissection. But, she reminded herself, so did the hotshot quarterback sitting next to her.

Later that semester she'd taken out the cat's heart and held it in front of Mr. Football's face. It was all just a matter of adjusting.

"The weekend anchor slot's a definite?"

Winters nodded.

"And if I don't take the assignment?"

Winters shrugged. "The bosses want you."

"Could you list the choices for me again?"

"Starting this afternoon or tomorrow."

"That's what I like most about this station. A constant stream of options."

Michelle met Bobby Lockhart at his cramped office at the Hall of Justice. "At least you have your own window," she said by way of introduction.

"Well," Lockhart said, "I sure don't have any window onto Becky Dirksen's death." He offered Michelle a seat across the desk from him. Lockhart specifically avoided mentioning Kelly Caldwell. The department hadn't released a final cause of death. The newspapers had raised the specter of two similar murders, but the department remained in a state of relative denial. "We don't have clue one. Ask me whatever you want. I don't know a thing."

"The station wants to run a story on the thin line between sadism and murder. They thought that you might have some insights, especially with your years in vice."

Lockhart shrugged. "I used to teach philosophy. I quit when nothing made sense. Now I'm in homicide. Can you imagine a man with a worse sense of direction?" He started to laugh, but stopped. "No. That's not funny," he said, as though reminding himself. "You sure you have the stomach for this kind of reporting?" he asked Michelle.

"That's the second time today that I've been asked. You didn't see *Silence of the Lambs*? We women are tough." But Michelle felt uneasy, her hands were getting sweaty. She hoped that Lockhart didn't notice.

"Ask your boss for a week off. In the long run you'll be doing yourself a favor. You don't need this kind of crap clogging up your mind."

"Could you tell me what you do know?" Michelle smiled at Lockhart. "About the case."

"You want to see the photographs of the apartment, or of the girl?" Lockhart motioned to his top desk drawer. "I wouldn't recommend it, but if you insist." He slid the drawer open a few inches. He paused a second and slammed it shut. "No. Don't look. It's sickening."

"She advertised in the sex papers?"

Lockhart nodded.

"And graduated from SF State. In anthropology?"

"You think she was doing graduate studies?" Lockhart said. "Some sort of fieldwork. Sure, that's it." Lockhart slapped his forehead with the palm of his hand. "Dumb me. Her murder was academia gone sour."

"I gather you're not wild about doing this interview." Michelle tapped her pencil on her note pad.

"Most murders are, in some particular sense, within reason. You get pissed at your wife or boss—there's a moment of rage, and boom. Most of my job is violent crime. And the occasional hit job done by some cool cucumber with the pride of a craftsman. Soulless mercenaries. But this is my first experience with sadism, with murder as pleasure. What's stranger, from what we can determine, it doesn't even appear to be primarily sexual."

"You have a department psychologist. What does he say?

" 'Good morning, Bobby.' That's what he says."

"You've discussed the case with him?"

"Discussed what? Ask some pseudoshrink who couldn't even make it in private practice why some men are evil? Please. We parade the good doctor around mainly for show. It satisfies the public to think we take motivation seriously, that we mull over the reasons behind crime. We stick him on the evening news. When the show is over, we shove him back in his office, lock the door, and turn out the lights. Sixty grand to stay out of the way."

"So I'm not going to get an interview?" Michelle rose from her chair.

"You just had it." Lockhart walked Michelle the first five feet to the door. "Honestly. I haven't a clue. If I sound frustrated, it's because I am. It's not personal. I like watching you on the tube. You do a good show. Give me a call in a week. Maybe there'll be something."

"It's not a show. It's the news."

"Right. News. Sure. Anyway, it was nice meeting you in person."

And Michelle was out the door. It was getting to be a habit, finding herself in the street without a clue as to what had just happened. Kate, Owen, Forester, now the interview with Lockhart. She felt as though she were deep behind enemy lines without a map or a weapon or even a clear understanding of who constituted the enemy.

She hurried back to the station, as though bright lights and the discipline of reworking tonight's copy would drive away the doubts that pounded at her temples and hid in the bunched-up muscles at the base of her neck.

TEN

FORESTER SAT IN HIS den, looking out into the garden. It was pitch black outside, the starry sky suggestive of a time before civilization and progress, before streetlights and VCRs. Before pornography and snuff movies.

He thought of Joan standing in the doorway, and of her pain and outrage. It was unspeakably cruel of him. He had loved her, he meant her no harm.

Forester took a bony finger and ran it along the parched edges of his mouth. Along his cheek. Michelle was going to hug him. Maybe even kiss him. He touched his lips. *My lips.*

What would Michelle think if she knew about the videotapes? They were grotesque, horrible, degrading. A year ago it would have been unimaginable that he would spend his nights in front of the TV, naked and erect, teasing himself.

He had done nothing wrong. They were just video pictures.

They were unspeakably sick.

It was a matter of point of view.

Earlier this week the *American Journal of Psychiatry* had featured back-to-back articles on the multiple personality syndrome. One said it was nonsense, just the fabrication of hysterics and psychopaths, the last defense of the clever murderer. The other gave case presentations that provided strong historical evidence for the diagnosis. Following the articles was an editorial that indicated that more research was needed, but that for the present time it was more likely than not that multiple personalities actually existed.

Contradictory aspects of personality was the norm, Forester thought. Inconsistency was human nature. Self-awareness was the balancing of the separate parts.

The articles had something to do with him.

Alan was not a bad boy. Dr. Forester was a good man. He just had developed a bad habit that should be no problem to break. Not watching the movies would be like giving up smoking. A little withdrawal, no big deal.

He touched his lips again. Michelle of the long legs, clear eyes, good heart, and strong, independent spirit. It was not by chance that she had come to see him. She had come into his life to rid him of the evil thoughts. It was a beautiful, unmistakable inevitability. There could be no doubt.

He had a flash of cold sweat. What if the bad feelings came back while he was with her? *No, I am stronger than what bothers me. As long as I can stay in touch with the parts, I will be greater than the sum of the parts.*

Which means that I have to know everything about myself. Everything.

He would talk to one of his colleagues. He would tell him everything, but present it as one of his patients, as though he were trying to get some professional advice. Nate Giles would be perfect. In the past they had consulted each other on troubling cases. Giles was the rare combination of a brilliant thinker and a good listener.

I will remember for him.

Nate Giles was a compact, wiry, gray-haired man in his late sixties. He loved tennis, the Forty-Niners, Kierkegaard, and sitting around shooting the breeze. Superheated battles of the intellect, or a good joke, it made no difference. He was the least judgmental of the senior analysts at the Institute. They met over dim sum at a Chinese restaurant on California Street.

"It's a tough problem. He's a first-rate doctor. As far as I can tell, there's no problem with his medical competency." Forester told of his patient describing the snuff films. He used Van Allen as the model, though he didn't mention his name, or give enough hints to allow for the possibility of identification by inference. "For the sake of discussion, let's call him A." Forester stuck strictly to the videos. "He wants to break the habit, but he says it's like someone else watching them. Someone he has no control over."

Giles listened patiently, swirling a pot sticker in the hot oil and vinegar. "You sure his fetish is just confined to the videos?" he asked when Forester finished. "My experience has been that this type of pornography is accompanied by other fantasies."

"Not that he's mentioned. He's very careful about what he says. I've seen him for three months and he hasn't said a word about anything else, except his partial impotence."

"Partial?"

"He needs pictures or videos to get aroused. Once he's up, he says it's okay."

"Is he worried about the videos, or that he's not satisfying his wife?"

"I suspect both. Twice he mentioned that she hasn't complained."

"Midlife crises tend to lean toward excesses of the same—younger women, more flirtatious behavior, that sort of thing. Not snuff films. That's serious." Giles ate the pot sticker, then wiped his mouth. "But you know all this." He looked at Forester. "We've known each other, how long would you say, twenty years? And you've always been straight with me. Now I get the sense you're holding something back. Is it something the man told you?"

Forester said nothing. He looked at Giles, trying to read what Giles was thinking. He wanted to talk, but Giles was so shrewd, maybe he would guess.

"Can we limit the conversation to the videos?" Forester asked. "So far, the other stuff has been only some vague ramblings disguised as dreams. I've pressed the point, but he's admitted to nothing else."

"Are they dreams of actually carrying out the fantasies?" Giles asked.

Forester nodded. "I'm worried about him. But there's nothing concrete. I've tried to have his wife come to a session, but A says there's no reason. She doesn't know about the videos and he thinks he's managing their sex life okay." Forester found the pseudonym A resonating in his head. He wondered if he had pronounced it without any unnatural emphasis or intonation.

"When your A talks about the person watching the videos, does he display much emotion or is he pretty distant?"

"I'd call it objective. He knows he needs the videos for arousal, and that part concerns him. Otherwise he describes the videos as though they were newsreels. But that could just be him. He's a pretty cold fellow."

"There's more, isn't there?" Giles said. He leaned forward in his chair. "You think he's dangerous? Or that the fantasies he's reporting as dreams actually happened?"

Forester said nothing.

"Oh, boy. You've really stepped in it this time. These new Tarasoff laws make it so difficult. If you even suspect a patient of being threatening to someone specific, you've got to report him to the police. If you don't, and something happens, you can be held responsible."

"But if they are just idle fantasies, and God knows we've all had them, then I'd be destroying his life."

"Do you think he's dangerous?" Giles said.

"Sometimes yes, sometimes no. Sometimes I get the feeling that there's another him, someone I haven't met. I've even considered the idea of multiple personalities."

"Is that something he's alluded to?"

"Not directly. Except that he occasionally refers to himself by his first name. And sometimes he gives me the creeps. I know that's not very scientific, but there it is. Normally I can get a pretty good handle on someone in a few sessions, but with him I feel that I'm still at square one. He tells me what he wants, withholds the rest, and expects me to save him."

"You can tell him that without his absolute candor that you can't help him." Giles paused. "No, that's ridiculous. Christ, can't you refer him elsewhere? No, that's not right, either, though it sure would be the easiest. Let me think. Perhaps you could tell him that it was a state law to report anyone who made a specific threat, and even if it wasn't specific, that you'd seriously have to consider turning him in. Which would mean three days in the county psych ward, under observation. That might get rid of him." Giles looked at Forester and shook his head. "No. That's worse, isn't it? You know, I've only done long-term analysis in the last ten years. Thank God, this hasn't come up. Alan, I'm not sure what to do."

"Can I just talk to you about the videos and the dreams? Can this just be confidential?"

"I should say yes, shouldn't I? But this kind of man is outside my experience. All I can say is that I'm glad that this A didn't come to see me."

"Some friend you are."

"Let me think on it. Maybe I can come up with something. Christ, I wish I could help."

"Sure," Forester said.

"So what else is new?" Giles said. "You all set for your talk?"

"I'm working on some new ideas. I think you might find them interesting."

Forester paid the waitress. The two men walked back toward the Institute. "I've got an errand to run. See you later."

"Right. Oh. Say hello to Joan for me. We haven't seen much of her around here lately. Everything's okay?"

"I'll tell her you said hello. And, Nate, thanks for listening. I'm sure it'll work itself out. There's really no need to discuss it with anyone else."

"Mum's the word. Like we didn't even have lunch."

"What lunch?"

"Right."

Forester watched as Giles walked to the corner and disappeared from sight.

As Forester turned and started down the street, a great wind howled past, causing him to tremble. His legs were shaky and the sidewalk undulated beneath his feet. The wind kept up, covering his face with fistfuls of smothering fog. He stopped and took a deep breath, trying to collect himself. At a great distance others strolled, oblivious to the elements, Lilliputian figures in a great cavernous corridor of roaring glass and stone. Forester braced himself, as though there might be an earthquake, but the earth was still, unmoving and unyielding. He was bracing himself against himself.

He had no idea what to do. He continued to the corner before he realized that his car was three blocks in the other direction.

That evening, after patient hours, Forester did his compulsory twenty minutes on the bicycle, then took a fast shower. He dried off in front of the TV. Michelle was on the evening news, interviewing a young girl with leukemia who was scheduled to receive a bone marrow transplant from her brother in the morning.

Michelle's soft friendly voice filled Forester's den. Forester had moved the large-screen TV from the living room to the den. The den was his. The living room had been theirs. Forester seldom even walked into the living room anymore. Somehow it had jilted him.

At the end of the interview, the camera focused in on Michelle, then faded to a wider-angle shot of Michelle with her arm around the little girl. Her face reflected sincerity and kindness. *If only that look were for me,* Forester thought as he flipped off the TV and the lights in the den. To his surprise, there was a peculiar shimmering blue tinge to the air. Not in the air, but to the air, as though the air around him had been made visible. Perhaps it was an afterimage of the TV, but it persisted. He closed his eyes and it was gone. He opened them; the room was charged with a bluish incandescence.

Forester panicked. Maybe it was his vision. He turned on the lights. Everything was normal. He checked each eye in turn, covering the other with his hand. Both were fine; his acuity was perfect. He turned off the lights. The blue persisted. It was quite subtle, a fine aquamarine aerosol.

Time was suspended; later he would not be able to say how long the light remained. Seconds, minutes; he was not sure. Reasoning failed. He trembled in fear, empty of thought. At some point the color was gone and the room resumed its darkness. His initial relief was almost immediately accompanied by a profound regret. Against his better judgment he half hoped the light would return.

The room remained ordinary.

It had been a moment of revelation and he had turned away in fear.

Great men like Aldous Huxley or William James would have observed, encouraged the vision. Puny Alan had checked his vision for defects.

He tried to reconstruct what had happened. He had been watching Michelle, he had turned out the lights, and the room was aglow. It was impossible to avoid the obvious message.

Michelle was to be his saviour.

He arose from his chair and paced the corridor between the den and bedroom. The hallway was too close, too confining. Still naked, he walked downstairs and out into his garden. It was dark and the high walls and trees kept him from being seen by his neighbors. The small pebbles of the pathway were cold and insistent against his feet. At another time the irregular stones would have felt uncomfortable; today he sensed nothing but their coolness.

Through the dense shrubbery to his left he could barely make out the dining room window of his next-door neighbors. The family was at dinner. He looked away. Above, the sky was faintly pink with city lights. Ahead and on his right was the near darkness of his formal garden. The urge to keep moving was irresistible. He walked briskly around the path that marked the garden's perimeter.

Though the night was cool, he was not chilled. He stopped and sat on a patch of damp grass, the blades prickly against his bottom. He drew his knees up to his chest, his arms around his legs, and sat motionless in the night, in nature's embrace. He ran his hand along the lawn, encountering a mound of dirt beneath a rosebush. He scooped up a handful and sniffed life and dirt and death inseparable in a single complex fragrance.

Life and death in every particle of earth.

He dropped the soil, wiping his hand on his thighs and chest. As a boy, before batting, he had picked up dirt around home plate, dusting his hands like Mantle and DiMaggio. Then he was someone else. Not now. Now he was primitive man in his primordial garden and there was no imitation. He was without social structure, not like that stock broker's family next door, so immersed in the everyday that they saw the sky as environment—analyzed, inspected, bought and sold as air rights.

Had the air really been blue, or had it been the effect of lighting? He could have performed a simple experiment, merely scooping up some of the air in his hands. If it had been the air, he could have seen the movement as he moved his hands.

It was too late now, but then, it was in the very nature of revelations to obscure their mechanics.

Of course it had been a revelation. Not to understand this would be nothing short of insane. Only a madman would doubt the clarity of the light.

Forester lay down and rolled over and over on the grass. The Big Dipper flashed down its greetings. Solitary stars, millions of miles from their nearest neighbors, yet still they twinkled and broadcast good cheer. "There's the Big Dipper," he would say as a child and be filled with awe. The Big Dipper was the very essence of grandness in isolation.

It was a model for mankind.

He remained on the grass for some time, until the cold shivered through him. He stood up and walked slowly back into the house. As he started up the steps he was aware of a pulling sensation between his shoulder blades. The pain quickly gathered intensity, hammering at his chest. *Relax, it's probably just a pulled muscle,* he told himself, leaning on the banister to catch his breath. Red veins flowed into view behind his eyelids. He tried to find his pulse, but his fingers were wet and clumsy.

Suppose it's a heart attack. You're old enough, and have been under enough stress. It could be the real thing.

He ran to the kitchen phone and considered dialing 911. The pain wasn't quite as bad. No. Yes. It was hard to be sure. The hospital was minutes away. He could drive there as fast as 911 could get to him.

He slipped on his trousers, shirt, loafers, and drove to

Memorial, his hospital. In the waiting room were the usual collection of lacerations and junkies and old folk on the way to nursing homes. The receptionist was looking at his bare ankles as she handed him the sign-in sheet.

"I need to see someone right away. I might be having a heart attack."

Moments later he was on a gurney in an examining room, a nurse hooking him up to EKG electrodes. A young physician came in and began asking questions. Forester started to say that he had been on the hospital staff for twenty years, but didn't. Instead he watched the EKG monitor, aware that he had forgotten even the basics of cardiogram interpretation. There really was no point in introducing himself as a doctor. It was like saying that he had run track in high school.

The pain was subsiding. The doctor ordered blood gases. A nurse swabbed his groin, then felt for his pulse. Forester watched her gloved fingers at the edge of his pubic hair, serious, purposeful, helpful. He wanted to tell her to stop, that blood gases weren't necessary. He didn't remember much, but he knew that he wasn't having a pulmonary embolism. He hated being passive, acquiescent, not in control.

"That's not necessary," he said to the nurse. "I'm feeling better already. It's probably only a pulled muscle." He rotated his shoulders to demonstrate. Quite unexpectedly his eyes filled with tears. He turned away and wiped his eyes.

"You okay?" the nurse asked. She was drawing blood, the needle protruding from his groin. She was done. Her fingers were applying pressure. It was all so incredibly casual, this complete stranger with her hand right there. He stirred slightly. "Looks like you're getting your color back," she said, withdrawing her hand. "Chest pain is always scary."

"It makes you aware of how fragile life is." Forester smiled weakly.

"You'll be just fine." The nurse pulled the sheet up to his waist. She was a pretty woman in her early thirties. Forester noticed the tiny cross hanging on her neck.

The sight of the cross triggered some ancient wordless memory. Before Forester could pursue it, Sol Rubenstein poked his head in the room. He was a cardiologist in his early sixties. He had been a fixture at the hospital for as long as Forester could remember. They had often had lunch together in the doctors' lounge. Sol was from the old school of house calls and self-sacrifice.

"You okay?" He took the cardiogram from the young doctor's hand. Then he was looking at Forester's face, his thumb pulling down the lower lid of one eye. Streaks of dirt on Forester's cheeks were crosshatched with trails of dried tears. "You're a real mess," Rubenstein said.

"There's something wrong?" Forester asked.

"Your cardiogram looks like your only asset." Rubenstein stood alongside the examining table. "Will you excuse us for a minute," he said to the doctor and the nurse. "We're old friends." The doctor and nurse left the room.

"What's the problem?"

"I was working in the garden. I didn't have time to wash."

"Christ, the airlines would charge you extra for the bags under your eyes. When's the last time you got a good night's sleep?"

"It's been a little rough lately. Joan's been going through some midlife stuff. I guess she's soured on me."

"I heard."

"But life goes on." Forester looked at the EKG machine and the strip of paper flowing out, curling up on the floor. It was a recording of his heartbeat, dribbling away on the tile. "It'll take some time to regroup."

"You think it'll be permanent?"

"Probably."

"That must be tough."

"I'm managing. I'd like to talk to you about it, but there's not much to say. It's good of you to stop by. I really appreciate it."

"We've known each other a long time. You can tell me and it won't go any further."

"I wish I could, but I don't know what to say. Besides, I've been talking with Nate Giles."

"You want, you come over for dinner some night." He patted Forester on the shoulder and left the room. In the hallway he said to the young nurse, "Dr. Forester's one of the best. And a damn good gardener, even if he does take half his yard inside with him."

The young physician entered the room. "You didn't say you were a doctor."

"I'm not. I'm a psychiatrist." The two of them laughed. A lab technician appeared with the blood gas report. Normal. He was free to leave. "Dr. Rubenstein's right. You look like you could use some rest." The doctor handed Forester a small packet containing four Halcions.

"You think it was an anxiety attack?" Forester asked.

"Everything checks out normal."

"Sorry I bothered you."

"It was no bother. You try to get some rest."

▪   ▪   ▪

It had been a strange day and he had much to consider. He felt like being alone in a crowd, his thoughts his companion. Since Joan had left, he often ate out, by himself, taking a book or a note pad. He was not embarrassed. Eating dinner alone was a sign of inner strength. Besides, he often had his best thoughts in public spaces, as though the movement at the periphery of his vision stirred him on.

He drove to North Beach and parked his car on upper Green Street. He decided not to decide, that he would choose his evening meal completely by chance. He would select the restaurant that spoke most directly to him. He began by walking up and down Kearny and Grant, then Columbus. At the intersection of Grant and Columbus was a pornographic theater that specialized in bondage films. Next door was take-out Indian food. Cumin, coriander, and grease hung in the air. On the other side the raw smell of recently cured hides announced a cheap leather goods store.

He stood in front of the store debating. It was time to eat; he had had only a salad for lunch. In the uneven reflection of the store window he could tell that he had lost weight. His face was more lined than the shabby coats on sale. He should have something solid, say osso bucco with fettucine over at Little Joe's. Put some meat on his bones. He recalled being hungry when he had started down the street. But not now. Where had his appetite gone?

He knew the answer.

His appetite had left him and had gone into the theater next door. It was already seated in the back, anonymously, watching the movies. He could eat anytime, but right now it was showtime. He could collect his thoughts in the animated darkness. He looked around; he knew no one. He was invisible, a stranger in a foreign land.

There were about two dozen men and two couples in the theater. He found the seat farthest from the weak aisle lighting. There were so many different types of illumination to light the way—there were the tiny bulbs along the aisles, the mercury streetlamps, automobile headlights. And there was the blue light that came without directions for its use.

The theater was awash in flesh tones. Sighs and moans quickly became white noise. The movie was boring and clearly simulated. Forester felt gypped. He was restless, the movie was Italian with endless grainy footage of Tuscan hillsides, the dialogue between two women dubbed. He would be better off eating.

Adjacent to the projection room was a book and video-cassette store. There was nothing of interest. His own home was better stocked. His eye caught a newspaper filled with sex ads—good reading material for the solitary meal. He envisioned himself at Ernie's or the Blue Fox, the paper folded subway-reading style in one hand while he ate with the other. "Is there anything else you would like?" the maître d' would ask. Forester would nod and point to one of the pictures. Now, that was living.

He bought the paper and shoved it in his coat pocket. He walked down the street to the City Lights Bookstore, where he bought a slim book of poetry. He ate pizza and salad at Calzone's, his book of poetry in his left hand, the newspaper hiding in his jacket, teasing.

ELEVEN

AFTER FILMING THE girl with leukemia, the camera crew packed up and left. Michelle had stayed to speak with the girl's mother. "If any part of the interview was bothersome, please let me know and we'll leave it out."

"No. It was fine. Isn't that right, Janie?" The woman turned to her five-year-old, who was standing with her IV pole, at the hospital window. It was getting dark, with the first of the evening stars.

"It was okay," the girl said. She was in her hospital pajamas and a plaid wool robe. What was left of her hair was pulled to one side in a frail, fuzzy braid. The braid said more about her precarious state of health than a thousand entries in her chart. The girl was smiling as another star appeared in the blue-black sky beyond the hospital buildings. She tugged Michelle's arm and pointed. "My grandma's out there, on that star. Isn't that right, Mommy?"

Her mother nodded.

"Soon I'm going to visit her. We'll be together, on that star."

Michelle recalled the conversation as she sat in the editing room at the station. Part of her was sorry she hadn't caught the conversation on tape; it would have made a perfect conclusion to her series. Mainly she was glad she hadn't. It was a private moment, and some things were better preserved by not being recorded.

"Michelle. Please. If you could just pay attention for a moment." It was Pete Weinman, the head of editing, nagging again.

"Send a letter." She stormed out of the room and went to her desk. She had plenty to do without being harrassed by some darkroom nerd. She buried her head in her hands, the little girl bigger in her mind than the six o'clock deadline.

But the deadline prevailed. Michelle returned to the editing room, watching her interviews skillfully spliced with shots of the hospital. Pete had done a good job of capturing the visual essence of the hospital. But there was more, between the frames, something both tragic and wonderful. She couldn't get Janie out of her mind, the girl pointing at the star as though it were her star, and her universe. It was the magic of childhood. Even in sickness the magic hung on, the children's best friend.

Dick Winters approached. "How about following up with Detective Lockhart. There's been a woman murdered out on Eighteenth and Valencia. Word is that she died during bondage. Bonnie Ringold's her name."

Michelle dialed Lockhart's number. One moment it was children with cancer, the next it was women tortured and murdered. Michelle held on to the receiver as though the firmness of the plastic handset was a clue to reality. She covered the mouth of the receiver with her hand. "You know what the difference between a schizophrenic and a news reporter is?" she called across the room to Dick Winters.

"I have no idea," Winters said with a look of frustration.

"Neither do I," Michelle said.

Lockhart answered. "No, we have nothing to say. Yes, it's awful. Yes, we're doing our best. And no, we don't have any suspects."

"This is Michelle Draper. From Channel Six."

"So?"

"So, I was checking in."

"Wonderful. Nice talking with you."

"That's it?"

"In its entirety. Sorry, but we've got nothing to say."

"Keep up the good work," Michelle said. "I'll be checking again with you tomorrow.

"It's your twenty cents." Lockhart hung up.

Michelle shook her head at Dick Winters, at the same time giving him a small shrug. Some insight into the three S and M murders would certainly be a coup for Michelle, but she had trouble concentrating. The whole subject was scary. Michelle had great difficulty even imagining how a woman could submit to being tied down and. . . . She resisted thinking further in that direction.

Yet the murders were her ticket upstream. Upper management was watching, assessing. A good performance and they would offer her increasing pieces of the sky.

But not the stars.

Her life had a hole in it big enough to drive a small family through. Forester had pulled back the curtains and shown her the emptiness.

After finishing the ten o'clock news, Michelle met Owen for a couple glasses of Chianti at the Cigar Store. The missing pieces of her life were particularly clear tonight. She was looking at downtrodden Owen, who looked like nine miles of bad road. His hair was curling over his collar, his blue denim shirt was thoroughly rumpled, and Michelle suspected that she smelled mildew. It could have been her imagination. Mildew naturally went with Owen's degree of dishevelment. She had to remind herself that this was the same Owen of the once bright blue eyes, quick wit, and big heart. Owen the charmer yet straight-shooting friend.

Michelle knew that she was, at least in part, responsible for Owen's shabby downslide.

"Where do we go from here?" Michelle said.

"Dubuque, Omaha, Petaluma?"

"I'm being serious."

"I know. It's just that I don't know how to answer you. It's like I don't have room for any more emotions. I know you think I'm obsessed. Maybe so, but labeling my mood doesn't make it any lighter. I must have put five hundred miles on these feet in the last month, pounding the pavement, looking in the cracks for an answer. All I can think of is Forester this, Forester that. I look at you. You're all I've got. And frankly I don't know what to do. I know that if I could resolve this Forester business I could get on with my life."

"I'm sorry I ever mentioned it. He's harmless. I swear it."

"That's it? You say it isn't so, and I'm supposed to let it drop, just walk away?"

Michelle nodded and squeezed Owen's hand, then let it rest on top of his. With her other hand she downed her Chianti, then waved to the bartender for another.

■   ■   ■

At the far end of the second floor of the San Rafael Civic Center was the Marin County coroner's office. Owen worried that he would faint. Fortunately the medical examiner's office was down the hall, a decent-sized room with a view of the parking lot and the Marin hills.

Dr. Whitelsey went over the papers. "You sure you want to discuss this?" he asked Owen.

"No, I'm not. But I need to know. Was there anything unusual, out of place?" Owen paused, cleared his throat. "Anything that might suggest . . ."

Dr. Whitelsey looked up, waiting for Owen to finish his sentence. But Owen paused. Whitelsey said: "Foul play? Is that what you mean?"

Owen nodded.

The doctor put on his reading glasses and read the autopsy summary, his voice low and respectful. With the turning of each page of the report, Whitelsey looked up to check on Owen. He concluded with the toxicology reports, which indicated a moderate level of alcohol and barbiturates.

"Did you do a complete screen?" Owen remembered a recent horror movie of a man poisoning a succession of secretaries. "For unusual drugs, cyanide, that sort of thing?"

"Mr. Carbone, there was no reason. Your wife fell three hundred feet." The doctor closed the file. "I'm sorry." The doctor glanced toward a picture of his wife and kids. "I know how badly I'd feel. But there's nothing out of place."

Owen drove to the spot where Kate had fallen. The shoulder of the road was covered with slippery ice plant.

Far below was the pounding surf. And the rocks. Owen stared down. "I didn't jump," the voice said. "I know," Owen said, his voice lost in the crashing surf. He was not surprised to hear Kate. He felt that in some obscure way she was directing him, showing him what to look for.

He stood in the wind, waiting for a clue.

Barbiturates. Doctors seldom used them anymore. Who prescribed them? Forester? Kate's only other doctor was Dr. Pritzer, a Mill Valley holistic gynecologist who believed in natural this, organic that. "Pack it with sea kelp," he used to say to Kate. Owen was sure she went to Pritzer partially out of amusement. "Any fool can do a Pap smear, you might as well get someone with personality," Kate would say, asking Owen if he would like to help her pack.

Owen phoned from the country store at Olema. "Of course I wouldn't prescribe barbiturates," Dr. Pritzer said to Owen. "Besides, she was allergic to them."

"Allergic?" Owen said.

"It says right here, in her chart, that she had trouble breathing when she had her tonsils out. Kate wasn't sure, but she thought the anesthesiologist said it was the barbiturates. She made me put a warning sticker on her chart, just to be on the safe side, in case she needed emergency surgery."

"You're sure?"

"I'm really sorry, Owen."

"Allergic." Owen hung up and stared out at the occasional car zipping along Highway One. Dr. Pritzer had said it all. One way or the other, Forester had given her the pills.

▪ ▪ ▪

"No, Mr. Carbone. I can understand your being upset, but I didn't give your wife any medications. Besides, barbiturates are sedatives. You wouldn't prescribe them to someone who's depressed." Dr. Forester watched Owen lean forward in the leather consultation chair. Owen had phoned earlier in the day, insisting that they meet. Owen's pressured speech and unkempt appearance worried Forester. He kept his distance, standing at the far side of the room.

"Her gynecologist, Dr. Pritzer, swears he didn't prescribe them. She didn't have any other doctors."

"Maybe she saw someone else. Many patients do."

Owen rose from the seat and walked over to Forester. "Cut the crap. Look me straight in the eye and tell me that you had nothing to do with Kate's death. Go on, tell me."

"Please, Mr. Carbone. I can appreciate your being worked up, but don't you think you're being a bit unreasonable?" Forester started to back away, but didn't, holding still and trying to look casual.

"You already said that. I want to hear you say that you're completely innocent."

"I already told you."

"Tell me again. Make me believe it." Owen reached out and grabbed Forester by his shirt. Owen felt buttons, fabric, and a hot, murderous urge. *It's him,* the voice inside his head insisted. *Him, him, him.*

Forester jerked his head back and tried to step behind his desk, but Owen's grip prevented him from backing away. The two men stood face to face. "Come on. Give me your best shot at sincerity." Owen's voice shook with rage.

"I don't have to stand here and listen to this nonsense.

I'm politely going to ask you to leave. Otherwise I have no choice but to call the police."

Owen took his hand from Forester's shirt and pointed to the phone. "Be my guest."

"Maybe you'd like to talk with someone, get some of this anger off your chest. I could recommend several good therapists."

"Maybe I can hire one of them to do to you what you did to my wife."

A red light went on over Dr. Forester's desk. He motioned in the direction of the waiting room. "I have another patient."

"After you show me Kate's chart." Owen reached out and yanked open the center drawer to Forester's desk. Forester rushed over and tried to push it closed. Owen jerked again, the drawer popping out and papers scattering over the floor. Forester squatted down and started scooping up his notes, at the same time reaching for the phone. Owen kicked the phone away.

"My wife's chart." He had his foot on Forester's right hand. "You tell me where it is."

"There's nothing to see. It's mainly billing information."

"No notes, huh? You sit and scribble in your note pad and then throw it all away?"

"Get off my hand." Forester was on his knees looking up at Owen with a combination of fear, anger, and surprise. Owen was six two, maybe six three, and well built. And out of control.

"It's a terrible feeling, being powerless. Not like the charge you get fumbling through someone else's mind." Owen transferred his full weight onto Forester's wrist, leaning into the pain on Forester's face. Forester tugged and grabbed Owen's lower leg with his other hand. He could not get sufficient leverage. With his clenched fist he hit Owen in the calf. Owen ground his heel harder into Forester's hand, feeling shifting bones.

"Get me her chart," Owen said.

"There's nothing there. You can see for yourself."

Owen shifted all his weight onto the edge of his heel. "Remember, this is just the beginning." He lifted his foot.

Forester made a point of not rubbing his throbbing hand, which was a blotchy red and purple. He rose and looked straight at Owen, trying to reestablish his authority. "It's my business to deal with the disturbed. There's no point in threatening me. And you can't scare me. I did what I thought was in your wife's best interest. Naturally I'm sorry it didn't work out."

" 'Didn't work out'? That's just perfect." Owen was inches from Forester. "Maybe I should kill you, then tell the lucky patient in the waiting room that you've been unavoidably detained. That's sort of like 'didn't work out,' isn't it?"

"You control yourself, and I'll get you her chart." Forester threw back his shoulders, and tried to look unruffled. But, to Owen, his eyes gave him away, cruel beasts pacing in their deep-set cages. "You don't know me," they said. It wasn't possible, but Forester's eyes gave off the rank stink of an animal that gorged on its own kind. "It's in the other room, in a file cabinet," Forester said.

"Let's take a look."

"Sorry. There are other patients' charts in there. I'll get it for you."

"We'll get it together."

"No. You'll have to trust me."

"Sure. You and Jack the Ripper."

"I said, these are private, and that's final."

"I'll stand in the doorway."

The two men walked to Forester's den. Forester pulled out Kate's file. There was nothing but billing information and a single page of notes about her background. There were no prescription notations. It was as though Kate had come for a single fifteen-minute appointment.

"Now are you satisfied?" Forester put the chart back in the file cabinet. The two men started down the hall to the small foyer that separated the consultation room from the rest of the house. "It's understandable, being upset."

"You say that one more time." Owen glared at Forester. "I'll figure it out. Don't you worry. Your ass is mine." Owen took his thumb and index finger and squeezed Forester's cheeks together. Their faces were inches apart. "Mine. You hear me, mine." He pushed Forester's head backward. There was a dull thud as it struck the wall behind them.

In the waiting room was a well-dressed man in his late forties. He was reading the *New England Journal of Medicine*. The man looked up and nodded. "You're better off throwing your money in the sewer than seeing this quack," Owen said.

The man smiled, a curious smile, as though he agreed but didn't want to say so. Owen was also aware that the man's front teeth were artificially bright and white, as though they had been excessively bonded. The man's smile quickly faded as Owen steamed out of the room.

"You'll have to excuse me for a minute," Forester said to Jim Van Allen. "I'm afraid the last hour was a little brutal."

"I gather. It looks like he must have gotten his first bill."

"Something like that." Forester left Van Allen in the consultation room. He went to his bathroom and washed his face. As he did, he thought of Kate's dead body broken at the bottom of some cliff. Fault wasn't the right word. He had tried and failed. Even though Owen was scary, he would try to be gentle with him. It's tough losing one's wife, Forester thought as he straightened his tie and prepared for Van Allen. With a little luck Owen's rage would blow over. It's just a case of displaced grieving, Forester concluded uneasily.

"You've been coming here for two months. We've explored your feelings about women. Do you think there's been any change in your attitude?"

"There's nothing to change. I am what I am. You think I've done wrong, that's your opinion. If you want to hear me confess, fine. I am an evil man, with evil thoughts. The Lord knows my sins, as he knows all our sins. He will be my final and only judge."

Van Allen sat on the ottoman, his chin in his hands, his elbows on his knees. Today he even refused to assume the stance of a patient. He flashed the same supercilious smile that never failed to inflame Forester. Van Allen was so smug, the words rolled off his tongue like greasy fake pearls. He was the personification of the new wave of televangelists, only he wasn't a preacher and he wasn't asking for money. He was a doctor who used his patients and those around him, and then threw himself into the arms of the Lord, always smiling and begging for mercy. It was a performance that made Forester sick.

"What do you want me to say?" Van Allen continued. "That I'm filled to the brim with sadistic impulses, that I wanted to torture these unfortunate women? Or would you prefer that I wring my hands, get on my knees, and confess that my actions are the thinly disguised sublimations of a murderous rage? You're some fucking therapist. All you do is sit there like some passive-aggressive know-it-all, trying to get me to say what'll satisfy your poorly concealed need to be Mr. Goody Two-Shoes. But your shadow is just as black as mine. If it's the darkness that bothers you, turn on the lights, but remember that down deep we all stink. Good and evil, whatever you want to call it, all steaming away in God's little broth of mankind. There's no reason to get uptight over our programming. It's like getting mad at having five fingers to a hand. Or two eyes. Go with the flow, man." Van Allen looked at Forester, his eyes brown bullets.

"No. We are not all evil. We may have urges, but we also have controls. That's what makes us human." Forester thought of the tape recorder rough-drafting Van Allen's confession. He would take the tape, edit, and transcribe it, and show the panel at the medical society what a truly horrid man Van Allen really was.

Forester was sorry it was such a small gesture. One more closed-doors humiliation for a man too insensitive even to care. It was a shame he couldn't give Van Allen a little sodium Amytal—a short-acting barbiturate once used to explore the unconscious. Forester had used it during his residency. He had been perpetually stunned by the sudden appearance of hidden agendas and long-suppressed feelings. But now Amytal was seldom used, and you needed a myriad of signed consent forms.

So Forester would have his transcribed notes for the medical society. Van Allen would get another smart little slap on the wrist, after which he would turn and laugh at him with those horrible extrawhite teeth.

The old rage welled up. Forester gripped his pen until he could feel the edge of the metal clip sharp against the flesh of his thumb. He imagined walking up behind Van Allen and hitting him over the head with a ballpeen hammer. He would drive the unconscious but still-living Van Allen out into a secluded forest glen where he could watch the animals set to work. That was what Van Allen really deserved.

Forester put his pen back on his desk and folded his hands in his lap. He was not going to let Van Allen get the best of him. He put on his most professional face and suffered through some more tirade.

"God, you're transparent. I hate to think what you're hiding. Maybe it's that Carbone girl. You must feel really accomplished, having a patient kill herself right in the middle of therapy. What happened? You try this holier-than-thou tack on her?"

Forester glared at Van Allen but said nothing.

Van Allen said, "I've done nothing, and you know it. At worst I played around with a few secretaries. My wife knows the whole story. She forgives me. I don't see why I need your blessings."

"Just once I'd like to hear you say you're sorry for the lives you've ruined."

"Ruined? I didn't ruin anybody or anything. They got what they wanted. Sex is sex, no big deal. So don't act like I killed them, or something. I have to laugh. There's a mass murderer loose in the city and you sit here accusing me of having too much sex with my office staff. Well, let me tell you one thing. It's not people like me that go around tying up women and choking them to death."

Choking? The papers hadn't said anything about choking. And why was Van Allen bringing up the deaths of the three women?

"Yeah. It's men who hate women, men who can't get it up, men whose wives leave them. You know the type." And there was that smile again.

"You don't have any sense of remorse, do you?"

"If I tell you I'm sorry, can we put an end to this charade?"

"If you mean it. Frankly I'm as tired of these meetings as you are. I don't believe I've ever met anyone more insincere, as devoid of even a single shred of conscience. You are completely hopeless. What I'd like is a handwritten letter of apology, so at least each of the women can feel that you are sorry. I'll let the medical society decide if that's adequate. A decent letter of apology, and we'll wash our hands of each other."

"If you promise to stop pouting. It's embarrassing seeing a man of your alleged qualifications getting so worked up over someone else getting laid. Try it sometime, maybe you won't be so cranky. The old in-and-out does wonders for the endorphins. Besides, only a fool would call what you do psychotherapy. If I did have a problem, you'd be the last person on earth I'd come to. Instead of having some compassion, all you've done is badger me. Frankly I find you pitiful."

"You are a horrible man," Forester said.

"I'll leave my judgment to the Lord."

▪ ▪ ▪

Michelle was interviewing Bobby Lockhart on the steps of the Hall of Justice. He acknowledged that there were some unexplained deaths with a similar pattern, but refused to comment further.

"Do you think it's the return of the Zodiac?" Michelle asked. Lockhart waved the camera away.

Forester pressed a button on the remote control switch. This allowed for a second station to be seen in the upper left-hand corner of the TV screen. The Channel Seven reporter was silently jamming a microphone into Lockhart's face. The remainder of the screen was devoted to footage of the city morgue attendants taking the body of Bonnie Ringold from her south-of-Market apartment. The name did not ring a bell. Forester had been introduced to her as Serena, her name in the ad. He was surprised to hear Michelle relate in hushed tones that Bonnie Ringold was from Manteca, a small town in the central valley. She had played clarinet in her high school band, worn braces in her junior year, had gone to Fresno JC, and briefly considered being a veterinarian.

The pictures of Bonnie Ringold's childhood continued as the main picture while in the corner box her body was again removed from the apartment. The juxtaposition of the two images gave Forester the peculiar sensation of having mental double vision.

He tried to recall the evening with Bonnie Ringold. It had not been pleasant. It had started out with Forester being annoyed that the woman was unnecessarily common, with a broad, flat face devoid of charm. The woman was horsey and direct; there was no teasing or intrigue. Forester distinctly remembered being disappointed.

He shuddered as the attendants closed the rear door of the morgue ambulance.

He had been with the dead girl. He stared out the window, sorting through his mind, trying to be honest with himself. Sometime in the last few days—he wasn't certain of the exact date—he had been in her apartment. But other than a vague recollection of the woman sitting on the couch, he could remember nothing.

His memory was getting dreadful. This morning he could not remember what he had had for dinner the previous night. And now there was a murdered woman on TV, a woman he had visited, and he couldn't recall a single shred of their conversation.

His throat was tight; he caught his breath coming in short bursts. Forester flashed on the horrible idea that somehow he might be the killer. It was ludicrous to think this way, but nevertheless his mind began to wander down this line of reasoning. So many killers claim amnesia. And there was always the possibility of multiple personalities.

The Channel Seven reporter was again asking noncommittal Lockhart whether it was true that the woman had died during bondage. Forester saw a woman paralyzed with fear, restrained by leather straps, struggling, trying to cry out, her voice muffled by the handkerchief stuffed in her mouth. Torture was commonplace experience—anyone who went to the movies, watched TV, or read your average thriller was fully conversant with all the gruesome details. It was no wonder they popped so easily into mind. Stabs of sizzling electricity charged his memory, jarring loose a wisp of vague remembrance. It was warm like perfume, with a round black shriek in its center. It was feminine and it yielded to him, anxious to please, happy to be the supplicant. It wanted him to be master.

Forester began to sweat. He wasn't the killer, why was he thinking this way? Was it because there's something of the killer inside everyone, a collective ability to maim and murder? And an insensitivity to violence that allows each person to so easily imagine himself playing the role?

The collective unconscious now included the role of mass murderer. It was a sick thought. One he might include in his lecture. Also it was an accusation of how far he had traveled since Joan had left. His mind had taken a wrong turn to conjure up this filth. It was time to take stock of himself seriously.

For a moment Forester did not want to leave behind completely the idea of multiple personalities. He had read cases that seemed to make sense. A group of strangers under one genetic roof. Perhaps. But it seemed doubtful.

The other night he had watched a program on Howard Hughes. Right on TV Farley Granger had said that his life would have been better off if he had killed Mr. Hughes, who had been his boss at RKO Studios. Granger had laughed and sucked on his pipe. It had been an idle comment. But in a way it was a leaking out of some hidden truth, the shadow voice slipping through the defenses. But there was no reason to think that Mr. Granger had multiple personalities.

The main picture switched to a drug bust in the South Bay, while the insert showed the county coroner's ambulance pulling away. Forester flipped off the set.

He had been off-balance since Joan had left, his life freewheeling out of control down a path not clearly of his choosing. His mind was filling up with unsolicited thoughts. It was about time to start paying attention.

He walked to his desk. The right-hand drawer was locked. He felt under the desktop for the key, which was fastened to the underside with a strip of Velcro. He opened the top drawer and looked at the mass of note pads, each filled with scribblings. Some pads had the name of patients. Others were unlabeled, perhaps for some future book. He began to read.

Mrs. Seifert:

. . . the epitome of passive-aggressive, her tongue is a sniper hiding in the grasses of ordinary conversation. A truly spiteful woman, almost impossible not to dislike. If I could feel something, anything, for her . . . But if I did, it would be nothing but my job. In my office compassion is no more than a tipped hat to a blind man.

On your way to work, on the freeway, a man suddenly cuts in front of you without signaling. He narrowly avoids hitting you. You honk, he gives you the finger. Fifteen minutes later, in your office, the man appears, a new referral. Your first response is: Does he recognize me? You are embarrassed until you are certain that he doesn't. The feelings of anger rise again. The man is inconsiderate, undoubtedly a brute at home, a bully at work, and insensitive. Very definitely he must be insensitive. You smile graciously, you will show him compassion in all its proud colors. You will be bigger than he is. You are above his pettiness.

You are a doctor, and a doctor heals without judgment. You will help this poor blighted man with his tortured psyche. Splendid.

You are nice to the man precisely because of, and directly in proportion to, your dislike for him. The greater the hatred, the more solicitous the manner. You are all smiling teeth, gentle nods, and welcome ears. You are a real whore with fake tears.

You are civilized.

And as obvious as Mrs. Seifert caught in the ecstasy of a whimper.

It is in the nature of smallness to feign empathy.

Take a walk down Market Street, and notice the wide assortment of souls coursing down the boulevard—all types, all manner of being. Look at each one and ask yourself the question: At first glance do I like this one or that one? Or does this one irritate me, make me step back, turn away, or want to bump into him? Be honest and take a poll. How many people you chance across are actually appealing?

Why should it be any different in your office or the doctor's lounge at the hospital, or at a family dinner? Why should the percentages vary?

Of course they do not.

The practice of psychiatry can be called a discipline—deserves to be called a discipline—in that it takes enormous self-control and self-denial to overlook the percentages and accept all comers as decent suffering souls. It is a noble struggle.

Even if your feelings are not real.

Dr. Forester caught sight of an old Peanuts cartoon that he had saved from medical school days. Lucy was laughing at Charlie Brown for saying that when he grew up he was going to be a doctor.
"That's ridiculous," Lucy said. "You despise humanity."
"Not at all," Charlie Brown said. "I love humanity. It's people I can't stand."

Forester slid the yellowed cartoon strip back in the drawer.

My patients drain my strength, especially the Mrs. Seiferts and the Jim Van Allens. It is an honest hatred, no different than what any one or all of you would feel. I have absorbed their collective poisons like some Hippocratic blotter. My anger oozes out, fills up the hours as a polluted fog. Still I listen, thirty-five hours a week, a Sisyphus chained to my desk. Their rocks are my eternity.

It is an ordinary hatred—I believe I repeat myself—but it is important to distinguish commonplace emotions from the other, the anger that contains joy as well as hostility. The other anger is a passion.

Somewhere in that other anger lies the answer. Retribution coats the feeling, but it is not the emotion any more than icing is the cake. Perhaps the true feeling is located on the same gene, not far away, a few nucleotides to the left. If only it were that easy.

Obsessive-compulsive, Tourette's syndrome, attention disorders—all a continuum of a morsel of DNA gone sour. If so, why not murder and mayhem? Perhaps they are only a few microns down the chromosomal road. Responsibility lies in the peptides. Free will is an illusion located on chromosome sixteen.

Forester hesitated, then opened the last notebook. It was unlabeled, and though it was of the same size and shape, felt different from the others. Inside were doodles and a stick figure of a flower, its stem snapped in two, the flower hanging lifeless. Underneath were the words "Ma Petite Fleur." Forester winced as he recalled the name of the perfume his mother had worn. It was very special and she saved it for Saturday evenings.

The bottle sat on her dresser, next to a grainy brown-and-white photo of her mother, a woman that Forester could only vaguely picture.

A short, dumpy woman in a black winter coat. Perhaps. She had been at the top of the cellar stairs when little Alan was passed on to neighbors. Her smallness could have been a matter of perspective and her sad, helpless odor. She smelled of the village, of mud and animals, and herring. She was not of the city. She was bewildered, you could see the confusion in her eyes.

Not like his mother, who was clear and determined, cool as that winter night. Cool as her fingers that touched his cheek and wished him a safe trip. She stayed behind, resigned. *Take me,* she said to the knock at the door.

He threw the note pad back in the drawer and slammed it closed.

Van Allen flashed that horrible smile and said that he was guilty, the smile erasing the guilt from the word *guilty*. He had no conscience, no inner life of ambiguities and ambivalences that generated anxiety. Minutes before, on the news, Donald Trump had said that his divorce had been emotionally trying, but that it had been good for business.

And was he, Forester, different? He'd had analysis, and he knew the lingo of self-investigation, but what did that really mean?

Nothing. It would be necessary to start from the beginning. But he was tired, run-down from the day's events. All he wanted was a good rest, a few days of peace and quiet.

Forester stood at the window, the lights in the neighborhood gradually coming on. In each of the neighboring houses families would be meeting over dinner. Forester was overwhelmed with the desire for simple coziness, the warmth of family, even the petty bickering and nagging that was the irritating rub of relationship.

He thought of Michelle on TV. He watched her nightly. She was resilient, with a strong moral sense. She didn't arouse any of the bad feelings. He ran his fingers along his lips. She had wanted to hug him. And she had lightly touched his arm. A gesture of gratitude and friendship. She was a good woman. She would never abandon her child. Never. She wasn't that type of woman.

"Help me," Forester suddenly blurted out. He was astonished to hear the words escape from his mouth like some foul gas. He could see them fog the window and his

view of his garden. "God help me. Please. I will be better.
I promise." The word "God" startled him. He had never
been religious. God wasn't part of his vocabulary. Yet here
he was, sounding like Van Allen. No, it was different. It
felt real, the word soft and comforting somewhere deep
within him. Though it wasn't something he had considered
in many years, at that moment he understood that God was
real, and that he had the power to forgive. Forester fell to
his knees, his forehead against the carpet. "I am sorry, so
sorry," he said.

Forester remained on his knees, rocking, sobbing, and
begging forgiveness until the sky was completely dark and
his garden had disappeared from view. *I am sorry and I
will show my repentance in good deeds. I will dedicate the
remainder of my life to goodness and retribution. I will
rise from the damned.*

Slowly there rose within him the sense of a subdued joy.
Soon he would be free of his bad thoughts. They had been
washed away in his tears. He could tell by the stars in
the sky that he would be forgiven. As long as he stuck to
the straight and narrow path.

He stood up and went to the back of his closet, to the
videocassettes. He took the bag of them and put them in
the fireplace. From the basement he brought a can of
lighter fluid. Soon the film was curling up in the flames,
the cassettes melting, the room filled with the raw but nevertheless pleasing smell of the acrid plastic.

The very denial of his urges would be an added demonstration of his renewed purity.

It was not too late.

TWELVE

THREE DAYS LATER A jogger discovered the body of Van Allen in his car, parked in a side exit from Tilden Park. Pinned to the passenger seat was a letter of apology. In an accompanying envelope was a taped confession. A gun was in his hand.

Bobby Lockhart smelled a rat. Van Allen's death was entirely too theatrical. From what he could gather, Van Allen was quite conservative in dress and lifestyle, with the exception of his penchant for women. He was from a prestigious Eastern family, had the appropriate Ivy League credentials, and normally wore traditional suits, or khakis and Topsiders. Melodrama was out of character. Lockhart listened to the tape again and again. Something didn't fit.

Perhaps it was the voice. Van Allen's apology didn't sound apologetic; there was an unmistakable note of sarcasm and no real sense of remorse. But Mrs. Van Allen had listened to the tape. She identified his voice, and yes, it did sound like him.

The note was in Van Allen's handwriting, on his own office stationery. The writing was clear and unforced. His wife could not completely account for his whereabouts at the estimated times of the three murders.

Lockhart checked Van Allen's office schedule. The night Kelly Caldwell was killed, Van Allen had been scheduled for a meeting at St. Joseph's Hospital. He was not listed on the sign-in sheet.

On the night of Bonnie Ringold's murder he had not been home from the office until eleven o'clock. He had told his wife he was dictating. The janitor of the building said that his office was empty.

His wife wasn't sure about the night of Becky Dirksen's death. She spoke with embarrassment. Lockhart saw a mixture of love and humiliation in her puzzled teary eyes. "He was a good man, and a good doctor," she said repeatedly. "He was working on his problem."

Lockhart went back to Dr. Setledge. "You sure this was a suicide?"

"Right down to the cadaveric spasm in his hand. His hand had to be on the trigger when he died."

"He was cruising along without leaving a clue. Van Allen would have known by the news blitz that there were no suspects. He was in the clear. If he had wanted to confess, you'd have expected him to make contact with the news, the police department, a priest. It doesn't ring true."

"You want he should stick to some script? You realize the distorted logic of expecting standard behavior from some sicko?"

"There are patterns."

"There are patterns in chaos, too, but that doesn't mean they can be extrapolated to the specific."

"Excuse me?"

"Chaos. You're the existentialist in the woodpile. Chaos has its own mathematics, or haven't you heard?"

"Please. Do you know how exasperating it is talking to you?"

"You've got a body, a confession, Spagliano is off your

back. You should feel like a million bucks. Okay, maybe not that good, let's say fifty thousand. That's more your speed."

"You're satisfied?"

"Personally—and you know what that counts for—I think the guy's a setup. The whole thing is too neat and tidy. But there's nothing in the autopsy to raise any medical suspicions. No drugs, nothing. Just a forty-five in his mouth, his hand on the trigger, and the back of his head misted onto the rear window. Forget it. If there are more murders you can start all over again. It's not like you're abandoning a bag full of clues."

One last stop and he would put his doubts to rest. The medical society showed Lockhart the depositions of Van Allen's office staff. They suggested he contact Dr. Forester for more information.

The entrance to Forester's home office set Lockhart's bitterness wheel in motion. It was a lovely old San Francisco three-story town house; it would cost Lockhart a lifetime in wages. Lockhart sometimes held to the theory of just compensation, a naive belief that wages should be commensurate with public good. He could understand why philosophers were paid next to nothing, and homicide inspectors little more. But a psychiatrist living in a house like this? It was a monument to cunning being of greater monetary value than intrinsic good.

Last week *The New York Times* had published an article on Freud suggesting that he had misrepresented several of his case studies. There was even the suggestion that he had encouraged two of his patients to divorce their spouses and marry each other. It was the worst kind of emotional tampering. Lockhart was glad to see Freud beaten up in the letters to the editor. He hated the idea that psychiatry and psychology posed on the doorstep of science. It was good for the world to see Freud as a brilliant con man and manipulator.

Forester's consultation room fueled Lockhart's resentment. Behind his desk were hundreds of books, including the complete leather-bound works of Freud, Erickson, and Karen Horney. The walls on the patient's side were empty except for the single picture of a mother cradling her child. Forester sat at his desk. The patient had a choice of couch or chair, both low and awkward to get on and off. It was the perfect setting for intimidation.

Forester was gracious, but cool. He acted as though he were doing Lockhart some glorious favor. He politely offered him the leather chair.

Lockhart refused. "Maybe I'll sit at your desk and you can lie down."

Forester stood beside his desk, waiting without expression for Lockhart to get down to business.

Lockhart remained at the window, looking out at the Japanese garden below. Though geometric and severe, the paths were covered with fallen leaves. It was as though the garden had been recently abandoned. It reminded Lockhart of the inside of an orderly but distracted mind.

It had nothing to do with his interview, but he enjoyed keeping his back to Forester. Lockhart's former wife had told him to see a therapist, to find out how to relate.

"Your problem is communication," she had said.

"I thought it was low salary," Lockhart had responded.

"Money makes people easier to understand," his wife

had said. It was her therapist who had dropped the big garbage bag of blame in his lap.

Shrinks. Lockhart thought of the slick-tongued hired guns who testified to diminished capacity, or mental aberrations due to eating Twinkies. He couldn't think of a scummier lot.

He felt Forester watching him. It was a delicious moment.

Forester cleared his throat.

"Your garden seems to be ambivalent," Lockhart said. He turned to face Forester.

"I haven't got all day," Forester said. "I presume you want me to tell you all about Van Allen. I'm sorry, but our conversations are confidential."

"Not when there's murder involved. Besides, I have a written release from his wife."

"You're sure?"

"Scout's honor."

"It's a long story, and I'm still trying to piece it together. You've seen the depositions at the medical society?"

"From my perspective, they're nothing special. Millions of men love to taunt women. I suspect it's our true national pastime. But that doesn't mean murder."

"Ambivalence toward women usually stems from faulty bonding. The man seeks the maternal love he never had, at the same time wanting to hurt mother figures."

"That's elementary psych. I thought you might have some additional insights."

"I have some ideas, but they're not well thought out. It's only been two days since I heard. This is the first time I've ever dealt with a murderer. It's a real shock. But you're right, it's important to sort through. As a matter of fact, I'm going to present some of my notes at a lecture I'm giving over at the Analytic Institute. Why don't you come? It'll be next Thursday at seven o'clock. Hopefully I can make more sense of it by then. If you have more questions, we can meet afterwards."

"You never had any idea, some suspicion?"

Forester looked down at his hands, then back at Lockhart. "You never really know about people, do you?"

"Thanks for the tip." Lockhart moved to the door. "By the way, it's a little strange that you can present your notes to your colleagues, but you feel it is confidential information and off-limits to the police."

"It's a medical subject. He'll be presented anonymously."

"A man kills three women and you think no one in the audience will recognize him from your descriptions."

"It's important to all of us to hash out the dynamics, but not dwell on the sensational."

"I can't wait." Lockhart stepped out onto the front landing. He was starting down the stairs when some queer trace of memory tried to assert itself. It was something he had read in the papers. While he was trying to remember he found himself asking Forester, "Oh. One last question. Have you ever had another patient commit suicide while under your care?"

"Excuse me?" Forester had the door nearly closed. He was looking out through the remaining crack.

"Suicides? Have you had other suicides?"

"No." Forester looked acutely uncomfortable.

"That's funny. I thought there was something in the paper. Recently." Lockhart couldn't remember the article, but he felt Forester's name swimming near the second or third paragraph. Lockhart sometimes kidded that he had a cheap Kodak version of a photographic memory. He thought he could see Forester's name and the picture of a pretty young woman.

"You mean Kate Carbone? The medical examiner said it was accidental. Though naturally the *Chronicle* made it sound like suicide. A very sad story. She was a lovely woman. And now, if you'll excuse me, I'm expecting my next patient."

"Two deaths in two months. One definite suicide and one possible. That must be close to the local analytic record."

"Is that all?" Forester asked.

"Sure." He knew he could index Forester in the department computer that logged all death certificates. It would be easy to see if there were others. If there should be a reason.

Lockhart was barely out the door before Forester dropped onto his couch and flipped on Channel Six. Michelle was summarizing Van Allen's childhood—his honors, scholarships, outstanding student awards. The implication was obvious—you can never know someone well enough to predict. Even the smartest, the most revered man could be a mass murderer.

Forester switched to Channel Seven. The local news was covering all the gruesome details of the three murders. Forester knew enough from this morning's *Chronicle* and the TV updates to feel he had been there. The camera coverage was so graphic it was as if each viewer were personally invited into the women's bedrooms. Forester specifically recalled Bonnie Ringold's dresser drawer, a deep burgundy laminate. It was the red of blood. He could even hear her muffled sobs.

It was easy to imagine Van Allen tying up each of the women, making them helpless, then watching them suffocate. TV made everyone an expert in violence.

Dr. Setledge was tying up his own loose ends. On the TV, Dr. Setledge was saying that each of the victims had low levels of barbiturates, but nothing that would cause coma or death. Death was by simple asphyxiation. There were no other details. Strange. Where did Forester get the idea that Van Allen had killed them by kneeling on their chests to prevent them from breathing? It seemed that he had heard or read about it somewhere, but Setledge was saying nothing of the sort.

Forester's head ached. He was confused as to what had happened, and even how he felt. Part of him was ecstatic that Van Allen had been uncovered for being the vicious animal Forester knew him to be. But another part wasn't convinced that Van Allen was the murderer. It was all so unbelievable.

And there was the ever-increasing sense of guilt. He had the distinct feeling that the three murdered women would still be alive if he had ... had what? He should have stopped him, that's what. He was paid to understand the mind. He knew Van Allen's urges stemmed from some deeper, more malignant pathology.

It was another example of his own self-absorption. It had been Kate, then Joan, and now the three women.

Forester paced the upstairs corridor, eventually opening the back door leading to the stairs to the garden. His eye caught a protruding floorboard at the head of the stairs. Joan had asked him a hundred times to nail it down. Always he had been too busy. Now the loose board stood as a sharp reminder of how preoccupied he had been.

The garden was a shambles, the geometric edges now more a demonstration of Brownian motion, the limbs going in all directions. It didn't take long—turn your head and nature resumed charge. It was as though you were given the reins for a mere second or two, to know what it would feel like to be in control. Then they were taken away.

His life echoed the wayward garden.

He couldn't imagine how he would pick up the pieces.

The phone rang. It was Michelle. "Not about me," she said. "It's about Van Allen."

"We can grab a cup of coffee," Forester said. "Though I've told the police everything I can remember."

"Maybe you can give me some impressions. Nothing official, and you won't be quoted."

"I'd love to."

The timing of the call was a sign.

It was a cold early November evening. As Forester approached Café Trieste on upper Grant he could see a wind-blown Michelle coming from the other direction. Even at a distance, with her hair wrapped across her face, she was beautiful. Special. The first Christmas decorations hung from telephone poles, flapping sharply in the wind, little claps of despair against Forester's ears. Michelle was the opposite, she was smiling and quietly inquiring about his health. She was not seasonal tinsel.

Forester spoke with enthusiasm about her interview of Van Allen's office staff, but seemed reluctant to provide his own insights. Michelle mentioned to Forester that two of the women were uneasy with the idea that Van Allen could actually be a killer. For the first time during their conversation Forester spoke with feeling about Van Allen.

"They want to see life other than as it is," he said forcefully. Almost immediately he lowered his voice, as though reining his emotions. "Of course, it's only natural. We all like to see ourselves as good judges of character. But it just isn't so."

"You're telling me," Michelle said.

"I'll second that. Even with all my years of professional experience."

"Yes?"

"You want to hear that even psychiatrists make mistakes? Well, of course we do, all the time. I knew Van Allen was sadistic, but I never dreamed. . . ." Forester paused. He looked downcast, beaten, as though his failings were now public knowledge. "I guess I really blew it. Maybe if I'd picked up enough clues those women would still be alive."

"And Kate Carbone?" Michelle was startled by her question. She almost blurted out that Kate had been her best friend. But she didn't. She was silenced by a subtle change in Forester's expression.

"Kate Carbone?" Forester's face narrowed. "I don't get the connection."

"I meant, it must make you wonder what you really know about anyone when you have two suicides in your practice within a short period of time." Michelle hadn't intended this line of inquiry, but there it was, the string of incriminating words jabbing the air between them. Now she sat watching herself, anxious to see the direction the conversation might take. And wondering why Forester was now so obviously tense, his shoulders rigid, parallel to the fixed furrows of his forehead.

"Kate Carbone's death was accidental. At least that's what I was led to believe."

"I thought the papers raised the possibility of suicide."

"I didn't see anything like that, but you know how the papers can be. No, I talked with the Marin County medical examiner. He assured me that her death was accidental." Michelle noticed that Forester was rubbing the knuckle of his right thumb with the tip of his index finger. It was a gesture that she had not seen Forester make before. There was a heightened intensity to his speech, as though Forester were searching for something. Or hiding something.

"But even the possibility of suicide, though that's not my understanding. . . . Well you can imagine how upsetting that is to a therapist. She put her trust in me."

Michelle wanted to pursue the questioning, unravel the meaning of the change in Forester's behavior. But the emergence of his nervous gestures and a stiff, formal manner could be nothing more than embarrassment and guilt. He was a prominent therapist who had had one patient exposed as a serial killer, another who had probably killed herself. It would be enough to destroy anyone's self-confidence. She looked for fake bravado or other signs of defensiveness, but the pain on Forester's face was suddenly obvious. He wasn't hiding anything. He was ashamed.

"I'm sure you did what you could."

"Obviously not." Forester looked out the window at the cars passing on Grant Street. He sipped at his wine, staring out the window. For a moment they sat in silence, avoiding each other.

He cleared his throat. "Maybe I haven't been all that astute lately. It's been tough since my wife left me." He spoke as though he knew that Michelle had already figured it out. "After my lecture I think I'll take some time off and regroup." Forester motioned to the waiter, who refilled his cup of decaf.

He continued talking about his wife, how it shouldn't be embarrassing to grow apart, yet it was, as though divorce were a public announcement of personal inadequacy.

Michelle found herself throwing in words of encouragement, comparing his situation to the recently divorced six o'clock anchorman at the station. "He's a good man, too," Michelle heard herself say. "These things happen."

"I've watched several of your recent programs. It's amazing how you make your subjects comfortable at the same time as you get right to the essence of what matters. Sometimes it even seems like you're providing them therapy. A chance to actually give something of themselves. Like right now. You don't know me, and you don't know my wife. Yet somehow you make me feel better. Maybe you should have been the one to see Van Allen. You might have gotten the message before it was too late. Maybe you could have even turned him around. A strong woman like you."

Forester sat with his hands in his lap, as proper as a school boy. Maybe it was just loneliness that made his eyes burn into her.

Michelle stood to leave.

"Since you've terminated therapy, do you think it would be out of line for me to ask you to a movie?" Forester's language was mildly stilted, old-fashioned. He moved to her side of the table and pulled out her chair. Though she should have anticipated some sort of invitation, she was surprised and caught off-guard.

Michelle shook her head. She meant to stop there, but found herself making an excuse, saying that she was exhausted from a series of twelve-hour work days.

"Of course," Forester said. "But maybe you could come to my lecture Thursday. I'm going to present my thoughts on Van Allen. As best I understand them."

"If I can get free from the station." She did want to hear the lecture, but right now she needed some fresh air.

"I'll look for you."

How lovely she was. And strong, too. He hoped she liked him. She had been a little cool toward the end of the evening. Maybe she was tired.

Forester walked along Grant until he reached upper Kearny Street. He had parked below Coit Tower. It was dark; the streets were nearly empty. Before he reached his car, he decided to walk farther. He turned the corner and headed back toward Broadway. The topless joints seemed made of plastic, the neon dull and blurry in the low fog that crawled in the street.

The fog was memory, formless, cradling blinking red lights and the invitations of plastic signboards. The fog promised obscurity and hidden pleasure. And hid the unmentionable past. Forester remembered, with some regret, having burned his videotapes. Too bad, tonight would be a perfect romantic night to curl up in front of the TV. No. He had been good for over a week—no thoughts, no urges. He had been preoccupied with his lecture and thoughts of this evening with Michelle. It was curious, being alone in a restaurant with another woman. It was the first time in over ten years. His only other contacts with women had been on a cash-first basis.

Women who let you enter their apartments and bodies without hesitation. They were the on-ramps to the sexual fast lane. What did they think, watching the scores of men drive through their bodies? Some moaned. All cried in the end. Forester's heart jumped into his throat. Wild screams roared down Broadway, whimpering, begging, pleading fragments of shattered heart exploding into the damp night.

He had been with Bonnie Ringold. Now she was dead.

It was the first time he had heard the stark terror. What kind of man could have provoked this chorus of fear jabbing at his ears?

Forester stopped in the street. A drunken tourist bumped into him, then wandered off into one of the topless joints. The doorway to the club was bright pink, the entrance was a dark curtain that a scantily clad woman pulled aside. Forester looked down the street at the collection of caves, a string of vaginas, with cash-only women drawing back the curtains.

The darkness inside corresponded to the darkness at the heart of man. Conrad used the African metaphor. Today he would have used Big Al's or Video Arcade.

Two tourists shivering in their seersucker jackets slipped into the Roaring Twenties. They were probably from Omaha, maybe bankers or farm equipment salesmen. Tomorrow they would be home with their wives.

An ambulance shot up the street, weaving in and out of traffic, its siren wailing. The sound of the siren slid inside the fading scream in Forester's head, a duet of suffering and help on its way.

A skinny woman in black lingerie and a loden-green car coat tugged at Forester's sleeve. "It don't cost to take a look." She pulled the curtain back a few inches.

"No, thanks."

"A little look won't kill."

"No, thank you."

" 'No, thank you,' " the woman said, her voice a mockery of Forester. " 'I don't believe I'll be having any sex tonight.' " She stuck out her tongue, rubbed it against her lips. Her hips moved slowly, in time with the saxophone growling behind the curtain. Then she drew back the curtain and slipped inside.

The siren faded in the distance.

Forester started down the street, relieved that he had not gone inside. A barker stepped out of an adjacent doorway. Forester waved him away, indicating with the downward swipe of his hand that he had better things to do, better women to see. He was not your ordinary man. He had Michelle.

Filled with renewed purpose, he turned back and walked briskly toward his car. Fifteen minutes later he was on his couch at home. He debated phoning Michelle and telling her what a wonderful evening he had had. *No. Play it cool. You've got all the time in the world.* He stretched out, under a woolen blanket, the telephone a pleasant weight on his chest.

One call wouldn't hurt. He held out as long as he could. He dialed her number. Michelle answered as though she had been asleep.

"Thanks for the evening," Forester said.

"Excuse me?"

"Sorry. I didn't mean to wake you. See you next week."
He hung up quickly, embarrassed at his own undisguised
need.

He phoned again first thing in the morning, this time
hanging up as soon as Michelle answered. Her voice was
enough to get him through the day.

His lecture was only days away. Originally it was to
have been primarily about religion and evil, beginning
with the Elmer Gantry syndrome and Van Allen's variant.
Now it was clear that the lecture would focus on the ultimate religious experience—possession. Religious fervor
was the attempt to possess God, incorporate His spirit. On
the other hand, religious possession—the act of giving
oneself up to God—was the ultimate religious experience.
Fake religious leaders possessed religion. True religious
leaders were possessed by God.

The two modes of experience were analogous to domination and submission.

Which seemed to Forester to be two primary poles of
human behavior. Everything in between, by definition, was
compromise.

There existed a natural hierarchy. Below religion was
love. Further down was sex. Van Allen hid behind the notion of original sin, the universal bruise of the heart that
tethered the soul. Religious possession was an impossibil-
ity and pure love was nothing more than a bad joke, a the-
oretical construct that left out one basic assumption. For
Van Allen religion was an excuse for domination, his evil
being no more than the expected expression of natural
man.

Forester looked at his notes, staring at the word *possession*. Material possession was what was left when you had neither religion nor love. Possession was also insanity, the devil's pitchfork firmly planted in the frontal lobe, as in the paintings of Hieronymous Bosch. Possession was fire and brimstone, harmony and transcendence. It was Neiman-Marcus and Bloomingdale's. It was slavery and bondage. It was cannibalism, the eating of the brains of the deceased to ingest the dead man's soul. It was the collection of baseball cards in order to identify, hold the players' spirit to your heart. It was capture the flag, as children or as nations.

It was killing women to conquer their spirits.

Obsession was possession. Indifference was another sort of possession.

The anguish of life came from the inability to capture beauty, love, a gorgeous moment. It was the failure of possession that led to the bitter-sweet nature of all things glorious.

Sadomasochism was the yin-yang of sexual possession.

Forester smiled. He was in possession of his faculties. It would be a brilliant lecture.

He phoned Michelle. Her answering machine clicked on. He hung up. He thought of phoning her at the station, but decided to wait until they could meet. She might think he was phoning just to show her how smart he was. That wasn't the point at all. He wanted to share his ideas about love. That was all. Nothing more.

THIRTEEN

FORESTER CONTINUED
to be media fodder: "FAMOUS LOCAL PSYCHIATRIST FAILS TO
RECOGNIZE PSYCHOPATHIC KILLER."

"I will not be part of a media circus," he responded, re-
fusing interviews. A panel show on KQED debated the
limits of a patient's right to confidentiality versus the therapist's obligation to the community. It was agreed that a
serious threat of violence against a reasonably identifiable
victim required police notification. The program tried to
define what constituted an adequate threat, but turned into
a succession of platforms for the participating psychiatrists.

Several of his patients demanded an explanation. Mrs.
Seifert seemed particularly pleased, showing up early for
each session and strutting into the consultation room as
though, at last, she had the goods on the man who suppos-
edly owned her mind. Forester adopted a policy of silence.
In another week or two he would be out of the papers. He
would learn to tolerate Mrs. Seifert's sneer. Besides, she
couldn't help it. It was the very nature of her pathology.

His lecture and the buffet to follow were sold out. Part
of him wanted to cancel; only two days away, he wasn't
nearly prepared. He could beg off, claiming that he was
too upset. But he was known as Dr. Reliable. Giving a

good lecture was important if he was going to reestablish his old self-confidence.

Forester figured that a half dozen points would be enough for a ninety-minute lecture. He would start with the religious theme and perhaps also touch on selective failure of memory, multiple personalities, dissociative states, fugue states, and psychogenic amnesia. There was more than enough material.

He wanted desperately to let them know of his guilt. A proper apologia would serve as a conclusion to this sordid period of his life. It felt right, confessing publicly. He would be among friends. They would understand.

Forester's spirits were immediately buoyed by the prospect of a complete new start.

He grabbed half of yesterday's hamburger from the refrigerator. He ate quickly, without tasting, instead aware of the looseness of his pants waist, and the jiggle of the wristband of his watch. He guessed that he had lost five pounds, though ten was possible. He probably should eat something else, but he wasn't hungry. He took some quarters from his dresser. If he felt hungry, he could play the vending machine in the basement of the Institute.

The Institute library was closed. Forester unlocked the front door and flipped on a single row of overhead lights. A chill came over him. He pulled his jacket tight against him, mildly annoyed that he had forgotten to bring a sweater. The Institute ran on a tight budget; the heat automatically shut off at five o'clock. Fortunately the library was on the third floor. The offices downstairs were cold even in the daytime.

The chill was augmented by the utter darkness that hung

in the high arched windows. The neighboring buildings were two-story and not visible through the windows. Normally the stars and the moon streaming into the library were a pleasant, even inspiring, sight. Tonight the moon was in retreat and the stars were hidden behind some high clouds. There was a sense of foreboding, some ominous possibility just out of view beyond the umbrella of darkened sky.

Forester went to the stacks and pulled out some standard texts on psychopathic behavior. He carried an armful to an empty oak table at the far end of the library. For twenty years this had been his table, his place of comfort. Several of his papers had been edited at this very spot. Forester wrote at home, but he enjoyed line editing in the library, where he might be seen by his colleagues. Sometimes he felt a little obvious, but so what? He was productive, turning out a book or a paper on a regular basis. He was entitled to a little sin of pride.

He spread the books out in front of him, the desk now covered with criminal behavior, from Jack the Ripper to the Hillside Strangler. Ideally he should trace the development of Van Allen's murderous trait, reveal childhood antecedents. But Van Allen had painted a rosy, untroubled youth—Forester knew nothing unusual about Van Allen's early years. It didn't say much for his expertise as a therapist.

He needed some childhood anecdote, which meant he would have to conjure one up. It might not be strictly truthful, but his colleagues would require some telling detail in order to accept the rest of the lecture. Forester started with Son of Sam and then Ted Bundy. There was a formidable amount of data. Forester read until the lines blurred. He took off his reading glasses and rubbed his eyes, holding both palms flat against his cheeks.

He could use the usual childhood deprivations: an alcoholic mother, a strict, overbearing father. Or there could be the hint of animal torture or early sexual ambiguities. But those were obvious and trite. He would prefer a single striking incident that could act as metaphor. It should be subtle, like being trapped in a church confessional box overnight. Or spending a week alone at sea. He stopped at this last thought, working his way around the image of the infinite ocean and the unchanging wafer of horizon. There would be the relentless sun, a searing white metal light, and the cruel distance of the evening star. The boy would be invisible in the infinity.

Van Allen had mentioned fishing with his father in the lakes of upstate New York. Perhaps he had even recalled the boat breaking free from its moorings, young Van Allen set adrift, without a paddle, in the aluminum dinghy. Yes, it was a moment of Van Allen's past.

Forester drew a picture of the boat and a stick figure of the little boy motioning to his father, who stood helpless, head down, on the pier. "Momma," the little boy called out, but there was no one to hear. Momma? Wasn't he calling to his father?

Forester pushed aside some distant memory. His own father had left home even before there were knocks at the door. Or had he been killed in the Resistance? Whatever gave him that idea? The Resistance? His father? Was that possible? Where had he gone? He struggled to bring the man into view, but he was not there. It was peculiar that he would now think of the Resistance. He had no proof.

No actual recollection. All he knew was that his father had not been there the day Alan was sent away.

He drew in the boy's little fingers. They were clutching the sky, trying to draw it down like a blanket. But there was nothing but thin air and the rasp of nails against emptiness. Forester looked down at his own hands, at their slender sinewy structure. This was not Van Allen's memory. It was his. But it was not his father on the pier. It was a neighbor who had brought him to the shipyard. It had been a bitterly cold day and the neighbor had given a single wave and trundled away, his hands deep in his own pockets.

Forester gulped and felt panic rise to his throat. It had been Van Allen's story, he was sure of it. And it was his.

He rose and paced back and forth between the library tables. He felt confused, disoriented. It could have been either of their memories. He tried hard to clear his mind but there remained an obstinate resistance to recall.

Who was the little boy in the boat?

Forester shivered and wrapped his arms around himself. It was the first time in many years that he had gotten close to the memory of the freighter, a solitary black dot on the vicious North Sea. He focused on the distant vague recollection, but the memory backed away, Forester trying, but unable to follow.

Had Van Allen mentioned the lake in upstate New York? For the purpose of the lecture it made no difference. He could make up the fact. The audience would grasp the significance. In this instance Van Allen and he could share a memory, a past. It was not verifiable, Van Allen's father was dead. The audience would have their metaphor.

He could even joke that the incident resulted in Van Allen acting as though he were without peer. No, this was no laughing matter and he scratched any idea of puns or double entendres.

But the question persisted. Whose memory was it? Forester was consumed with a sudden dense nausea. Man was the sum of his past, and now there was a serious question where he ended and someone else began.

He thought back to their sessions. Van Allen had definitely mentioned his father and that they had gone fishing together. This he remembered distinctly, and, yes, he had named some lake near Wells. Forester specifically recalled the town, priding himself on knowing where Wells was. So they had been on a fishing trip. But had Van Allen been set adrift, or was it Forester's imagination, or was it Forester on the North Sea?

Forester tried to remember the freighter, but could not. Not one detail or impression yielded itself. It had to have been a boat; he did not fly until he was a teenager. But the image of the voyage was nowhere to be found. It had to be there somewhere, and Forester sensed the urgency of finding it. Memories were necessary. They served as personal walls to block out the memories of others.

Nature abhors a vacuum, and does what is necessary to fill in the blanks. Van Allen was sneaking up onto the very edges of Forester's personality.

Forester glanced down at a book relating psychopathic behavior to multiple personalities. He stopped at a particularly interesting experiment. A patient with diagnosed multiple personality disorder was given IQ testing. The tests involved tasks that would become easier with repetition. Each personality, tested in succession, demonstrated improved scores, which strongly suggested that all of the personalities had access to the material. The tests were repeated on ten patients with multiple personality disorder; the results were identical.

Forester stopped and mulled over the data, partially hoping it was wrong. But he could find no flaw in the paper. He nodded his head. The experiment had been well conceived and executed. The conclusion was unavoidable: regardless of how strongly the patient denied it, there was communication between the various personalities.

So it was possible to know and not to know at the same time.

Which meant that the absence of memory was no excuse. He could not hide behind what he did not remember.

The nausea intensified. The hamburger could have been bad. He swallowed repeatedly as he rose and walked toward the small bathroom at the back of the periodical section. It wasn't necessary, walking to the bathroom, he wasn't going to be sick. But he was. For some time he knelt at the toilet bowl, his hands clutching the icy porcelain sides.

The nausea passed. He stood, his knees shaky, and rinsed his mouth. He put a flowered hand towel to his mouth, but pulled it away again, aware of the faint floral scent on the towel. He held his hands under the warm water, but he could not shake the cold. His teeth chattered. He turned the hot water on further. Even with the steam rising up, and the water nearly scalding, his hands were like ice.

The nausea had been replaced by a tight burning knot at the pit of his stomach. He turned off the light in the bathroom and returned to his seat. He would rest for a few minutes. He put his head down on the desk.

When he opened his eyes the room was bathed in blue light. It was not in his eyes, but in his mind, as though the light had been poured in through an opening in his skull. It was the color of the sky in a Turner landscape—Forester prided himself on knowing about art history—and for a brief second, the placing of the color distanced him from the horror of the fact. The color was not a vision or some majestic revelation. It was a hallucination.

He circled the perimeter of the library, walking through the bluish haze. The oak-paneled walls were a sickly brown against the aqua patina. There was the sensation of green moss covering the walls at the interface between the actual wood and the superimposed color.

It will pass, he told himself. *It is a momentary disruption.*

It did not pass. Time trudged through the blueness, each second a lifetime. The air was charged with silent accusation. He could not get a handle on the warped blue space that screamed at him, crawling along his skin and the inside of his skull like some insidious burrowing creature. The words *temporary insanity* came to mind. The words meant nothing. They were a defense, not a description.

Take a deep breath, close your eyes, focus yourself. He sat down in his chair, which no longer had the same sense of familiarity. He looked down to be sure it was his favorite, which it was, though now it seemed devoid of any recognizable quality. It was just a chair in a room called a library.

Ted Bundy was looking up at him, from behind bars. There was an evil grin on his face. Forester turned the page to a snapshot of clean-cut Bundy at law school graduation. This photo was worse, more ominous because

nothing was out of place. Alongside Bundy were stick figures of a man on a pier, and a little boy lost at sea. He
tried to remember why he had drawn them, but could not.
He knew that it had to do with his thoughts about Van Allen, but he could not find the threads of reasoning that had
led to the drawing.

He felt the tremendous weight of his brain.

Suddenly there was the sound of screaming, the smell of
cheap perfume, and the flashy redness of fingernails tapping at his hands.

"Those are not my memories," he said out loud. "They
are Van Allen's."

His arms ached with fatigue, as though they were carrying the burden of his buried memories. He held his hands
out in front of him, opening and closing them, testing
them. He wiggled his fingers. There was a strong downward pressure on his forearms. He leaned forward, as
though he was about to relieve himself of some great
weight. He found himself surprised to realize that his arms
were empty.

And that he was falling. He lurched and grabbed two
bookshelves for support. The familiar feel of the books
was comforting; his mind focused. It was a section on
Freud. His right hand was on *Selected Essays on Hysteria*.
He yanked the book from the shelf. It was the case of
Lucie R. in which Freud talked about the intact nature of
forgotten memories.

He turned directly to page 38. Forester remembered the
quote verbatim.

The real traumatic moment is that in which the (emotional) conflict thrusts itself upon the ego and the latter

decides to banish the incompatible idea. Such banishment does not annihilate the opposing idea, but merely crowds it into the unconscious. When this process occurs for the first time, it forms a nucleus for the formation of a new psychic group, separated from the ego, around which, in the course of time, everything collects which is in accord with the opposing idea. The splitting of consciousness in such cases of acquired hysteria is thus desired and intentional, and is often initiated by at least one arbitrary act. But as a matter of fact, something different happens than the individual expects; he would like to eliminate an idea as though it never came to pass, but he only succeeds in isolating it psychically.

His recall was perfect. His mind was working just fine. There was no reason to get alarmed. A few hours' sleep was what he needed. It was sleep deprivation and the anxiety of his lecture that had overwhelmed him.

Mrs. Ralston, the head librarian, kept a small electric heater behind the check-in counter. Why hadn't he remembered that before? No matter. It was there, along with several unclaimed umbrellas and a plaid cap that Forester recognized as belonging to Nate Giles. Everywhere there were signs of innocent failures of memory. See, forgetting wasn't always intentional.

He considered unplugging the heater and bringing it back to his desk. As he bent over, he noticed a small patch of oriental rug where Mrs. Ralston stood. It was her own two-by-three feet of luxury, her own tiny office. Immediately beyond the perimeter of her office was the library cart that Mrs. Ralston used for reshelving the stacks of books that were piled on either side, several feet high.

A large hand of fatigue pushed Forester to his knees. He rolled over onto his side and curled up on the rug, his back against the library cart, his ankles and feet extending onto the adjacent linoleum. The heater sizzled near his face. He moved it a few inches away, his face and chest now warm in the friendly, maternal glow of Mrs. Ralston's hot coils. Nestled behind the four-foot-high counter, Forester had the momentary pleasing thought of being shielded from the vast remainder of the library, and from what loomed at his desk.

The overhead light stared at him, upsetting the delicate balance of his calm. He arose and walked to the front door of the library and switched off all the lights, then, guided by the campfire glow of the heater, made his way back to his small pen.

From his position he could see the tops of the high arched windows. The moon was so far away that it seemed an afterthought hastily painted into the sky to complete the picture.

He was not sure when it had disappeared, but the blue light was now gone. It could happen to anyone. *We've all had our moments.*

He would grab a moment's shut-eye before writing up an outline.

He awakened to the sound of a vacuum cleaner in the hallway. Early morning light clothed the library in soft shadowy gray. Forester scrambled to his feet and quickly walked to his desk. He grabbed a pen and pulled on a professional demeanor, just as the custodian entered the library.

"I always knew you guys worked better in the dark,"

the tall, scraggly-haired janitor said. "The unconscious is easier to see, or something like that?"

Forester pictured the janitor twenty years ago, stoned, with a crown of flowers, the Grateful Dead breaking up his synapses at one hundred twenty decibels. Forester smiled. "You can flip the lights on." Forester made a point of noisily gathering up his notebooks and papers. He closed the lids on Ted Bundy and Sam Berkowitz, the two men rejoining history. He hurried out of the library, aware that he had no place to go.

He drove around the awakening city, struck by the amount of traffic for the hour. San Francisco was no longer a sleepy backwater town. The buses were crammed with financial players on the way to their international monetary casinos. Forester disliked business types, and the brief cynical pleasure he felt watching the crowded bus roar down the street was momentarily reassuring. Small ordinary thoughts of habit were the nuclear matter of sanity.

Forester went home, slipped off his clothes, and jumped into bed. It was Wednesday morning. There would be no problem with the lecture. He would go back to his original notes on religion, domination, and humiliation. In a way, this was more professional. Not talking about Van Allen, except by inference, would remove any criticism of exploitation.

Unmentioned Van Allen would be the hidden agenda.

Forester pulled the covers over his head, to block out the sun. He had four hours until Mrs. Seifert, who, for the millionth time, was mulling over the remote possibility of leaving the mister. It would be an easy hour, followed by lunch and an empty one o'clock so graciously vacated by

Van Allen. Two midlife crises of modest proportion would round out the day. He would manage. An abbreviated day, a good night's sleep, the lecture, and he would be back on even keel.

In the distance there was a high dry sound, like someone screaming against cellophane. *It's just the wind,* Forester told himself, clenching his hands and jaw. *And I'm safe here under the covers.*

FOURTEEN

THE SERIES ON VAN
Allen was not going well. Viewer response was reasonably
enthusiastic, but there was no significant rise in daily rat-
ings. Winters not-so-politely suggested that Michelle find
some obscure facet of the case that might catch the view-
ers' attention. But her sources totaled a complete zero.
Even interviews with his medical brethren yielded nothing
of interest. She quickly found that Van Allen's flirtatious,
taunting behavior was common knowledge among his hospital cronies, and that it was dismissed by most of them as
a healthy case of overexuberant libido. One cardiac surgeon
had the nerve to say, "He taunted them because he knew
they loved it," dismissing with a single wave of his hand
the dozen smoking depositions at the medical society.
Michelle hated the surgeon's self-satisfied cockiness. The
man was insufferable and, worse yet, reminded Michelle of
her recently collapsed romance with the orthopedist.

Surgeons. All that cutting must go to their heads. Perhaps Van Allen was a surgeon in internist's clothing. In
which case his behavior could be seen as conforming to a
particularly cruel set of social norms.

Power men. Hot shits. She fumed, realizing that her irritation was in part driven by failure to come up with a
provocative conclusion to her Van Allen piece.

She toyed with the idea of ending with a collage of Van Allen family pictures, the centerpiece being the good doctor holding his young daughter aloft in his arms. Smothering her with kisses. The pictures would say it all.

But even this modest moral—that serial killers can look like ordinary men—had been usurped earlier in the week. NBC had run a two-hour documentary on child molesters. At the end several of the offenders told the camera that they were ordinary folk, just like anyone else, that they had no clear idea why they did what they did. The program finished with the face of a serial child killer awaiting execution. "I could be the man next door. Or your family doctor."

And he was right.

Which meant that Michelle had no wrap-up for the series.

She finished her segment of the six o'clock news and walked back to her cubicle at the far end of the newsroom. Forester's lecture began at seven. She'd tidy up a few loose ends and drive over.

But there was an attractive blond woman standing at her desk, hands jammed in the pockets of a fashionable navy blue blazer. She was in her late forties but seemed younger, her figure trim, her movements quick and youthful. Only a certain slump of her shoulders and a grayness under her eyes reflected recent fatigue.

"Sorry to bother you," she said to Michelle.

"I'm just on my way to a lecture. Can it wait?"

Mrs. Van Allen shook her head. "I'd hoped it wouldn't be necessary, but if you're going to continue with the series. . . ." She sighed and looked at Michelle's chair.

"You mind if I sit down? This will only take a few minutes."

Michelle pulled out her chair and motioned to Mrs. Van Allen. She grabbed two cups of coffee from the nearby Mr. Coffee and handed one to Mrs. Van Allen, who was now perched on the edge of the chair, her body rigid, her small matching blue canvas purse tightly clutched.

"It isn't at all like it seems," Mrs. Van Allen began. "Can we talk off the record?"

"Mrs. Van Allen. You know I'm still working on the series. It's hard to promise before I know what you're going to say."

"It's not about him, exactly. It's more about me, our family. There are things you should know, but only as background. Maybe it'd change your slant. But what I tell you must be confidential."

Michelle nodded.

"And call me Ellen. Mrs. Van Allen sounds like you're about to deliver more bad news." She smiled weakly, then looked away at a bank of news monitors. "I knew," she said quietly.

"About the killings?"

"Of course not. I knew about the women. We didn't have secrets. That's not it at all. We talked about his problem. He was trying."

"You mean all his playing around?"

"Uh-huh. He couldn't help himself. It was like binge drinking. He'd be wonderful for months, then it would be some office secretary, an EKG technician. Broom closets, after-hours in some smelly laboratory. Sure he'd hide it while it was happening, but later, he told me everything.

"You'd understand if you knew his mother. A tough Bible-packing Presbyterian. Always criticizing him. No matter what he did, what he accomplished, it was never enough. Sometimes he understood her effect on him. He had his moments of insight and regret. But life isn't a straight line. The women usually happened when he was upset, tense, worried."

"And angry?"

"Sure. That too. He may have played games with them, but never, never would he have hurt anyone. I can vouch for that."

"You went along with him, with his 'games'?"

"They weren't much. A few harmless fantasies."

"So, in a way, he had your approval?"

"These weren't exactly affairs. He loved me. You might find this hard to believe, but Jim was a good man. He was always there for the kids. The oldest is starting med school, wants to be just like her dad. And the boy is in grad school in archeology. They both adore . . . adored him. You can't imagine how this makes them feel."

"You talk like you really believe he didn't commit the murders."

Mrs. Van Allen took a piece of paper from her purse. "This came in the mail today. A certificate for completing an advanced CPR course. Strictly voluntary. It was held the same night that Becky Dirksen was killed. I phoned the hospital; the class was over at nine-thirty. The police say she was killed around eleven. So it's useless as an alibi. But can you imagine practicing saving lives, then going out and killing someone? It doesn't make sense."

"Detective Lockhart tells me that the evidence is pretty conclusive."

"I tried to talk to the police, but they say the investigation is closed. Anyway, I'm not here to discuss his guilt. What I'd appreciate is that you try to paint our family with a sense of respect. It'd mean a lot to my kids. Maybe you could spend a few minutes interviewing the children. They could talk about their dad, how much he meant to them. Instead of focusing exclusively on his problem."

"You keep saying 'problem,' like he had a bad hip. Or bit his nails. Forgetting the murders for a moment, do you think pushing women around, humiliating them, do you think that's right?" Michelle was surprised at her sudden anger, but the idea of Mrs. Van Allen's apparent complicity infuriated her.

Mrs. Van Allen's eyes welled up with tears; she tried to blink them away. Immediately Michelle was sorry for her harsh questioning; worse yet, she shuddered as she thought of her own disgruntled acceptance of the demeaning, condescending manner of the orthopedist. Complicity was a matter of degree. So was eating your pride.

"You're not married, are you?" Mrs. Van Allen stood up. "Sometimes we do things, put up with things." She straightened her jacket, then buttoned it. She pushed away the chair and started to walk away. Then she turned back to Michelle.

"Jimmy could be very arrogant, particularly if he felt threatened. Once in a while he'd recognize it, talk about it. Like his effect on the psychiatrist he was seeing."

"You knew about his visits with Dr. Forester?"

"Sure. Even how much Forester despised him. Sometimes Jimmy laughed and figured that the medical society knew exactly what it was doing, pitting the two of them together. Other times he'd come home furious, raging about how Forester spent all of their time hounding him, instead of letting him ventilate. I think he really wanted to talk to someone, but Forester wasn't the man. From Jimmy's description, Forester sounded like he was the one that needed help." She again tugged at her jacket. "Anyhow. Whatever you can do, we'd appreciate it."

"Have your children give me a call."

"I thought you'd understand," Mrs. Van Allen said. "It can happen to any of us."

As Mrs. Van Allen walked away, Michelle checked her watch. Forester's lecture was probably finished by now. She looked up to see Dick Winters waving a telephone receiver at her. "It's the police. They want you down at Central Station."

An unexpected rainstorm deluged the city. At Fillmore and Sacramento streets a storm drain was clogged, and a great pool of muddy water slowed traffic at the intersection. Of all nights, Forester thought, drumming his fingers on the steering wheel. It meant wet feet, dripping hair, and short attention spans. He eased his car through the water, aware of the lack of traction, his wheels at the very edge of friction. Clearing the intersection he pumped his brakes, the drums groaning against the soaked disc pads. Carefully he drove the remaining few blocks to the Institute.

He was pleasantly surprised. A cluster of collapsed umbrellas dribbled away in the foyer. The auditorium was already half full. There was the smell of damp crowd. *They are coming in out of the rain to listen to me,* Forester thought.

He was still groggy from the three Halcions he had taken last night. Before the pills he'd had two sleepless nights. The Halcions gave him twelve dreamless hours. Or at least as far as he could recall. He had not awakened until five this afternoon. Then he had taken his time, stretching his stiff body, spending extra time shaving and making himself presentable. He even splashed on some aftershave.

Though he detected nothing—he had just showered—he could not rid himself of the notion that he might have some odor. His body felt uneasy and off schedule, a minor queasiness perched in his throat. Maybe it was the beginning of a cold. Or it could be nerves.

He realized that he had not eaten since yesterday evening. Forester grabbed a slice of turkey from the buffet setup in the main conference-reception area. He also took a couple of strawberries from the dessert tray. He was surprised to see a smudge of redness on his fingers. It was several seconds before he traced the bloody tint back to the strawberries. He jerkily wiped his hands with a napkin, and started toward the auditorium, trying to ignore the pounding in his chest.

Nate Giles and Dorothy Lindholz stood near the drinking fountain in the corridor behind the auditorium. They were trading psychiatric jokes, the two of them laughing and poking at each other. Giles saw Forester enter the corridor and motioned for him to join them.

"You look fine. How am I?" Giles laughed.

"Very funny," Forester said. "Can't you see I'm a nervous wreck. Two hundred hungry, wet souls waiting for me to hand them the word."

"I don't think they're that optimistic." Giles laughed again. "After all, this is psychiatry, not life." Giles turned to Dorothy. "Will you excuse us for a second?"

"Sure. The women shouldn't hear the really filthy

ones." Dorothy Lindholz laughed and walked off toward the auditorium.

"I just want you to know that our conversation was completely confidential. What with all your recent publicity over the Van Allen matter, I presume he was the case you mentioned to me."

Forester nodded.

"Don't take it personally. There was no way you could have known."

"Thanks. That's what everyone says. Maybe so, maybe not. I was worried enough to mention it to you. Maybe that should have been a clue."

"It's over with. Now go out there and give us ninety minutes of your usual brilliance."

The two men entered the packed auditorium. As Forester moved toward the podium he searched the audience, looking for Michelle. Instead he caught the eye of Bobby Lockhart sitting in the last row. Lockhart nodded. Forester thought he returned the gesture, but wasn't sure. He was glad to reach the podium, the wooden sides comforting. He spread his notes, a series of three-by-five cards, on the lectern. He shifted his feet, but couldn't find a comfortable stance. His wool slacks, slightly damp from the rain, were suddenly itchy. He tugged at his pants and looked up to see Lockhart staring at him. It was not a look of intellectual curiosity. He had something on his mind.

And there was his little mocking smile.

Forester gathered himself together, and again scanned the auditorium. Michelle wasn't there. Maybe she was late, he consoled himself, easing himself into the history of pathologic states associated with excessive religiosity. He covered the increased incidence of religious content in the lives of patients with temporal lobe epilepsy. "Geshwind at Harvard believes it is more common with left temporal lesions," he said, giving his lecture the flavor of science.

He touched on the biological basis of self-destruction, ranging from hair pulling to the head banging so common to brain-damaged children. He discussed the inherited basis of self-mutilation seen in children with the Lesch-Nyhan syndrome, a metabolic disorder in the urea cycle. Even though the institute was predominantly Freudian, it was important to tip his hat to the biological movement in psychiatry.

Then he moved to the blackboard to discuss his theory of symbols. He drew man and woman and the cross. He presented the ideas as though they were a patient's, though he knew that most in the audience would presume they were the thoughts of Jim Van Allen. He shifted his gaze from the blackboard to the audience, taking in the power bestowed upon him by the rows of attentive eyes. He was in charge.

He paused and gave a weary nod, implying how troubling it had been for him to deal with the unmentioned man, the anonymous subject of his lecture. He ran his eyes up and down the rows, letting each colleague know his anguish at not having recognized Van Allen for what he was.

He put down the piece of chalk and moved forward to the lectern. "I hadn't planned on interrupting myself, but there's something important I have to say. All of us here tonight believe in the power and the good of psychiatry. We spend our days working with the minds and hearts of those who trust in us, and despite the frustrations, the boredom, the repetitious nature of the work, we continue. Because somewhere down deep we believe that we can effect changes. When we do, we are validated. And when we don't, when we fail, we blame the patient, the method, the lack of time, social circumstances. As a rule we blame anyone but ourselves. Perhaps that's understandable, particularly when we know, down here," Forester pointed to his chest, "that real change is rare. And that psychiatry would be a very questionable field if we kept honest statistics.

"Yet it's what we do, because, whether or not we can prove its value, we believe in psychiatry, and by extension, in ourselves. As you can imagine, the recent weeks have been very trying for me. It is difficult to admit failings to yourself, let alone to your colleagues, but there is no other explanation. It is important that you all understand that I did not recognize the extent of Dr. Van Allen's psychopathology because of his inflammatory effect on me. There were subtle references that I might have pursued, but my goal was to use psychotherapy as humiliation. In short, I wanted to make Dr. Van Allen cringe."

"Alan. This isn't necessary." It was Nate Giles speaking up from the back of the auditorium. "We all understand how difficult this has been. But there's no reason to apologize. We'd rather that you continue with your talk."

Dorothy Lindholz stood up and said, "Strike up the symbols, Alan. If we all start confessing how we didn't really try to understand a patient, this will turn into a mass *mea culpa* and we won't be out of here for years."

"I just wanted to make myself clear." Forester went back to the blackboard and continued, talking and reading from his notes. After a few minutes he stopped and wiped his brow. He checked his watch. He was on schedule.

"In light of recent events I also thought it would be

worth discussing the general subject of amnesia and crime. As you know, there are multiple organic causes for forgetfulness, ranging from Alzheimer's to Korsakoff's. But I would like briefly to touch on the functional amnesias, those without any biological basis.

"Amnesia is frequently reported after the commission of a violent crime. In a variety of studies, between thirty and forty percent of convicted murderers claim that they could not remember their crimes. Up to sixty-five percent of individuals charged with homicides claim amnesia. By contrast, amnesia is extremely uncommon in nonviolent crimes.

"A number of studies suggest that memories are acquired in a particular mood state, such as happy, sad, or angry, and are more readily recalled in a similar affective state. I have given a great deal of thought as to why we can see a patient week after week in our office and never get the memories that matter. Naturally there are the conscious motives such as avoidance. But there remains the additional problem that it can be extraordinarily difficult to retrieve memories established during an extreme state of emotion unless that state is recreated.

"If the patient is without access to memory, there is no starting point to analysis. This phenomenon may well explain the failure of psychiatry to unravel the underlying realities in the situations of mass murderers. It is important to remember this when we are called to examine such individuals."

"Forget mass murderers and your bullshit apologies!" someone from the back of the room screamed. A large disheveled man burst into the room carrying a movie-poster-sized placard. In bold red letters was printed: "Forester Killed My Wife."

Before he could be stopped, the man ran to the front of the room. He shoved Forester aside and leaned the placard on the blackboard.

"What do you think you're doing?" Forester said to Owen.

"You want me to tell you? No, I'm going to tell them." He pushed Forester again, and grabbed hold of the lectern.

"My wife went to see Forester because she was depressed. The next thing I know, she's dead, and the coroner says it was an accident. Not a chance. This maniac killed her. I can prove it." Owen reached into his spotted Harris tweed jacket and pulled out a copy of the coroner's report. "Listen, please. You have to listen," he said to the audience. But two large security guards had arrived and were grabbing him by the arms. "Please," he hollered as the men tried to pull him from the lectern. "Forester is a murderer. I know it. She would never have committed suicide! She was allergic to barbiturates!" The guards were half dragging, half shoving him toward the door at the rear of the auditorium.

Forester stepped back from the podium, uncertain what to do. Nate Giles came to his side, saying nothing. They stood side by side watching the security guards usher Owen into the foyer just beyond the rear door of the auditorium. Some of the audience remained in their seats, watching and talking with each other. Others followed the struggling men out into the foyer where they stood in a tight semicircle. Watching.

One woman told the officers to be gentle.

A third guard arrived and called the police on his cellular phone.

"She was loaded with barbiturates! Forester had to have given them to her," Owen shouted. One guard had Owen's arm twisted behind his back. The other was trying to grab Owen's free hand.

Lockhart stepped up to Owen and showed him his police badge. "Calm down," he said. "Just take it easy and no one'll get hurt."

"You'll hear me out?" Owen asked Lockhart. For the moment he stood with his arms at his sides, not struggling. "Please."

"You'll behave?"

Owen nodded.

Lockhart motioned to the security guards to release their grip on Owen.

"Here, read this and see what you think." Owen reached into his jacket pocket and produced a photocopy of the autopsy report. He handed it to Lockhart.

By now two uniformed policemen had arrived.

"His wife died and he's distraught," Lockhart said to the policeman nearest him. He felt uneasy, as though he were looking at the solution to a question, but wasn't sure exactly what the question was. "Murderer," the raggedy man had hollered. Why would Forester be involved in so much controversy all at once? Lockhart watched Forester as he approached, cautiously moving up the aisle. His face registered more than fear and embarrassment. Something devious. Lockhart could not put his finger on it.

"Can I have a word with you?" Forester said to Lockhart. The two men moved away from the others, down the corridor.

"This is the second time. The first time he threatened me at my office. Can you get him to stay away from me?"

"You can get a temporary restraining order."

"That means that he'll be subjected to hearings, and so on?"

"Usually. But if he doesn't show up, the judge'll probably issue it on your statement."

"A hearing would agitate him that much more. It wouldn't help anybody."

"Why's he so insistent that you killed his wife?" Lockhart looked down the hall at Owen, who was showing his driver's license to one of the policemen. There was a soft, pained look to Owen's eyes, the haunting befuddlement of a victim. Owen was not a malicious madman. Lockhart felt his pain, the grief of losing one's wife. In contrast, Forester had that smooth, controlled inflection that poked at your innards like a thousand slivers of glass. Lockhart realized that he detested psychiatrists and that he could be overinterpreting Forester's solicitous manner. But he didn't think so.

Forester was a bad man. Lockhart could feel it in his bones.

"Maybe you could talk with him, tell him I'd be happy not to press charges if he would stop harrassing me. Tell him I really don't want to make trouble for him."

Lockhart returned to Owen. "You got yourself together now?"

Owen shrugged, then nodded.

Forester cautiously came toward them. Owen waited until Forester was within arm's length. He caught Forester full on the jaw with a straight right. Forester started down, but not before Owen connected with a left to the midsection. Forester was sliding toward the ground, while Owen was trying to hold him up by his shirt. Lockhart and the two policemen wrestled with Owen, pinning him against the corridor wall.

Owen was handcuffed and locked in the backseat of a patrol car. In the foyer psychiatrists milled around. Giles came up to Forester and put his arm around his shoulder. "We'll finish the lecture another day." Several other nearby psychiatrists nodded in agreement. "These things happen," Giles said.

"No. I'd really like to complete what I started." Forester spoke grimly, carefully moving his jaw from side to side.

"It's not necessary," Giles said. "Come on. Let's grab a drink." Giles nudged Forester in the direction of the buffet.

"In a minute," Forester said. He walked to the police car and bent down to the level of the window.

"I had nothing to do with your wife's death," he said to Owen through the closed patrol car window. A blast of rain fell from the sky, pelting the car and Forester. His jaw throbbed as he spoke. "Honestly. I swear to God."

Owen continued to glare at him, struggling against his restraints.

"You'll have to come down to the station to press charges," one of the officers said to Forester.

Forester was frightened. Owen looked seriously disturbed, capable of. . . . Forester felt the rain at his neck. He didn't want Owen loose on the streets. He ran his finger over the beginning swelling at the angle of his jaw.

"That's not necessary."

"You sure?" one of the policemen said.

"Yes." He leaned toward the car window. "Believe me, Owen. I'm really sorry about your wife."

Owen's face remained knotted in anger, his eyes burning into Forester.

Forester turned to the policeman. "What are you going to do with him?"

"A few hours in the tank will cool him off. You think about it. It'll only take a few minutes for the paperwork."

"He's already had enough grief," Forester said. The words were right, but the tone? Lockhart wasn't convinced.

The two officers slid into the patrol car. Moments later Owen was a shimmering reflection in the slick streets.

Several of the senior analysts tried to convince Forester to present the remainder of the lecture another day. Forester refused. He resumed the podium. "Where were we?" he said, trying to smile, shuffling through his notes. "Ah, yes, we were talking about religion and suffering." Forester continued on, his voice hollow and forced. The audience was uneasy. There were looks of embarrassment. When Forester finished there was polite applause, but no questions.

Forester stepped from the podium, his legs rubbery as though he had run up a thousand flights of stairs. Giles took him by the elbow.

"Too bad this had to happen. You had some really impressive ideas. I guess we were all too shaken up to take it all in. Perhaps another time."

"No."

"You get it off your chest?" Giles asked.

"It's been very disturbing. The lecture should have been the perfect opportunity. Now, I don't know."

"How about taking a vacation? A week or two on the beach somewhere. Hot sand and no thoughts."

"Sounds great, but I've got patients."

"I'm sure they'd understand. I'll be glad to see any emergencies."

Forester and Giles had reached the buffet table. An analyst's wife spilled some red wine down the front of her white silk blouse. Forester stared at the stain. Someone suggested rubbing her blouse with salt. "I'll be glad to," said another analyst. There were scattered laughs. The spotted woman was not amused. She looked at her husband as though the mess required someone being at fault.

The red blotch sat like the state of Texas between the woman's breasts. Forester felt light-headed and held onto the edge of the buffet table.

"You okay?" Giles asked.

"Maybe a little fresh air?" someone else said.

"I'm fine." Forester took a glass of white wine and two slices of sourdough French bread and sat down at an empty table. Giles joined him. So did Bobby Lockhart. "You don't mind?" Lockhart asked Forester.

"Of course not."

"That man was really fired up," Lockhart said. "But I imagine you get lots of threats and outbursts from irate spouses. I'll bet they accuse you of everything under the sun." Lockhart sipped at his wine. It reminded him of all the university cocktail parties that he had despised.

"I'd rather not talk about it anymore," Forester said.

"And your lecture. I guess I was expecting something different," Lockhart said. "Id, superego, that kind of stuff. I didn't expect symbols in the house of Freud."

"We haven't been introduced," Giles said to Lockhart. "You new in the community?"

"Not exactly. I've been in vice five years and now five in homicide."

Giles looked to Forester for explanation.

"Detective Lockhart was investigating the Van Allen murders. I invited him tonight." Forester started to take a sip of wine, but quickly put down the glass. His face was pale except for the dull red bump at the side of his jaw.

Lockhart bit into a prawn, pulling off the tail and ceremoniously dropping it into a nearby ashtray. "You plan to do more work on Van Allen's case? I mean, write it up for a journal article?" Lockhart asked.

"I don't have any plans."

"If you do, I'd love to have a reprint. There are some aspects of the case that don't hang together. I'd appreciate any ideas you might have."

"I'll keep you in mind."

"I'm sure you will." Lockhart rose, knocked back the rest of his glass of wine, and left. It wasn't necessary to be nasty, but it felt good.

Back in his car Lockhart looked at Kate Carbone's autopsy report. The cause of death was listed as accidental. Owen had said murder. Allergic to barbiturates.

He continued to stare at the report.

"We've got the kid in the drunk tank. It's the only space available," the desk sergeant said.

"Let me talk to him a few minutes," Lockhart said.

The police settled on a misdemeanor—disturbing the peace. Michelle brought the two hundred and fifty dollars and paid Owen's fine. "Come back with me," Michelle said once they were outside the station. The rain had stopped and the street smelled of wet leaves and humidity. "I've got a pull-out bed. We can roll it into the living room." She brushed a curl of hair from his forehead.

"You don't have to."

"I want to." Michelle had tears in her eyes. She slipped her arm through Owen's. "I'm so sorry," she said as they walked toward her car.

A sputtering neon sign showered Owen with pink, his eyes briefly luminescent with sadness and anger. Michelle held Owen tighter. "Maybe you could talk to someone?" she said, her voice barely a whisper.

"Oh, yeah. I'll trot right down to the corner therapist and buy a pint of happiness and ten pounds of understanding. 'Put it in the trunk, next to the shotgun.' " He clenched both fists. Michelle took one hand and stroked it in the way that you would coax a baby to open his hand.

They rode to Michelle's in silence.

Owen gulped down a double shot of brandy and stretched out on the couch in the living room.

"You want a shower or a bath?" Michelle asked. "I've got a fresh razor and a clean bathrobe. You'd be more comfortable."

Owen waved her away. He turned his face toward the back of the couch, his large hands clasped between his thighs. Michelle sat on the edge of the couch, stroking his neck. His hair was long and greasy, curling under and over the streaked collar of the same denim shirt he had worn the last three times they had been together. There were strands of gray that she had not noticed before. Michelle sat at his side until he was asleep. She covered him with a light blanket and went into the bedroom.

As Michelle was sliding into bed, the phone rang. It was Forester. "You have a minute? It's been a strange day."

"Not right now. It's very late." Michelle slammed down the receiver. A minute later the phone rang again. Michelle turned off the ring volume. She heard the answering machine click on. She turned off the volume of the answering machine.

She was exhausted, yet she couldn't sleep. The answering machine blinked on again. She tried to think the evening through, but there was no line of reasoning on which to hang the various events. And now Forester was pestering her. Of course it was understandable that he'd want to talk. She toyed with the idea of answering the phone, but the light blinked off.

And on her living room couch was a desperate, angry man who didn't want to talk. Michelle had no idea what was happening with Owen. On the street, with the pink neon in his eyes, he had seemed capable of anything, even murder. And all because of what she had told Owen after Kate died.

Once again she went through Kate's descriptions of her meetings with Forester, trying to sort out fact from intuition. It had been nearly two months since Kate's death and already memories were elusive, as though they stepped in and out of sunlight, the sunlight too blinding, the shadows too deep.

She could hear Owen shifting on the couch. A sudden chill caused her to rise up in bed. What if he killed Forester? What if Owen slid all the way to San Quentin?

She remembered interviewing the San Leandro man who had stalked his wife's mugger. The woman had required reconstructive surgery, in stages, over a year, and she was still left with scars and a sightless eye. The mugger had plea bargained and served eighteen months at Santa Rita, the county facility. A year after the man's release the husband located the mugger and shot him point-blank through the head. The judge commented on the need for laws to prevent anarchy and lynchings in the street. Then with a look of apology she sentenced the husband to five years.

Michelle had interviewed him at San Quentin. "They call this justice," the man had said to Michelle, his face a mass of rage. "But let me tell you, I'd do it again."

Michelle remembered thinking how profound love could be, but realized that more than love, it was revenge. The man knew he would be caught, but that was less important than righting his tilted world. "No one fucks with my wife," he had said, concluding the interview.

She would talk with Forester one more time, sort out the details. She might even tell him that the therapy had been staged, see his response. Maybe that was a good idea, maybe it wasn't. She would sleep on it.

But she couldn't sleep. Instead she watched the sky lighten. And heard Owen stumble to the bathroom. For a moment she had the fatigued fantasy of Owen living with her, that he belonged with her. She jumped up, put on her robe, and slipped into the kitchen. Moments later the two of them were sharing the small kitchen counter, sitting on adjacent stools and drinking coffee. Owen had aged ten years, his face was lined, his once-springy step now more of a trundle. He sat stoop shouldered, holding his coffee mug in both hands.

"You think you can let it drop?" Michelle asked.

Owen didn't answer.

"What's it going to take? You can't shoot the man." Michelle was immediately sorry she had let the thought slip out.

Owen smiled, a distant, scary smile, as though pleased by some inner musing. "Thanks for bailing me out last night."

"Owen. Look at me. I'll do whatever I can, but you must pull your life together. And forget about Forester." She worried that her words didn't sound convincing. They certainly didn't convince her.

"Eye for an eye. Soul for a soul. Simple math, not even as tough as percentages."

"There's no talking to you?"

"We're talking now."

"Is there anything I can do?"

Owen rose from his stool and held out his arms. "Yeah. You can give me a hug."

Owen put his arms loosely around her waist. Michelle had her hands at the back of his neck. Owen was hesitant, his back arched away from her. He looked at her, his eyes confused and glistening. Then he leaned forward and drew Michelle tightly to him. Michelle felt the sting of his bristly unshaven cheek and the desperate pull of his arms. They stood, neither moving, for some time. Then Owen drew back.

"I'll be all right. You'll see." He started to say something else.

"Yes?" Michelle said.

"Later. It can wait."

FIFTEEN

SETLEDGE READ KATE Carbone's autopsy report while Lockhart marveled with disgust at the human skull tastelessly displayed on Setledge's desk. Setledge had filled the inside of the skull with soil; a handful of impatiens grew out of each orbit.

"Modest amounts of barbiturates and alcohol. Massive head injury. She could have jumped or fallen."

"Or been struck in the head?"

"True, but if she was hit in the head first, we're not going to be able to prove it. Not with these." Setledge showed Lockhart the photos of Kate's crushed skull and the fragments of rock ground into the brain tissue.

"I see what you mean," Lockhart said.

Setledge shook his head. "I thought you were done with the Van Allen matter. And this Carbone case isn't even in your jurisdiction."

"It just seems strange that Forester's name would be involved with Van Allen, and then with the incident at the Institute."

"Well, it's not here." Setledge handed Lockhart back the report.

"Nice vase you've got here." Lockhart pointed to the skull.

"It's my idea of the visual representation of inspiration," Setledge said, waving Lockhart away.

In the last month there had been a curious lull in the city's homicide rate. Lockhart's desk was unusually clear of unsolved crime. There had been the expected flock of reporters—"crime vultures" Spagliani called them—but interviewers had dwindled away, some even disappointed in learning that there was no new Zodiac killer loose in the city.

Lockhart reported in, took off his coat, and hung it over his chair. As he sat down, the Kate Carbone autopsy report, still rolled up in his jacket pocket, poked him in the ribs. He took the report and started to drop it in his waste basket. But he didn't. Everything was too neatly in place. Even the quiet unpressured hum in the homicide division was all wrong. He smoothed out the rolled-up report and tucked it partially underneath the left-hand corner of his desk blotter. The exposed portion slowly started to recurl. Everything has its natural shape, and three S-and-M murders followed by a suicide was not one of them.

In San Francisco a little kinky pain wasn't particularly out of the ordinary. The local educational station had even run a one-hour special on a Folsom Street S-and-M club. The low-key interviews gave the program the same sense of dignity as discussions of child care. Lockhart had watched with a combination of repulsion and fascination, especially the segment featuring the woman "pain specialist" in her black leather mask. "During the day I work on Montgomery Street. I'm an institutional investor." It made sense. On public television, validated by hushed tones and serious reporting, anything went. Even necrophilia might be seen as little more than excessive respect for the dead.

A walk down Folsom Street would be enough to make Krafft-Ebing blush. Hard-On Leathers. Studs and Rivets Bar and Grill. The Florence Nightingale Bandage and Merthiolate Society. Pain as sexuality was available everywhere.

Lockhart sat in the still homicide room, his wheels spinning. It wasn't sex that the killer had been after. It wasn't just domination, for he could have had that for a hundred bucks, two hundred tops.

He went back through the three autopsy reports. None of the victims had any traces of semen in them or on them. There had been no sign of forced penetration.

Van Allen loved sex. All the complaining women had told of his constant arousal. None had mentioned impotence. Quite the opposite, he was a man who lived up to his constant leer.

He could have worn a condom. There would be no traces. Given the intenstity of the moment, it seemed unlikely, though Van Allen was known to be neat and meticulous. Maybe the murders weren't primarily sexual.

Lockhart considered himself sophisticated. Five years in vice had shown him more than he cared to see about depravity and the extent of degradation humans could tolerate, no, even desire. But he realized that experience didn't equal understanding, and no matter how flippantly he might chat with his co-workers, he didn't really have a clue as to why.

Over coffee across the street from the frame shop, Mi Mi told Bobby that most sadists she had met were driven by a feeling of power. Beyond that she begged ignorance.

"That was never my thing. I always considered myself

a romance counselor, a Cartier for the gonads, not a punching bag."

Lockhart told Mi Mi what he knew of Van Allen's sexual practices. Mi Mi doubted he would be a killer. "It sounds to me like he enjoyed knowing that he could humiliate a woman and have her continue to work for him, say 'yes, sir,' do the dictation, that sort of thing. Sure, down deep, he might hate women, but it's a different sort of hate, one mixed with pleasure, rather than pure anger. The pure hatred ones—mind you, this is second-hand information—tend to be impotent."

Lockhart felt himself settling into his seat. He could easily spend the day with Mi Mi. She was gorgeous. Even the lines around her eyes looked strategically penciled in, as though age was doing everything within its power to be gentle to her. He loved the smooth sound of her voice. He had to remind himself of how many men had had the same thoughts, had left their business cards and hundred dollar bills stacked on her nightstand.

"Is that it?" she asked. "Nothing else on your mind? A movie, a play, the Shakespeare festival at Ashland?"

"The frame shop. It's going okay?"

"Pretty good. It's too bad. All those men. It made me feel like a someone. To be honest, I was the one who got off on the power, the looks they gave me, knowing I could tow the senators and tycoons around by their little pink handles. Then when someone decent comes along, like you, I've got nothing but back alleys and broken dreams on my breath."

Lockhart put his two hands on hers, which were wrapped around her coffee mug. "Would you like to have dinner tonight?"

"Thanks. But I can't stand kindness. If you really mean it, phone me in a week or two. If nothing else, it'd be nice to be your friend."

"If you hear of anything, think of something that might convince me one way or the other on this Van Allen thing, please phone." He gave her his police card, then hastily wrote his home number on it.

"Just a thought. Kelly Caldwell once gave a seminar for the local psychiatric association. Maybe they have some tapes. You might get an idea." Mi Mi rose from her seat. "I've got to get back." She gave Bobby a quick peck on the cheek. "Thanks for the caviar," she said from the doorway.

Lockhart was again alone with his coffee and a sour taste. Van Allen didn't fit the bill. Which went to show how little he knew about human nature. The case was officially closed. He should let the whole thing drop. But he knew the look on Owen Carbone's face, the look of betrayed trust, of footing the bill only to be double-crossed. He had the pleasing notion that in some way he could incriminate Forester. If nothing more than showing that Forester knew Van Allen was dangerous and failed to report him.

Thinking about fucking over Forester lifted up his spirits. He looked up to see Mi Mi across the street, showing a gold-leaf frame to a customer. Next week he would give her a call.

The medical society referred him to the Maimonides Medical Library—it had the tape cassettes of all recent educational seminars. Kelly Caldwell's course on S and M wasn't included. "If it's sex you're after, try the Institute," the librarian said.

The Institute head librarian, Mrs. Ralston, remembered the seminar. "Sure. It was standing room only. You know how these Freudians are. Strictly intellectual curiousity, mind you." She sorted through a drawer full of sign-in sheets. "The meeting was worth three continuing education units," she said as she searched for the right paper. "Here it is. Everyone who attended. Maybe one of them could help you. Who knows, maybe one of them even taped the talk."

Halfway down the page was Alan Forester. *I'll be damned,* Lockhart thought. "You think he'd be a good one to ask?" Lockhart said to Mrs. Ralston, pointing to Forester's name.

"Probably the best. As I recall, he's even written some on the subject."

"There wouldn't be any reprints here in the library, would there?"

"Sure. We keep all the members' articles. Come on."

Minutes later Lockhart was seated at a library table with a half dozen of Forester's early papers.

Civilization requires the voluntary subordination of its citizens. Whether it be to achieve the kingdom of heaven, the greater good of the majority, or merely to provide maximum efficiency, each must be willing to sacrifice his personal interests, even on occasion his personal freedom. It is as necessary as and in many ways comparable to the domestication of livestock. In animals this is accomplished through breeding. Human beings require the combination of guilt and the invocation of grander, higher motives. Passivity, submission, loss of individual will—these are the prerequisites for social order.

Lockhart yawned. He'd had no idea that Forester was so pedantic. He started to skim. As he flipped from page to page, his eye caught a peculiar syntactic error.

During the Holocaust many Jews marched passively to their deaths. This was the ultimate expression of our humiliation, the degree to which they abandoned self-determination, and, in consequence, gave up themselves and their children.

Our humiliation? Was he referring to the human race or to himself? If himself, then why did he say *they*? Perhaps it meant nothing, but it was an odd sentence, out of keeping with the otherwise impersonal academic tone of the article.

He browsed through the remainder of the articles. They all dealt with technical aspects of masochism, ranging from guilt as a personality trait to the pleasures of hypochondriasis and martyrdom. There were references to the thanatos principle, man's pull toward death. The smell of Freud in these passages overwhelmed Lockhart. It was as though he had passed by a psychiatric stockyard, the stink of rotten theory as thick as the big black flies circling for hidden meaning.

Lockhart dialed Forester from the pay phone outside the library. The tape said Forester was on vacation and that he would answer his calls as soon as he returned. Lockhart left word that he had some unfinished business to clarify before he could conclude the Van Allen investigation. It was necessary that they meet as soon as possible.

Lockhart would bring the article. If nothing else, he wanted to see the expression on Forester's face when he pointed out the words *our humiliation.*

On a bench in Washington Square Park, two old Italian women in black chatted and knitted. Though in direct morning sunlight, they both huddled deep inside their heavy woolen coats. Owen sat across from them, alone on his bench. He recognized the women, not by name, but from their location—they took the same positions on the bench each morning but Sunday, when they would not arrive until after services at the nearby Church of St. Francis of Assisi. The two women were park fixtures, as reliable in their presence as the statue of St. Francis hovering behind them on the grass. Though they were never with their husbands or children, the two women represented permanence and roots amid the parade of generations in this once predominantly Italian neighborhood.

On the other side of Columbus Avenue, Martinez, the Spaniard with the acquired Italian accent, cobbled shoes in the window of his small repair shop. He spotted Owen and waved. Owen nodded. Kate loved shoes; Martinez sang songs from Catalonia while he resoled at a twenty percent discount.

" 'Cuz you're neighborhood," he would say to Kate with a gold-toothed grin.

Owen was uncertain how to proceed with his life. He had made a few bucks on the World Series, enough so that he didn't have to find a job immediately. He could continue booking, though he suspected that a real job with regular hours and co-workers might help him snap out of his depression. He tried to consider alternatives, but he could not get beyond Forester and the answering machine that said he was out of town for a week. Owen couldn't imagine how slowly a week could pass. It seemed like an eternity. He wasn't sure he could wait.

He closed his eyes and saw Forester begging and pleading, his mouth dribbling apologies, the last ounce of pride drained from his arrogant, smug face. And then, when there was no more fear to be extracted? Owen ran his fingers over his father's pistol nestled in his jacket pocket. He would shoot him, at first in the hands and feet, maybe a toe at a time. Maybe his shin first. Each time he tried to think of an additional, more intensely felt, pain.

But would he actually shoot him? Owen was agitated by his own uncertainty. The urge was overwhelming, but there was a portion of his mind that continued to nag at him that he could go to prison. They had him on record at the Central Station. He would be the first suspect, even if he hired someone else. He shouldn't have barged in on Forester's talk. He had told himself he wouldn't, right up to the moment when he had stormed into the lecture hall.

Owen's brief pleasure in imagining Forester's punishment quickly dissolved into the bitter realization that he might not do it.

He could feel himself edging away from the charged space of uncontrolled anger at the center of his being. One moment he was emptying his gun into Forester, the next he was taking the gun from his own hand the way you might take a dangerous object from a child.

He despised his own indecisiveness.

He recalled Michelle's expression when he had left her

apartment. She cared for him, worried about him. She was constantly telling him how childishly he was behaving.

When they were together she made perfect sense.

But when he was alone, it was Forester who burned in his brain.

No one else could understand. For a moment Owen wished he had buried Kate. He wanted to visit her, feel her presence. Instead he had had Michelle make arrangements with the Neptune Society. Kate had been scattered to the wind. At the time it had seemed appropriate. Now he wanted her someplace where he could visit. A spot that would be theirs. He would bring flowers, though he hated the idea of cemeteries and burials. He was filled with a vast emptiness, Kate scattered through space, everywhere yet nowhere, dust to dust. He needed a home. He needed to talk to Kate. He sat waiting for her voice, but there was only the muffled chatting of the two women, and the background hum of buses pulling away from the curb, cars, others.

There was no choice. He owed it to Kate. Not to shoot Forester would be the real crime.

The cold morning sun glared but did not warm. Owen held his face up to the pale disc, gathering up the heat of his anger. He sensed the great beauty and purity of what he would do. His heart was infected; his mind was no longer in charge.

He drove over to Forester's house, parking his car at the end of the street where he had a good view of Forester's front stairs. It was noon; there were no lights on in his study. He sat staring at the building, not making any specific plans, just watching as the angle of the sun shifted across the brick stairs, the shadows lengthened, and the fog rolled in.

It began to rain, big drops rolling down his windshield. The downpour continued: the day passed. Owen could not recall any specific thoughts, unless you call constant seething a thought.

It was midafternoon, but Forester was still in bed. Since the lecture he had slept only for a few minutes, up to an hour at a time. He was exhausted, but each time he closed his eyes a flood of frightening images assaulted him. He had spent the day following the lecture convincing himself that the bad thoughts were countertransference, that he was feeling so guilty about Van Allen that he actually was assuming some of his memories.

It was the only reasonable explanation for the horrible screams that continuously prodded him from sleep. It made sense, but it did not stop the muffled choking sounds, the whimpering and the begging. And the pulsing sensation in his hands.

He had the week off, he didn't need to follow a schedule. He could sleep when he wanted. If he could. One day he had walked along Ocean Beach, but all he had felt was fatigue and annoyance at the sand gathering in his shoes. There had been no romance to the ocean, no beauty in the surf. Everything in his sight was a monochromatic gray. Even the eucalyptus trees marching down to the beach were sticklike bits of wood.

He tried Halcion and earplugs. Right now he was in his kimono and wearing a sleep mask, the covers up to his chin. There was one benefit from his profound fatigue. He was slightly less anxious. He didn't have the energy.

Which made him all the more surprised when he awakened this afternoon to the rain and an erection. It was the first he could remember having had in weeks. He searched the tail end of his dreams, but there was no object. He was startled and puzzled, as though confronting the mistaken thought that his sexuality was behind him.

There had been a recent article in the *Chronicle* on middle-aged men, often married, who had joined a monastery in Napa, embracing celibacy. Not a bad idea, Forester thought, though it was a little late. But it certainly would have made life easier.

He looked down at his still nearly erect penis with profound disgust. The two of them had been places, done things, unspeakable things. And still it wanted more. He thought of patients who had emasculated themselves with razor blades, the very idea raising the hair on his neck. It was the height of psychosis, yet the thought seemed almost reasonable.

His erection began to dwindle, though he retained a heightened sexual awareness. Michelle came to mind. She was gorgeous. Perhaps with her it would be different.

He jumped into the shower, keeping the water ice cold. Afterward he stood at the mirror, examining his face. He had no characteristics of his adopted father or mother. He could not remember the faces of his true parents. He had no brothers or sisters. He resembled no one.

Michelle would give him comfort. He could lie beside her and feel warmth. He could feel whole again. And decent. He would treat her like a princess. And she would be his new family.

The phone rang. It was Lockhart. Forester listened as the speakerphone relayed Lockhart's message. Lockhart was still investigating. Why? Forester felt jolts of electricity up and down his arms and legs. He tried to calm himself, to think of benign bureaucratic reasons behind Lockhart's call. But his heart was pounding. Lockhart was onto something.

Forester looked in his desk; every drawer was filled with notebooks and scraps of paper covered with scribbles. Some were initialed; many were not. He picked some at random and read them, often confused by the abbreviated comments, not even sure which patient had prompted the observation.

Though he was not exactly sure why, he saw the scraps as clues. Perhaps there were notes on Van Allen that he had forgotten. Or maybe Lockhart wanted more information about Kate Carbone.

He picked up the notebook that contained "Ma Petite Fleur." On the next page was the single word "Katestrophe." The *K* had been written over, now a capital *C*, but the indentation of the original letter was still apparent. Even with the *C* it read "Katestrophe."

Forester felt a tapping sensation on his hand. It grew more insistent, then it faded. He rubbed his hand, as though it had gone to sleep. The tapping returned, then faded again. The room grew dim, as if Forester was looking into some long dark tunnel. It was not a tunnel, though. It was the trunk of Kate's white Volvo, with its spare tire and neatly arranged traffic flares.

Forester shook his head, trying to dislodge the image. It had been an accident. He had done it for Kate. She had agreed. Not only agreed, insisted. She said it was going to be her last visit, and that if he couldn't make her better, she would solve the problem herself.

It had turned out wrong. But he needed to know exactly what had happened in order to be prepared for Lockhart. His hands were wringing wet. He wiped them repeatedly on his thighs. He was dreadfully afraid to look back. The memories would haunt him forever.

For a moment he had the reassuring notion of explaining everything. Free himself of this terrible burden. But that would be craziness. They might take his license away. No, he would keep the information to himself. But he did need to know everything—and that meant all the gruesome details.

He came up with the novel idea of creating a second personality, someone who could acknowledge the memories, then disappear from view. He could look at himself impersonally, assign the hidden memories to a temporary inhabitant, someone who had momentarily assumed control, then retreated again. It would be the equivalent of a drunk man cheating on his beloved wife, remembering nothing in the morning, the memory lashed down to a transient aberration. Or the man who loses his paycheck in Las Vegas and returns home with no clear recollection of what transpired. It happened all the time, errors of the spirit sidetracked onto lost weekends, shunted out of sight. Sure the lost paycheck had the man's name on it, but it wasn't *him*.

Everyone did it. Even Joan had gone on a buying spree after receiving final word of his infertility. It wasn't until the bills arrived that she realized how many dresses and pairs of shoes she had purchased. Forester remembered her look of surprise when he had totaled up the amount. "Me?" She had seemed incredulous. "That's not possible. There must be some mistake." She had actually phoned the department stores to complain, even while Forester pulled the clothes and shoes from her closet.

Hidden others inside ourselves.

If he were treating himself as a patient he might try free association, hypnosis, possibly even drugs such as Amytal. But first he would just sit and sort through the scraps of paper. The memories were down there, somewhere, he could feel them trapped far beneath the surface like oily bubbles beneath a great Arctic ice cap. He knew enough to be careful. The extraction was as dangerous as delicate surgery. An extra memory, a loose association, the inadvertent simultaneous scooping up of an unexamined feeling—all could upset his fragile balance.

It had been almost a week since the blue light and the rush of dread in the Institute library. He had purposely avoided mulling over the implications of that evening. Temporary aberration of a stressed mind, he had written in the margin of his self-awareness. There had been no recurrences, though he could sense threatening forces hovering at his periphery. Now and then he caught himself turning suddenly, as though he were being watched or addressed. There were odd sounds in his quiet house, creaks and groans that appeared without apparent cause.

He told himself it was just the foundation shifting along invisible fault lines.

Evening lights were coming on in his neighbors' windows. It was family time, pools of related genes puddling together for the evening meal. This had always been Forester's worst hour, the time of his greatest longing. There was the taste of cinnamon in his mouth. And something sweet, like cake frosting. Forester pursed his lips and ran his tongue across his upper teeth. A moment's thought and he could place the impression. The sensation was there, unaltered by more than fifty years. Even down to the hot-from-the-oven warmth. Zooming into view were his mother and grandmother holding the pastries on a hot metal tray. "Don't touch. Wait until they cool," his mother said. There was the period of expectancy, Alan reaching out toward the cinnamon buns, teasing his mother, who flashed him the look of mock annoyance. It was their little game, just the two of them, his grandmother back at the sink washing the pan.

Forester was stunned with the clarity of the recollection. He could see the red and yellow flowers on his mother's apron, feel its raised pattern. It was his hand on her apron, her soft lilting voice teasing him to wait.

He held his fingertips together, looking down at them as though some of the fabric might have clung to him over the years. His fingers tingled. He held them to his lips and blew lightly on them.

Cinnamon buns were on Sunday. Perhaps the recollection was so vivid because it had occurred dozens of times. Sunday lunch, around two in the afternoon. Cooking in the morning, then the family together in the front room. His grandmother sat to his left, next to the birdcage in the corner. She fed the crumbs to her pet canary, sometimes lifting the bird from its perch and holding it on her index finger. He could see her finger with its deformed knuckle and wide splayed fingernail—the result of an unspecified farm accident. For effect she would wag her finger at him—You see what happens when you don't pay attention.

Initially there was a man across from his grandmother. The picture was blurry, as though the man had been there at one time, then wasn't anymore. There was a period of sadness, the picture sagging, his grandmother in tears, his mother leaving the room without explanation. There was crying. But he could not place the man. Then there was his grandmother's face, very big, very close, the smells of age hot against him. She was telling him to be a big boy. And that his father wasn't coming back.

Forester tried to fill in the seat once shaped by the shadowy figure. But eventually the chair was taken away. The hole in the picture had been covered over.

The yellow flowers were more rough-edged than the red, as though they had been sewn by two separate tailors. That puzzled him, especially if the apron had been machine manufactured. Perhaps the yellow required double stitching.

He looked down at his desk, startled to see the name Kate Carbone scribbled on one of the scraps of paper. "I wish I were dead," a voice rose up from the paper. It was a self-accusing but attractive voice of someone accustomed to being happy, now bewildered by the surprising intensity of her recent grief. She did not listen to reason, each week she went over the same data, learning nothing, concluding nothing other than that she could have done something. Something. He could hear her insistence.

She could not be reassured. Something dramatic was needed. He saw her hands pulling at a handkerchief, once reasonable, efficient hands reduced to useless gestures.

He wanted to look further, to hear their interviews, but he pulled back. Instead he stared out the window at the gathering night, at the shadowy leaves flickering in the quiet autumn breeze.

He had been this way before. There should be no problem in returning to the charged memory. He already knew what it contained, even if he couldn't say it or hear it directly.

But he couldn't. Instead he was poised to deny everything, should someone ask. He looked around the room, half expecting Lockhart to emerge from the shadows. There was no one but himself. He was the one asking. A huge lump rose into his throat, followed by a surge of anger.

It wouldn't be this way except for the confidentiality laws. There was no one he could confide in. Nate Giles had turned him away. He would have to confess to himself.

He reached into his desk drawer and pulled out his Lanier voice-activated tape recorder, the one he had used with Van Allen. He would talk unedited into the machine, no one listening, then play it back, listening as the critical observer. He would be sure to destroy the tape once he had the information.

He flipped on the machine, the red eye flickering as he rustled the papers on his desk. He stretched out on the couch and closed his eyes. For a long time there was nothing. Then there was the taste of herbal tea. Cinnamon and ginger. He tasted from Kate's glass; there was the suggestion of something sharp and burning to the lips. He added some honey.

She didn't really want to kill herself. It was a damaging figure of speech, the words falsely fueling her depression. So many mistakes in psychiatry arose out of the wrong choice of words. Take depression, a clinical word, as opposed to grief, a natural harmonious word. One was the product of a disordered mind, the other of compassion and love. It was important to stay away from damaging figures of speech and self-destructive phrases.

" 'You don't really mean you want to kill yourself,' I told her.

"She insisted that was what she felt.

" 'You don't really mean that.'

" 'Yes, I do.'

"I came up with a little experiment that would convince her that she was a victim of her mischosen words. Once she could see that she felt badly, but that she had no desire to die, her depression would have been easy to treat.

"So I gave her the tea, and the medication, which helped her to relax. She said she trusted me, she was in complete agreement. I told her she could just tap my hand anytime she wanted me to lift the pillow. She was in complete control. A tap on the hand meant she wanted to live.

"It made perfect sense.

"Maybe I misjudged her. Maybe I underestimated her grief.

"We all make mistakes.

"She promised to tap."

Forester flipped off the tape recorder. There was something he wanted to say, but could not. The bitter taste of her tea lingered in his mouth. He recalled the smell of her perfume even after he had cleaned out the trunk of her car. It was not the scent of someone anxious to die.

It was an unorthodox experiment, yet something out of the ordinary had been necessary to snap her out of her depression. Yes, he should have worked harder, even given her some antidepressants, though she was against pills and it was unlikely that they would have worked.

It was a horrible mistake, of his making. And the reason for the terrible guilt that clouded his every moment.

Suddenly he was deluged with images, as though a very bright white light had been turned on in a darkened room, each object over-illuminated, giving off not only its own image, but an added dimension of brilliance.

Everything from that forgotten day shot out from the darkness like so many white-hot stones of memory. Forester jerked his head backward, burying it in the soft woolen pillow at the head of the couch. He held his arms around his chest, then put his hands to his head, the assault pounding at his temples, roaring at his ears. Had he wished to, he could have looked around inside his mind and seen all the gruesome details like so many items in a well-lit meat counter.

But he didn't; instead he rocked and held his breath, his eyes squeezed shut. He summoned up all his mental forces, concentrating on ignoring the horrible images that washed over him. He focused on his good deeds, like volunteering at the local homeless shelter, scooping out mashed potatoes for the less fortunate.

"I am a good man," he said to himself, again and again, over the soft gurgling sound unlike anything he had ever heard before. "A decent man. A man who helps the sick. Not a bad man. Not like Van Allen. No. A good man."

There was the piercing jab of silence. The terror of the silence pushed Forester to speak more loudly, filling his room with his cries of innocence.

"I am good, good, good," he repeated endlessly until his memories began to fade. "No, no, no," Forester chanted, long after memory had retreated, the sounds and the silences gone.

He was soaked, his kimono clinging to his back and upper arms. A sound rose in his chest, halfway between a gag and a cough. He gripped the edges of his couch until the nausea passed.

He rose unsteadily and glanced around him, as though someone might be in the room. He had no idea why, but he felt as though he were being watched. Which was ridiculous. He was just overwrought. Nate Giles was right. He should take a vacation, sit in the sun, get himself together.

SIXTEEN

THE PHONE RANG. FORester hadn't planned on answering it, but he had a hunch.

It was Michelle. She was sorry to bother him, but his comments would make a logical conclusion to her news piece on Van Allen. She would be by as soon as she could wrap up a few things at the station.

Forester threw on some clothes, turned on the lights in the front room, and walked to the top of the back stairs leading to the garden. There was an overhang from the third floor; this shielded him from the steady rain. He kept his ear cocked to hear the buzzer at the other end of the corridor that connected the front stairs with his consultation suite and the back stairway to the garden.

It was more than coincidence that Michelle would have phoned at that exact instant. Her voice had been intense, urgent. She wanted to get together with him. He felt a stirring in his groin. There was a high-pitched sound far off in the neighborhood. Forester strained to hear, then tried hard not to. It was a woman's weak cry for help. It was muffled, as though there were a hand at her throat and mouth. He felt his hand tighten, curling against itself inside his pants pocket. His fingernails pressed into the flesh of his palm.

The arteries in his neck pounded as though they might

burst. He counted his pulse at one forty. He closed his eyes and took a deep breath.

It was raining heavily, the front stairs slippery and treacherous in the thin light of dusk. The recessed entrance was deep in shadows. A damp overhanging vine brushed Michelle's face, catching her just beneath the eye. Raindrops ran down her cheek and under her coat collar. She impatiently jabbed at the illuminated buzzer. Forester's voice came over the intercom, inviting her in.

The wind rose as she hurried into the dimly lit waiting room. As she reached behind her to close the front door, there was a particularly strong gust. The latch did not engage completely, but Michelle was already moving across the room before the fact registered. She was anxious to get out of the draft, and continued into the small foyer leading to a second flight of stairs.

The dampness of her clothes and the creepy feeling of the downstairs waiting room and stairway made her both irritated and somewhat unnerved. She took a deep breath and ascended the long narrow staircase.

Forester was standing at the far end of the hallway, framed by the tall window that looked out on his garden. He was dressed in a plain white longsleeved shirt and slacks. Michelle realized that it was the first time she had seen him not wearing one of his customary gray suits. Without his uniform he seemed naked.

Exposed.

And different.

"I love listening to the rain in the darkness. It's very peaceful. Especially when you're alone in a large house like this." His body was only partially turned to Michelle; briefly he looked her way, then back out to the garden.

"Besides, the flowers can use the rain." Slowly he turned and walked to the entrance of his consultation room.

"Have a seat," he said, entering and standing at the window.

"Thanks, but I've been sitting all day." Michelle stood across the room, leaning against one of the bookcases. She was at eye level with Freud and Jung and all the others. She wasn't sure how to proceed. Forester was never what she imagined. At first sight he had been frightening, a stranger. Now, only moments later, he seemed a lonely, brooding romantic huddling in the shadows from his Japanese garden.

"I realize this is an awkward time for you, so I'll try to make it brief."

"There's no hurry. Would you like some tea, a drink, mineral water?"

"That's not necessary. What I would like is a wrap-up on my Van Allen series." Michelle was going to say that she wasn't convinced of Van Allen's guilt, and neither were his family and medical associates. But, at the mention of Van Allen, Forester's eyes narrowed, and a sour, disappointed look came over him. She waited.

Forester stood in silence at the window, looking at his feet, the bookcases, out into the garden, then finally at Michelle. "I missed you at the lecture."

"I got hung up at the station."

"Yes. Those things happen. I guess it was just as well. The evening was a real disaster. A former patient's husband broke up the lecture, even socked me in the jaw. I was mortified. All my colleagues watching and he's hollering that I had something to do with his wife's death. He's got me really worried. I think he's very disturbed. The police want me to press charges but I think that might agitate him even more."

"Why would he be so upset?"

"He thinks his wife committed suicide because of my therapy."

"Is that a possibility? I mean, we've all heard stories about therapy having the wrong effect." Michelle was careful to keep her voice low, her tone casual.

Forester looked away. He rubbed his hands against his slacks, but an insistent throbbing persisted. He pressed them firmly against his thighs, the pressure blocking out that other sensation.

"I hope not," he said. "It's always a concern with depressed patients." He heard the words; they were correct. But he listened closely, as if he might be about to say something else. Michelle was strong and understanding. He could tell her of his failed experiment. She would listen, not judge. She was logical, the experiment was logical. It would be such a relief. But he was talking in a pedantic professional manner about the dangers of unrecognized transference, especially with vulnerable, susceptible patients.

"But with your experience and training, certainly you would know if therapy was going sour."

"I thought she wanted to live. I never expected. No. I thought she was stronger." His hands were heavy, filling up with unclaimed responsibility. He held them at his sides and tried to ignore their presence. "She never told me how violent her husband was. Perhaps he was a factor."

Michelle saw the direction of the conversation. If it wasn't Kate's fault, then Owen was to blame. And Forester was rubbing his hands, as though wiping them clean of any responsibility. She saw the fading bruise on Forester's lower cheek and was sorry she hadn't done it herself.

"No," she said, surprised at the conversion of her thoughts into speech. And at the forcefulness of her voice. "Owen is one of the gentlest men I know. Or was. Before all this."

"Owen?" Forester stared at Michelle in amazement. "I don't understand. You know Owen Carbone?"

"We're best friends. Kate Carbone and I met in college. We were like sisters."

"And you came to me after she died." He stopped, looked out the window, then back at Michelle. "Why?"

She had gone this far. She blurted out the whole story.

She expected Forester to show anger, resentment at her betrayal and duplicity, or at least some indignation. But Forester seemed lost in thought. He stood motionless, listening. When she finished he said nothing. She expected anything but silence.

He took a step toward her, rubbing his hands. They were ice-cold. He felt as if he had been working in the garden in the dead of winter. His back was stiff and his fingers ached. He looked down, expecting to see garden soil under his nails. There were some blackish spots on his palms. He briefly picked at one with a nail, but stopped, now carrying his hands in front of him, half-cupped as if holding two large candles. Or clubs.

"That's funny," he said quietly, "for a moment the shadows from the tree looked just like dirt spots." He looked up at Michelle as though surprised to see her standing there.

"So you came to see if I'd treat you the same way as Kate. Is that it?"

Michelle nodded.

"And?"

Forester was clenching his jaws, and the veins at the side of his neck were now clearly visible, even accentuated by the uneven lighting coming from the floor lamp at the corner of the room. Much of the room remained in shadow. Instinctively she stepped backward.

"You tried to set me up, to prove that the psychiatrist didn't know what he was doing, maybe do an exposé on the news. Is that it?"

"Kate was closer to me than any family. It's just hard for me to imagine her jumping off a cliff."

"She was very disturbed." Forester took another step closer.

Michelle felt herself backtracking, moving along the wall toward the open door leading to the hallway. She had no reason to be frightened. Forester was a beaten man trying to save face. But that wasn't true at all. Both hands were now curled into fists.

Forester saw Michelle staring at his hands. He unfolded them and held one index finger under his nose, sniffing at it. There was the smell of cinnamon and honey, it was very strong. Forester wondered if it was on his hands. It bothered him seeing Michelle terrified like that. Because he was a psychiatrist and could see into her mind. It was a shame. He wasn't thinking bad thoughts about her. She was a strong woman. She had stood up for her friends. Yet she was backing up, moving away from him. *Don't do that. There's no reason to be afraid. It isn't necessary.*

She stepped out into the hallway, but Forester followed, interposing himself between her and the stairway leading back to the waiting room.

"You must have more questions."

"Not really. I've got to get back to the station."

"It was your idea or Owen's?" His arms were now folded across his chest, his hands tucked under his armpits. It was too bad she was so suspicious. Confession was now out of the question.

"It seemed like a good idea at the time." Michelle knew that she should apologize, but she didn't.

"You wanted to get to the bottom of her death. Out of love and friendship. I understand." There was a new, more controlled, tone to Forester's voice. "I guess you expect me to be mad, hurt, resentful. On the contrary, I think it's wonderful that you could care for someone that much."

He stepped closer. "Very admirable," he said, as though talking to himself. "You're a woman of great strength. And loyalty. I like that." He ran his tongue over his lips, as though tasting something, or thinking, remembering.

"Now that everything's out in the open, we could start over. Not as doctor and patient, because it wasn't really, was it?"

"Stop. I've got to go now."

"Sure. I understand. But before you go, do you mind if I hold you? It'd be my way of saying that I did everything for Kate that I could, and that I . . ."

Forester started forward, his arms reaching toward Michelle.

"Hold it," said a voice from behind Forester. Owen emerged from the shadows at the front of the hallway. He started toward Forester. In his right hand was his father's gun.

"Owen, wait!" Michelle yelled.

He motioned her back inside the consultation room. "Thanks for leaving the front door open. I've heard enough—bullshit lies and mumbo-jumbo excuses. But we're going to change all that, right now. Come on," he said, waving the gun at Forester. "They say a dying man feels better confessing."

There was a clap of thunder. Forester retreated to the end of the hallway. "My God, don't." Forester's voice broke.

"Say your prayers, asshole." He jabbed the gun into Forester's chest.

Forester jerked backward. His heel caught the loose floorboard. He stumbled, losing his balance. He fell backward down the flight of stairs, landing heavily on the path below. There was an audible snap. Forester let out a cry and reached for his leg. It was dark and hard for Owen to see, but it appeared that Forester's shin was poking through his pant leg.

"Not having a good day?" Owen said as he started down the stairs.

Michelle stood on the landing at the top of the stairs. "Owen. Leave him alone. It's not worth it." But it wasn't at all clear what she really wanted. A minute before, Forester had been reaching toward her. In what? A gesture of affection or anger? He had seemed half-mad. And Owen looked completely crazed. For the moment she stood transfixed, unsure what she was watching. And what she wanted Owen to do.

Forester held his leg with one hand and tried to back away. He was on his side. With his good leg and his hands he pushed himself along the gravel path, then through some low shrubs onto a square of lawn. There was another flash of lightning and Owen could see Forester's muddy trail. Owen walked slowly, savoring the slithering sound of Forester retreating through his own precious garden. In his left-hand jacket pocket was a small halogen flashlight. He pulled it out and focused it on Forester's face.

"Maybe I'll just watch for a while. See how much fright you can muster up. This is a moment I'll want to remember for a long time."

"You must be crazy," Forester said. "I didn't do anything to you."

"And I haven't done anything to you. You're lucky I came along when I did. I'll bet you were getting pretty cold and damp, lying out here all night in the rain." Owen stood several feet from Forester, who was now curled up on the lawn. Forester was running his hand around the edges of his fracture.

"Put the gun down." Michelle was alongside Owen, her hand on his right forearm. "Please."

Owen pulled his arm away, ignoring Michelle. "What's a couple little bullets between friends, no, more than friends, my wife's doctor?" he said to Forester. "My wife wanted help. She trusted you. A broken leg is nothing compared to what you did to her." As Owen spoke, he realized that he still did not know exactly what had happened. But it made no difference. Not now.

"I didn't do anything. It's all a mistake," Forester said. He blinked. The glare was blinding, he had trouble making out Owen's features, though he could see the outline of Owen's right arm, and the gun. "I'm expecting company any minute now. You can leave and I won't tell anyone."

"Tell them what? That you're so nervous and paranoid

that you literally jumped backward down a flight of stairs? Personally, I'd be embarrassed if I were you. All those years of analysis and you're still afraid of shadows. Not much of a testimonial, if you ask me." Owen looked up at the sky. The rain had temporarily stopped; the moon was peeking down between clouds. "Are you a religious man?" Owen asked. "If you are, now's the chance. Come on. Give God a little beg, let's hear a couple rounds of shabby explanation for your worthless life." Owen flipped off the safety. "I'll give you two minutes."

"Owen, please," Michelle pleaded. But she stood at some distance down the gravel path. Anything was possible. "This is craziness," she said to Owen. But he wasn't listening.

Michelle ran upstairs and dialed 911. All she said was that a man had been seriously hurt.

Owen flashed a vicious smile at Forester. His hand gripped the chilly pistol handle; he worked his index finger comfortably onto the trigger. It was time. But he did not shoot. Instead he stood frozen, glaring down at Forester and the splinter of moon-whitened bone. Forester lifted himself onto one hip and began to drag himself farther into the garden.

Owen was confused. At the very instant of his triumph he found the murderous edge of his anger elusive. He had imagined Forester resisting, denying, then begging and pleading. He had not foreseen Forester shriveled up like some shattered animal, not even protesting, just trying to hide. He was so pitiful.

"I'll bet that hurts a lot." He walked up and poked Forester's broken leg with the tip of his shoe. "Physical pain is bad, but the other kind, mind pain, you know how much worse that is? Do you really? Do you know what it's like to have someone you trust tell you how disturbed you are?" He gave Forester a hard kick. Forester let out a cry, groaned, and pulled himself toward the rear of the garden, gaining traction on the wet grass by gripping the limbs of the low shrubs. A small branch came away in his hand.

"Careful, look what you're doing to your yard," Owen sneered, squatting down on his knees, his face inches from Forester. "I loved my wife. You were supposed to make her better." He searched Forester's eyes for the haughty arrogance that might spur him on. But all he saw was cringing fear and pain—a pathetic mockery of a man.

He stood up and walked to the front of the garden. He had not given up the idea of shooting Forester. He watched the clearing sky, the moon making an intermittent appearance. He looked at Forester's trail—the torn-up path through the grass, the mangled shrubs—and then at the more distant sight of Forester, now resting on his side, his eyes fixed on Owen's gun.

"Help me," Forester said.

"As in shoot the wounded animal? It'd be my pleasure." But the moment had come and gone. Owen was overcome with a bone-weary exhaustion. The weeks of restlessness and sleeplessness crashed in on him. Even as he walked over to Forester he could feel his momentum sag and gather around his legs like heavy shackles. His knees ached, his will was being sucked from him, and for a second he imagined the cool comfort of his bed.

"The barbiturates? What was that about?" Owen asked.

"I didn't know she was allergic, and I doubt that she was. They were part of a simple medicine—Fiorinal— that I gave her for some tension headaches. The last time we talked, you were so upset I didn't think I could explain."

In the darkness it was difficult for Owen to see Forester's expression. Owen's weariness grew into a light-headedness and a tightness at the base of his neck. He was no longer sure that he had ever planned on killing Forester. He had wanted to. Perhaps that had been as far as he had gone. To want to. Owen was embarrassed by the confession. But Forester's humiliation was no justification for shooting the man. Michelle was right. His grief had made him obsessed. He had no hard evidence, no smoking gun. He had to concede that sniveling Forester was no murderer.

In the distance was the sound of sirens.

"I can't stand the sight of you. I wish you were dead." But he dropped the gun back in his jacket pocket and went upstairs.

Dr. William Spurling, the orthopedist on call at Memorial, offered Forester a choice of local anesthesia or a spinal. "We can give you plenty of sedation, make you real high. You won't notice a thing."

"You mean, something like Amytal?" Forester felt panicky. Amytal was the last thing he needed now.

"Something like that, only more modern. You won't remember a thing."

"No. I'd rather have general anesthesia."

"That's not necessary. There's no reason to take the risk."

"What is it? One in ten thousand?" Forester asked. He felt a curious sense of pleasure that he still remembered some medicine.

"Even so. We normally do this with a spinal. This way there's no intubation, no possible atelectasis, aspiration, that sort of thing."

"I'd just feel better with general. I've always had a thing about spinals."

"I'd rather a spinal," Dr. Spurling said.

"Humor an old fart."

"If you insist." Dr. Spurling acquiesced. Forester signed the necessary papers and was wheeled off to the OR.

"This will just take a second," the anesthesiologist said. She started an IV and injected the preoperative sedative into the tubing. Forester watched her complete the injection and step behind him. Her hands were cool on his neck. She was positioning his chin.

Forester closed his eyes, anticipating the relaxing effect of the sedative. But there was something wrong. The anesthesiologist's hands were holding his lower jaw in position. They seemed unnecessarily forceful, as though she were trying to choke him. He tried to open his eyes, but his lids were heavy. He struggled, gaining a blurry glimpse of a large female face hovering over him. She was smiling, a peculiar, cruel smile. He expected harsh laughter, but there was only the sound of metal equipment scraping on the tile floor.

"Relax," the woman said. "You're doing perfectly fine." But she was sneering. And the grip on his throat was so intense. He tried to reach up to take her hands away, but his arms were fastened to arm boards. "Take a few deep breaths," she was saying, her voice right up against him.

"Trust me." The voice was different, deeper, huskier.

He couldn't see her anymore, not the anesthesiologist. The woman was younger, with blond hair and wide eyes. The voice was not hers. It was coming from somewhere closer, from his own throat. His hands were heavy, filled with something soft yet dangerous.

"Trust me," he remembered himself saying, looming over Kate Carbone. Yes, it was Kate. Now it was perfectly clear. He had the pillow over her head, each of her hands on his. "Tell me when you've had enough," he heard himself say, at the same time feeling the increasing pressure in his forearms. There was an enormous sense of unleashed power, anger, retribution. His arms were shaky from the effort, muting the tapping at his hands. The tapping gradually died away. He remembered lifting the pillow and looking at her lifeless face. The pillow had left rows of wrinkles on both cheeks.

He pulled at the sides of her mouth until her skin was again smooth. His arms were heavy from carrying her from the trunk of the car to the edge of the cliff. Heavy and sore from the effort.

Hands were positioning his chin. He tried to wiggle his fingers. "No. Don't," he thought he said. But now the voice was soft and childlike. She was pleading. "I'll do anything you want, but please let me up." He was sitting on her chest, running his hands through her hair, along the base of her neck. Her breasts were immediately beneath him, but he had no desire to touch them.

"How could you?" he heard himself say. He wanted to hit her, choke her, but that would leave marks. No, he would kneel on her chest, as though praying, his weight boring into her chest, and watch the growing look of fear on this woman he knew only as Mistress Diana. Mistress

Diana? The words burned his brain. He saw her face clearly, her head whipping from side to side, trying to avoid him. But there was more. There was the smell of cinnamon and the soft pained eyes of his mother watching him crawling out the basement window. Milky sad eyes bursting from their sockets. Belated tears. And that sickening lonely silence.

He tried to turn away from the vision of the women, each tied as he was now, each unable to speak, as he no longer could. And for the first time he saw them as helpless, his mother as helpless.

He had misunderstood.

He wanted to run, but his legs were leaden. He tried to speak, but there was a mask over his face.

Kelly Caldwell, Becky Dirksen, Bonnie Ringold. And Kate Carbone. Each loomed up. Every detail was woven into a giant tapestry of terror that hung in front of him, suspended in clotted time. The terror was flowing from them, to him, filling him with the knowledge of the horror of what he had done. There were bodies and screams and silent pleas. There was the scent of chardonnay and the faint lament of Edith Piaf in the distance.

There was something heavy in his hand. A hammer. He was behind Van Allen, who was mocking him. His arm was descending, moving against something firm yet giving. The hammer became a pistol, the bullet obliterating the rear of his skull, and with it the evidence of the hammer blow.

And in that moment he knew with blinding clarity the awful truth. He was consumed with its enormity, which now rose in his throat, the bitterness of evil burning his mouth. He gagged and tried to spit, but his lips refused him. He wanted to scream, to apologize, to explain. But most of all he wanted to confess. To confess and be forgiven. But he was too deep inside the horror, so far beneath its surface, his voice silenced by the blackness.

SEVENTEEN

AS MICHELLE WAS WALKING out the front door of the station she got the call.

"Is it serious?" she asked.

"Your name was in his wallet, to be contacted in case of an emergency," the nurse said.

"I'll be right there."

Forester was spread-eagled in bed, both arms extended outward on IV boards. Wires ran to the EKG monitor, an arterial pressure line emerged from his groin. Several doctors were gathered around the bedside. Michelle stood at the entrance to the ICU. The nurse told her that Dr. Spurling would be with her shortly.

From the doorway she could see Forester in the nearest bed. His leg was cast to the midthigh, the whiteness of the cast accentuated by the harsh overhead lighting. His face was smooth and innocent in sleep, the wrinkles of the past month erased by the anesthetic.

She reminded herself that he had tripped. But she knew that it was the sight of Owen and his gun that had sent Forester down the stairs. Which made them responsible. Michelle was trying to shake this thought from her head when Dr. Spurling emerged from the ICU.

"It was like a premonition, me telling him not to have

general anesthesia. This is the first time in my twenty years."

"What happened?" Michelle asked.

"One of those flukes. He vomited and aspirated during induction. It could have been the barbiturate. I'm not sure. We were right on him, but he still hasn't come around. Dr. Slader thinks there might be some brain damage. He'll be out in a minute and you can talk to him."

"We won't know the extent for a couple days," Dr. Slader said moments later. He was tall and very slender, like a marathon runner, and spoke with a slight British accent. Somehow, though she had never met one before, Slader acted as she imagined a neurologist might. He was cordial and precise, but with a slightly detached manner. Brain damage was his bread and butter. "Perhaps we'll have some idea in the morning."

Michelle could not sleep. She was back at the hospital shortly after sunrise.

Forester was no longer in the ICU. "What a catastrophe," the head nurse said. "He's down the hall with a private duty nurse."

Michelle poked her head in the room. "Kate?" Forester said. He seemed puzzled. There were a series of fresh scratches on one side of his face. He rolled down his lip and opened his mouth, as though trying to look inside and see what was wrong with his words. "Kate Carbone?" he said again, without any hint of recognition.

"It's Michelle," she said, moving closer. A young nurse was sitting down, writing in his chart. She looked up, her head averted from Forester, held her index finger to her temple and made a circular motion.

"Kate," Forester said. His fists clenched and opened as he struggled against the thick leather restraints that were fastened at the wrists and the elbows.

"Has he been this way all night?" Michelle asked the nurse.

"He didn't say anything until about an hour ago. Since then it's been the same words, over and over. It's spooky, especially when he says 'Mistress Diana.' His eyes get all weird and he tries to pull at his face. Those scratches are his. We had to tie him down for his own safety."

Michelle stood staring.

"Don't take it personally. If I step out of the room for more than a minute or two he doesn't recognize me at all. I keep reintroducing myself to him, and all he says is 'No.' "

Forester shook his head and let out a horrifying scream. Michelle flinched and jumped back from the bed.

"It's all right, Dr. Forester," the nurse said, trying to smooth down one of Forester's fluttering hands. "You're going to be all right."

"No, no, no. Momma mistake."

Dr. Slader appeared, along with two neurology residents. He saw Michelle and gave a terse smile. Forester watched, his eyes darting back and forth from Dr. Slader to Michelle. He bared his teeth and hissed. "Kate," he said to Dr. Slader.

"Perhaps it would be easier if we stepped outside," Dr. Slader said to Michelle.

"I was just explaining to the residents," Dr. Slader began once they were in the corridor. "We call it posthypoxic encephalopathy, but I'm not sure that's entirely accurate. Usually that presents as a generalized confusion, but Dr. Forester seems to have an unusual combination of aphasia and Korsakoff's syndrome. In other words, he has difficulty talking and comprehending speech, as well as an inability to lay down new memory."

"Is there any special significance to what he *is* saying?"

"With aphasia the words that are most commonly preserved are those with the greatest emotional content. Swear words, highly charged names, that sort of thing. Unfortunately this is compounded by his not retaining new information. Old memories are all that come to mind. Even these are difficult to hang on to when you're this aphasic."

Michelle was speechless. She had a million questions to ask, she didn't know what to say.

"Sometimes a patient will fixate on something in his past, and go over it endlessly. Sometimes, if you pardon the bluntness, he'll sit all day in bed, saying 'fuck' endlessly. It's curious how that word often is the last to go." He gave Michelle a little smile, one of the residents grinning behind him.

"And he can be experiencing emotions without words to describe the feeling, or even a verbal recollection of the event that triggers the emotion?" Michelle asked.

"Precisely. Though sometimes there are internal images. Patients can sometimes see what they cannot describe. It all depends. You don't know unless they recover and you can ask them. Sometimes they'll relate having seen vivid moments from their past, though they occur without words or names." Dr. Slader's expression softened. "Are you a close friend?"

"Not exactly. I was just concerned about him."

"He has a wife, children?"

"He's separated. There aren't any children, as far as I know."

"What a disaster. Frankly, this is one of the worst scenarios in neurology. As you know, memory really is the essence of man. It establishes his identity, his reality. Now Forester is limited to the emotionally charged fragments of his past. The present is elusive, like running water sliding through your hands. It's like living inside a nightmare."

"You sound like this is permanent?" Michelle said.

"The aphasia may improve, but Korsakoff's tends to be permanent. At least this variety. But we'll know after we get an MRI scan. I think tomorrow or the next day will be soon enough to show structural changes. But you should brace yourself for a long-term problem. I wouldn't wish this on my worst enemy."

There was a high-pitched scream from Forester's room. "Yes, no, yes, yes. Now, no, yesterday, yes, yes, Mistress yes, Momma no."

Dr. Slader stepped up to the nurse, who was wiping Forester's brow with a damp cloth. "I'll order more Thorazine. If that doesn't touch him, we'll switch to Haldol."

As the nurse turned to Dr. Slader, Forester jerked his head, grabbing the washcloth with his teeth. He tried to pull the cloth inside his mouth, chewing rapidly, the nurse tugging.

"Here," Dr. Slader said. He grabbed Forester's cheeks and squeezed them sharply together, causing Forester to release his hold on the cloth. Some spit gathered at the corner of his mouth. It was pink tinged. Forester had split his lip.

Forester turned to Michelle. "Mistress Diana? Becky? No? Yes?"

"He keeps saying the same names over and over. Do you have any idea who they are?" Dr. Slader asked.

"I'm not sure," Michelle said. She couldn't believe what she was hearing. She wanted to run out of the room. She wanted to talk to Owen. She wanted to phone the police.

She did all three.

That afternoon Lockhart sat beside Forester, his tape recorder running. He read Forester his rights, for the tape, but realized that it made no difference. Forester did not recognize him. Lockhart knew that nothing Forester said could be used in court. There was no question that he was incompetent. But he could use the tape as sufficient indication of suspicion to justify a search warrant. If he could get inside Forester's house, there must be something.

Did he know? Lockhart wondered. Was he aware of his predicament? Partially aware? Or was he completely lost inside his mind? Lockhart sat all afternoon and into the evening, listening to the fragments and names, watching Forester tug at his restraints, bite his lip repeatedly, his lips now sore and bleeding. The nurse rubbed them with glycerin, but Forester wiped it off by pulling his shoulder across his mouth, at the same time giving the nurse a wild look that suggested primordial hate and fear, all rolled into one.

His IV clogged up. The nurse loosened one wrist restraint, to get the tubing out from underneath his arm. Forester's hand shot out, striking himself in the chin. He continued hitting himself with his closed hand until the nurse, assisted by Lockhart, could refasten the leather strap.

The nurse was exhausted. Lockhart offered to watch

Forester while she went downstairs for a coffee break. The nurse nodded and stepped out of the room. Lockhart closed the door behind her.

"Just tell me you did it," he said to Forester. "Tell me about Bonnie Ringold, and Becky Dirksen, and the others. Come on, you'll feel better."

Forester's good leg rose up under the sheets, as though he were kicking someone. He struggled against the restraints, writhing and twisting. "No!" he hollered.

"You killed them, didn't you?" Lockhart said again, his voice quiet and determined. One yes would guarantee him the keys to Forester's house. He thought of faking a tape by splicing it, if he could just get Forester to say yes. Splice the tape? It would be a snap. Rent a couple tape recorders, do some fancy editing. It wasn't court material, but it would do the job. Some vague notion stirred in the back of Lockhart's mind. But Forester was not cooperating.

"You killed them. Tell me you did."

Forester looked at Lockhart as though he had never seen him before.

Lockhart returned to the Institute library. *Who's Who in Psychiatry* listed Forester as having been raised in Toronto. He phoned the Toronto PD. Ten minutes later he knew that Forester was a Polish refugee of the Holocaust, Forester his adopted name.

He went back to Forester's original articles. Guilt. Sadomasochism. The words swam in front of him. So did the images of high-stepping Nazis. And concentration camps. Lockhart closed his eyes and tried to imagine how it must have been, being a small child sent to a new country, without parents, family, or friends. He had seen it a thousand times on the news. Orphaned children lining the war-torn roads, their big sad eyes weeping into the camera. Vietnam, Central America, the Middle East. For Lockhart it was always the children who brought home the horror of war.

For a brief moment he pitied Forester and his nightmare fate. Then he recalled the ligature marks on Kelly Caldwell.

Lockhart sat at the library table trying to reconcile the conflicting images of the little boy walking away from his home and family, and the image of Forester alone with the murdered women.

The standard homicide division phrase came to mind. *Sick bastard.* It was the policeman's way of acknowledging the murderers' pain, at the same time as his essential evilness. And it was a way of recognizing the human in the otherwise impossibly sick behavior.

That afternoon Lockhart started at the south-of-Market shops, then Castro Street. His last chance was Polk Street. In one magazine and video store, a girl with IUDs for earrings recognized Forester's face from the book jacket photo Lockhart handed her. She studied the photograph, then nodded.

"Yeah, I think so." She snapped her finger. "Sure. That's the guy that bought the *Architectural Digest* a couple months ago. We sell about one copy a year. A purchase like that I don't forget."

"You use them as decoys?" Lockhart said, smiling.

"Excuses."

"You remember anything else about him?" Forester asked.

The woman thought for a second. Her face suddenly turned sour. "I completely forgot," she said. "I gave him Kelly Caldwell's number."

"Say that again."

"Kelly Caldwell, the girl that was murdered by this Van Allen character. I gave this guy her telephone number."

"And you'd be able to recognize him if you saw him in person?"

"Naturally."

Lockhart submitted his tape of Forester's few words, the sworn statement of the girl from the porno bookstore, and photocopies of Forester's early papers on guilt and sado-masochism. Judge Connolly gave him the go-ahead.

Lockhart understood when he saw the two high-tech VCR's hooked up in Forester's study. Forester had manufactured Van Allen's taped confession the way he had wanted to manufacture Forester's. Supporting this idea was the voice-activated Lanier tape recorder in the den. Lockhart packed all the unlabeled VCR and audiotapes into several evidence bags, then filled several others with the contents of his desk drawers.

After the bags were in the trunk of his car, Lockhart returned to the house, to Forester's consultation room. He scanned Forester's book collection. He was struck by the entire shelf devoted to Kafka. Forester had several editions of *The Trial*, ranging from a heavily underlined paperback to a handsome leather-bound copy.

Another entire shelf was devoted to ethics and medicine.

Lockhart sat down in Forester's upright chair adjacent his desk and tried to sense what Forester had seen. Lockhart imagined a steady stream of troubled people sitting across the room in that black leather chair, pouring out their hearts. One chair for the therapist, stiff and upright, and one chair for the patient, soft and comforting. As though the patient was somehow more needy, even of simple comforts. It was easy to imagine the enormous power that psychiatrists must feel. He was surprised that Forester's chair was not on a platform, elevated above floor level, as in a throne.

Kate Carbone had trusted him. And somehow he had destroyed her. Lockhart was not sure what had happened, what the details were. And, unless Forester's mind returned, he might never know. At the moment the actual facts didn't seem necessary. It was the presence of evil that gripped Lockhart, the sense of unrestrained domination that oozed from every pore in the room. And particularly from Forester's chair. He rose and went to the window that looked out on the garden. Lockhart could see traces of Forester's muddy path through the shrubs and the lawn.

He wanted to see Forester on all fours, scurrying like some trapped animal. Let his patients stand at the window and watch him crawling on his hands and knees, no larger than a hyena. Let them pelt him with stones and the regurgitated humiliation of their treatment. Open the window wide and let them bellow out the last laugh, loud enough for all the world to hear.

He prayed that the evidence bags contained enough to nail the son of a bitch.

He also prayed that Forester had enough brains left to understand what was happening to him.

The tapes had all been erased. Lockhart was certain that Forester had fabricated Van Allen's confession. He phoned a wiretap expert who referred him to a sound man who told him that you could check the tape for indexing. The man explained that if the editing had been done on a new high-quality VCR, each time the videotape was set to record again, there would be an index marker embedded in the sound recording. Even if the tape was then dubbed to ordinary cassette tape, there would be a residual subliminal distortion of the sound pattern at the start of each new recorded segment of tape. The distortion was not audible, but could easily be seen on a spectral analysis. It was similar to looking at the wave patterns of a person's voice. There would be the additional frequencies of the index marker.

Forester and the sound man watched the oscilloscope as they started up the cassette of Van Allen's confession. The sound man smiled as he pointed to the sudden low-frequency blips that peppered the confession.

The scraps of paper from his desk linked Forester with each of the victims. But the details of the murders were completely unclear. Lockhart knew that the district attorney would require some more specific piece of evidence.

He went back to Forester's house and looked again. Of course, Lockhart thought to himself. Of course the answer would be in Forester's dirty laundry. At the bottom of the laundry hamper was a black medical bag with the name Alan Forester, M.D., engraved in gold block letters. It was the bag old-timers used for house calls. *How far we have come,* Lockhart thought as he opened the bag. Inside the medicine bag was a half-empty vial of Ketamine HCL, along with syringes and needles.

Over the phone Setledge explained that Ketamine was an agent used primarily as an animal tranquilizer. In low doses it produced sedation as well as a dissociative amnesia for the event. In higher doses it produced unconsciousness and even death. It was commonly used in animal experiments and in subduing large animals that needed to be transported.

Setledge added that it was not a drug normally included in the routine forensic toxicology screen.

Blood samples from Becky Dirksen, Bonnie Ringold, and Kelly Caldwell were still stored at the Hall of Justice pathology lab. Within the day all revealed traces of Ketamine HCL.

Mel Boston, the district attorney, accompanied Lockhart to the hospital. There had been no change in Forester's condition. Boston read Forester the charges, speaking as though Forester understood. Forester watched intently, his eyes focused on Boston's lips. A soap opera played silently on the overhead TV. The nurses set it at the beginning of each shift. Forester never changed the station or turned on the sound.

"You are under arrest," Boston said. "Do you understand me?"

Forester said nothing. He acted as though he were waiting for Boston to continue.

"You have the right to counsel."

Forester let out a frightening forced laugh, as though he

were trying to be sociable. "Mistress Diana?" he said to Boston. "Yes?"

Lockhart met with Dr. Slader in X-ray. Forester's MRI scan was on the view box behind Dr. Slader.

"What are the chances he will recover?" Lockhart asked.

Dr. Slader pointed to the dark areas in both temporal lobes. "I'd say it was nil. You see these areas of atrophy? They control the laying down of new memory. And here, on the left. The speech area is clearly affected. Based on the scan and his minimal improvement over the last several days, I'd say that he's going to remain like this."

"So there's no chance that he will ever be able to stand trial?"

Dr. Slader shook his head. "I don't know what you do with suspected criminals who are brain-damaged, but I suggest you make some long-term plans. He's going to need custodial care indefinitely."

"Can you tell what he understands?"

"Not with certainty. Judging by his agitation I suspect he has a pretty good sense of his condition. It's even possible that he has full understanding, but can't verbalize it. It's also possible that he understands intermittently, then forgets what he's figured out. It may be a process of understanding and forgetting and understanding again, without the ability to express or to remember what he's figured out. In cases like this, you never know."

"So you can't say whether or not he knows that we've found him out?"

Dr. Slader shrugged.

"Shit."

"You're not satisfied knowing that he's condemned to a lifetime alone inside a broken mind, unable to communicate, twenty or thirty years or more in some custodial facility?" Dr. Slader looked over his reading glasses at Lockhart.

"I want him to know he didn't get away with it."

"Believe me, he didn't get away with anything. I'm sure if he had a choice between this pseudoexistence and the gas chamber, he'd be the one to drop the pellet."

"Maybe so. But I'd just like to see the look on his face."

"You mean you want him to look worse than he already does?"

"Yeah. I know you're thinking 'Have a heart' and all that sort of thing. I guess this is why I went into homicide and you went into medicine."

Dr. Slader put down his glasses. "He really killed those women and Jimmy Van Allen? You're positive?"

"Cross my heart."

"Off the record?"

"Sure."

"My wife went to Forester. She says he was marvelous. Kind, empathetic, concerned. She has nothing but the highest praise for him. She refuses to believe that he's guilty."

"Take my word for it."

Dr. Slader felt the heat of Lockhart's intense frustration. He turned to the MRI scan. For several minutes he said nothing, as though sizing up Forester's guilt or innocence in the pattern of the cerebral convolutions. Then he looked to Lockhart. He nodded his head.

"I'm sure he knows," Dr. Slader said.

▪ ▪ ▪

Owen took Michelle to Thanksgiving dinner at the Savoy-Tivoli. He was clean-shaven, his hair freshly cut. He even wore a suit and tie.

It wasn't until they were seated at the dinner table, the wine served, that Michelle spoke up. "I'm not much for prayer, but somehow it feels right today. The first is for Kate's soul. May she now be at peace." Owen stared at his lap, then closed his eyes and slowly nodded.

"And the second is for you." Michelle started to say something else, but instead said, "Welcome back, Owen."

After dinner they walked down Grant to Union, then up to Telegraph Hill. They were holding hands. When he reached the front of her apartment building, they both paused. Michelle considered inviting him in. Owen considered asking. Michelle spoke first.

"There's no hurry. Let's wait until we're both comfortable."

"I'd like that," Owen said.

As he walked back down Union toward Columbus Avenue, he found himself humming a tune that he couldn't name, but that he recognized as being one of Kate's favorites. He thought of Kate and of Michelle. With tears in his eyes he continued home.

Forester was transferred to the medical facility for the criminally insane. The chronically ill were housed in an ancient granite-and-stucco building annexed to the main facility. Forester was in the middle of an open ward crowded with a dozen brain-damaged inmates. Those who had been beaten while in prison, or those who had had strokes or Alzheimer's disease.

The ward reeked of stale urine and the sweet stench of the incontinent demented. There was a constant background of moans, cries, whimpers, and the occasional scream and rattling of the bed rails.

In two weeks Forester had lost another ten pounds. His face was gaunt and lined. Often he refused to eat, even if he had been previously sedated with intramuscular Thorazine. He had no desire for food, for company, for anything except relief. He struggled to find words to make sense of what had happened. Occasionally he could think of a word that seemed as if it fit, though he was not sure, and a minute or two later it would be gone, deep inside the darkness of his shattered memory.

Once the words *Kill me* came to mind. He became terribly excited and began to bang on the bed rail with his mittened hands. Yes, this was what he wanted more than anything. He tried to say the words, but nothing came out. He reached down into the swirling nothingness of his mind, trying to hold on to the words, bring them up into the light. He searched and groped but already the phrase had slipped from view. He was like a toothless man bobbing for apples in a great dark space. Each time his mouth came away empty, the tantalizing, taunting taste of words on the tip of his tongue.

He opened his mouth, pursed his lips, ran his tongue around his teeth and lips, as though there might be a crumb of a new word hiding in there somewhere. But he remained with the limited vocabulary of the first few days.

Three nurses approached his bed. One was the regular staff nurse, two were student nurses, seeing Forester for the first time. All three smiled. Miss Gould introduced the others to Dr. Forester. Forester looked up, not recognizing any of them. Yet they seemed vaguely familiar in their white starched uniforms. He had seen their shapes before. "Mistress Diana?" he said.

The women looked at each other.

No, that wasn't it. Forester shook his head.

The women nodded.

It was something else. They were some . . . some what?

The three women drew closer, watching, saying nothing. Forester caught their glances, his eyes traveling between them. They were doing something. . . . They were thinking.

He started to scream. He was on trial. Becky and Bonnie and Kate standing there. Passing . . . He knew the word. Everyone knew the word. It was what happened at the end of your life. He banged the bed rails again and again, at the same time screaming "No, no, no."

"Relax, Dr. Forester. There's nothing to worry about. We're here to help you."

Help? Becky and Bonnie? Help him? No, they weren't Becky and Bonnie, they were three women in white. The phrase *angels of mercy* bobbed into view for a split second. Yes, yes. They were here to take him away. They were all smiling and moving their lips, talking to him with such lightness and concern. They understood. He could feel new words forming, then breaking up and floating away. He wanted to tell them "Yes, please. Do it."

"Do you think you can eat a little more today?" Miss Gould asked. "If you do, we may be able to cut down on the Thorazine. If you understand me, try nodding your head."

The lady was smiling and talking. Forester smiled back. They understood and were going to do it.

"Yes, yes," Forester said.

"Wonderful." Miss Gould turned to the other women. "It's important to maintain eye contact with an aphasic. Often they can read your facial expressions even when they don't understand the words. It's like talking to a foreigner." She turned back to Forester. "We need to get some meat on your bones." For emphasis she patted Forester's knobby shoulder.

They're taking me now, he thought. His eyes filled with tears of gratitude. Deep inside was the vague warm sensation of hope that he would be relieved of this terrible nameless burden.

"Today is meat loaf, mashed potatoes, and string beans. Sounds good to me." Miss Gould ran her tongue over her lips.

Kate? Is that Kate? He had forgotten the thread of his thoughts. He shuddered, closed his eyes, tried to grab the lost thread. They were watching him, they wanted something. He had that warm feeling again. They were here for him. He felt the inexpressible pleasure of having retraced a thought. He dropped his head back on his pillow, his eyes closed.

Do it now, he thought. *Now.*

He opened his eyes. Miss Gould had motioned to a tall burly man pushing the food cart down the center of the ward. The man stopped at his bed, reached down, grabbed a full tray, and approached Forester. There was the nauseating smell of greasy meat. It grew stronger, the food was directly under his nose.

Forester shook his head.

"Try it, you'll like it," the man said. His voice was deep and gruff. He had fifty men to serve and he was impatient.

Forester jammed his lips together like a petulant child. He shook his head from side to side. He looked up at the three women. They were supposed to be helping him. Fragments of words jumped onto his tongue, then out into the air.

"O dog, hell me."

"That's wonderful, Dr. Forester. You're beginning to talk again." The other nurses nodded. The orderly stood waiting for Forester to take the first bite.

This wasn't what he wanted. "O dog hell me," he said again, more loudly.

"After you eat your lunch," the orderly said.

"Please!" he screamed. "Now."

"Go on, Dr. Forester. Take a bite. It's good for you." Miss Gould pulled down his jaw while the orderly dropped in a square of meat loaf.

"Chew," said Miss Gould.

"O dog," said Dr. Forester, his eyes watering, his mouth moving against the strange meat.